About the Author

Ted Winter studied Modern Languages at Manchester University and taught French, German and Spanish for twenty-seven years before taking up writing. He had two A-Level study guides published before the lure of light-hearted fiction proved irresistible. His previous two novels in the Bear Hoskins series, *The Enigma of Four* and *To the End of the World...and Beyond*, have both been published by Olympia. When not writing, he enjoys travelling, country walks and tennis. He lives in Dorset.

The Curious Pathways of Persistence

Ted Winter

The Curious Pathways of
Persistence

Olympia Publishers
London

www.olympiapublishers.com
OLYMPIA PAPERBACK EDITION

A CIP catalogue record for this title is
available from the British Library.

ISBN: 978-1-80439-247-8

This is a work of fiction.
Names, characters, places and incidents originate from the writer's
imagination. Any resemblance to actual persons, living or dead, is
purely coincidental.

First Published in 2023

Olympia Publishers
Tallis House
2 Tallis Street
London
EC4Y 0AB

Printed in Great Britain

Dedication

To Keira

Acknowledgements

I would like to thank my wife Wendy for giving me the nudge to follow my creative instincts in the first place and casting a critical but encouraging eye over the work. Thanks also to Edward Atkinson for introducing me to Basel, great hospitality and many inspiring memories of enjoyable times in the region.

Chapter One

Constable Country

'It has to be in the best two or three, pushing hard for top spot,' was Christine Warmsley's unhesitating answer to her colleague's question. As the school minibus left the outskirts of the pleasant Suffolk riverside town of Princewood, the driver nodded in acknowledgement as the Head of Art continued, 'if you're lucky with the weather, of course, which we have been, so far, touch wood…' She tapped her forehead in a mock-superstitious gesture. 'Both times we've gone it's been glorious, and the staff are so knowledgeable and inspiring, take the students off your hands, you just have to blend into the background and watch them paint and take in the scenery. It really feels like a day out, which is not the case with some school trips.'

Bear Hoskins had asked Christine how she rated the excursion on which they were embarking in comparison with other outings that she had overseen in her career. As a historian, he had participated in his share of trips in the seven years he had taught at the independent day and boarding establishment, Princewood School.

Today's excursion saw him assisting another department. As the school had invested in a new fleet of minibuses, they had to be driven by staff who had got around to taking, and passing, the rudimentary test comprising a brief circuit of the town. Whereas neither Christine nor her fellow art teacher Linda Porter had achieved such status yet, Bear was one of the few teachers to have found the time to secure the school's internal authorisation to drive the vehicle. Hence, he was invited to step in to drive Christine and nine eager Lower-Sixth art students on the one-hour journey westwards to the Constable Centre.

As Christine was familiar with the route, she hardly needed to refer to the sketch map and directions supplied by the Centre along with the confirmation of her group's slot in the calendar. She was happy to answer Bear's curious enquiries as to the unusual set-up of the recently established arts training venue.

'And it's not been going that long, you said?' asked Bear.

'It's in its third year,' confirmed the art teacher. 'We were very fortunate. When it was first opened, they sent out invitations to schools and colleges in Essex and Suffolk only, Constable having been born in Suffolk. I thought it would be an interesting venture, so I applied straight away. The first visit went well, and we got first refusal on a date same time the following year. And we certainly weren't going to refuse.'

'So it's been at the end of June each year?'

'That's right, which fits perfectly with school exams being finished and the Head being keen to have lots of trips out that go beyond the usual classroom experience. Mind you, this time round they were a bit more pressing in getting me to confirm our interest early. It seems they have a growing reputation and a lengthy waiting list. And all that's happened in three years.'

Bear was suitably impressed. 'I imagine it must be more fun than a visit to the National Gallery.'

'Oh, don't get me wrong,' Christine responded. 'The children learn a lot from those trips to London, and there's a lot to do making sure they see what they should and make the most of the day. But it's always demanding on your concentration, especially with a large group, making sure no one gets lost. Today is a complete contrast.'

Bear could acknowledge the veracity of that statement just by keeping an ear open. The volume in the minibus was limited to animated, but only moderately loud chatter, punctuated by the odd outburst of laughter. Here were some serious students of art, keen to experience something new, whereas with larger parties in the younger years there was always a combination of the committed, the disengaged and the clueless. Today a positive, enquiring energy was in the air.

After a half-hour following the dual carriageway across from Suffolk through the flatlands of Essex, the minibus turned off to pass through narrower country roads into Dedham Vale. On Christine's direction Bear spotted the promised sign to the Centre's car park with space for perhaps a dozen vehicles. Three private cars were already on site as Bear parked the minibus and the group disembarked. The car park was enclosed in deciduous woodland and there was no indication that a cultural centre was in the vicinity, but Christine led them on over a bridge, and to their left the compact but impressively modern 'Constable Centre' was suddenly evident in striking silver-grey stonework. Outside was erected a sandwich board with the face of the famous artist and opening times and prints of a couple of John Constable's landscapes were visible in the windows as appetisers.

The Princewood party was greeted warmly as Christine

13

reported to the reception desk and was welcomed back, obviously remembered from her previous visits. Gisele was announced as their guide for the day, and Christine recalled, approvingly, that the same expert had taken charge the year before. Gisele duly appeared and began the promised tour of the building. She was a bubbly, bustling woman in her mid-forties, bursting with a hostess's enthusiasm as if welcoming guests to her own secret treasure trove. The Centre was constructed on a single floor, with a studio and several exhibition rooms, but began in a mini-cinema where the students sat on padded benches and took in a short film of Constable's life and work and were encouraged to look out for certain techniques and patterns as they followed Gisele's subsequent tour of the premises. As the group made its way from room to room, being directed to prints, and a few originals on loan from major galleries, Bear was aware of an imposing nineteenth-century flour mill on the opposite riverbank. Its importance would be evident later on.

Gisele was experienced at delivering this enticing lecture, pointing out the subtleties of Constable's brushwork, his eye for detail and eagerness to depict the built and natural environment. She knew just how much to encourage her listeners to hone their skills to be young landscape painters with the excitement of being able to exercise their talents after the tour had been completed. Impressive, mused Bear, makes me almost want to pick up a brush myself, although he knew his limitations in that direction.

The tour finished where it had begun as the group was seated to listen to a few concluding remarks by Gisele. Before the visitors were released to attempt some painting, she drew their attention to four pictures lining the wall to their right.

The accompanying information board read: 'Constable's legacy'. Four landscapes from a slightly later period in the nineteenth century adorned the walls. All were by French painters. Gisele timed her remark to perfection as she related that Constable was far more popular in France than in Britain; indeed, he had sold only twenty paintings in his home country in his lifetime. However, he had inspired a group of French artists that met at Fontainebleau, not far from Paris. Did any of the students know the name of this particular school? At this point Christine maintained an amused silence. She knew the answer, of course, and was sure that she had mentioned it to her pupils at some point. Blank looks were exchanged between the Sixth formers, which persuaded Gisele to put them out of their misery.

'No idea?' she continued, 'well, I'll tell you, it's—'

'The Barbizon School,' a voice from the back of the room interrupted her.

'Give that man a gold star!' exclaimed the guide extending her arm in the direction of the answerer in joyous acknowledgement.

'Oh, well done, sir!' some of the pupils added.

'You must be an art teacher too?' Gisele asked Bear, who shook his head.

'No, it's... just something that stuck in my mind,' Bear answered sheepishly.

Gisele concluded with an explanation of the four painters influenced by John Constable. Three were known to at least some of the students, and even Bear had heard of them, although the fourth artist explained was not a name with which he was familiar. He was intrigued why Jean Duclos should be included on the same platform as the three illustrious fellow occupants of the wall. The painting depicted an austere, functional farm building in the background with two labourers pausing for a momentary exchange of remarks amid a warm afternoon's toil. Gisele compared Duclos' work to *The Gleaners* by Millet which showed women working in the fields but with their faces obscured. Duclos, she noted, was known for introducing more facial expression than some of the better-known members of the Barbizon School. He was also closer to Constable in style and content for his inclusion of the built environment. Like the English landscape artist, he did not rely on the natural scenery but blended in the realities of working, mainly agricultural life of the period.

Experience had enabled Gisele to anticipate the likely question of her audience as to why a supposedly lesser artist was included in the centre's exhibition. She had delivered this talk often enough to know how to convey mystery and a sense of wonder. 'Duclos is nowadays being thought of as an underrated artist. It seems from documents recently discovered, from correspondence with the artist, both business and personal, that there may be other paintings that have been lost or have not yet come to light. One in particular that he describes in a letter apparently depicts the flight of persecuted Huguenots leaving France for the safety of Switzerland in 1685.'

Bear nodded thoughtfully at this point. He was acquainted with the notorious Revocation of the Edict of Nantes by the enigmatically named 'sun king' Louis XIV, by which the Protestant believers were denied citizenship rights and forced into exile. Gisele accurately summarised their plight.

The structured part of the visit was concluded. The group was free to make use of the centre's café which overlooked the river for lunch, which they did so. They occupied several chairs outside but did not linger long as they were scheduled to be met by another staff member, Bertrand, who was to supply them with painting materials. As the weather was set fair for the afternoon, the sixth-formers were led out on to a terrace with a fine view of the riverside scene that faced the mill encountered earlier, the bridge and several trees, including an overhanging willow and a silver birch. Plenty for the young latter-day would-be Constables to get their teeth (and brushes) into. While Bertrand was getting the group started at river level, Christine and Bear were able to cast a watchful eye on proceedings from the café as they finished off their cups of coffee. Supervision, as Christine had learned from previous visits, was minimal. The students were left to paint while the teachers observed every now and then in extremely agreeable surroundings.

Conversation centred on school trips they had embarked on in the line of duty. For Bear, the obligatory visit to the Viking burial site outside the town of Princewood with the fresh intake of Year 7 pupils each autumn and regular exploration of the ruins of Roundham Castle to evoke the turbulent atmosphere of the English Civil War had been regular excursions.

Occasionally he had made up the numbers on ventures organised by other departments, most memorably when responding to a late call to replace an injured colleague on the school's annual exchange trip to Germany with exploration of the former communist East included in the itinerary. Christine recalled Bear's eleventh-hour response to the appeal for help and said that she was grateful for his filling in on this occasion, albeit one of much shorter duration.

17

Their discussion inevitably turned to what the accompanying teachers would have been doing back at base. Bear said he normally taught both the Upper Sixth and Year 11 that day of the week, and as both groups had been taking public examinations, and therefore, had been on leave for weeks, there were naturally some gaps in his timetable. However, as they both recognised, so-called 'free' time at this time of year could often be taken up by having to cover for colleagues themselves absent on trips, and they both knew from experience that having to supervise groups where work had been set could be hazardous. Some teachers provided rigorous instructions as to what was to be completed in their absence. Others were more vague, causing the unfortunate substitute to be obliged to respond to a flurry of pupils' questions as to what they were required to do. Hence, Bear was pleased to take a break from such challenges at the time of year. He had made a point of issuing clear directions for the classes he had left behind, lest any accusation of hypocrisy be laid at his door.

'So you know about the Barbizon School,' Christine remarked. 'You *are* a dark horse. Didn't know you knew your art history.'

'I know a few bits. I wouldn't say I'm an expert,' Bear replied. 'I just knew someone who was quite well informed, and it seems some at least has sunk in.'

Christine turned away to gaze at the group now established with their easels and canvasses on the terrace, ready to begin their artistic challenge. She deduced that Bear was not about to elaborate on the source of his knowledge, and she was right in that assumption. Bear had surprised himself by his utterance earlier during Gisele's talk and

18

reflected that it had been some time since he had had cause to dwell on the person who had shared her knowledge of the history of art with him. It had been a stimulating, emotionally stirring period in his life that he had left behind, he assumed permanently.

The afternoon proved relaxing for the accompanying teachers and students alike.

Christine and Bear sauntered down to the painters' level to observe their progress. Christine responded to a few queries, while Bear was content simply to respond to the occasional pleasantry.

'You should give this a go, sir,' encouraged Sarah Blake, an extrovert member of the group as she turned momentarily away from her work, 'especially now we know you're an expert on art.'

'I wouldn't call myself an expert, Sarah,' Bear replied cheerily, 'I just know a little bit about art history, that's all. My word, your painting is coming along nicely...'

'But seriously, sir,' Sarah persisted, 'did you study history of art at uni or something?'

'No, you wally,' Helen Watson answered before the teacher had a chance to do so. 'He studied history, of course. He's a history teacher!'

'Well, his course could have included some art...,' continued Sarah. 'Where did you learn about art history, sir?' she probed.

Bear was struggling to give a thorough, convincing answer without relating a significant phase of his private life. 'It's just general knowledge, Sarah. Things you pick up as you get older, as you progress along life's journey,' he explained, resorting to the mystery of maturity being the clue to life's

19

secrets, usually a sure way to end unwanted banter with younger students but in this relaxed setting with curious sixth-formers, less likely to deflect further questioning. 'I just happened to—'

'I know!' exclaimed the usually laconic Matthew Bourne without looking up from his easel, 'Mr Hoskins did a bit of modelling in his youth.'

There followed whoops of amusement and a ripple of laughter from those students within earshot and a few puzzled queries from those further away.

'There are certain secrets which everyone is entitled to preserve, Matthew,' Bear responded enigmatically, at which the painters exchanged intrigued looks as if the history teacher had revealed a tasty morsel concerning a dissolute youth. He immediately regretted his choice of phrase, but fortunately Christine was on hand to remind them of the limited time available and the changing light which meant that they needed to take advantage of the next half-hour without allowing themselves to be distracted by idle chatter. There was considerably more brush work and much less repartee for the rest of the afternoon, which concluded with Bertrand casting an expert eye over the group's efforts, which all showed an awareness of proportion and colour, given the limited time available to test their landscape painting talents. The work was gathered up to be transported home for completion with a view to being displayed around the school's art studios in due course.

'It'll be interesting to see what changes the centre makes by this time next year,' observed Christine as Bear drove away from Dedham Vale eastwards. 'I gather there's a major exhibition planned at the National Gallery about the Barbizon

School. It's a major anniversary since the school was founded and it should prove popular.'

'Should be worth a visit,' Bear responded politely.

'They were impressed with your knowledge,' she added, referring again to his timely answer to Gisele's teaser at the beginning of the day, 'I mean, Gisele and Bertrand, not just our lot. You can certainly come again.'

'Well, I have had my sources,' confessed Bear modestly. On an impulse he added, 'who was it said, "There is a history behind every painting, not just a history of art"?'

'Mmm… I'm not sure, but it sounds spot on. That *"Flight of the Huguenots"* has certainly got a history to it if it can ever be discovered.'

Bear was unsure of the origin of the quote but recalled full well who had passed it on to him, inevitably speculating what she was doing now. They hadn't been in touch for years. Little did he suspect that the answer was to be forthcoming in a matter of days.

Chapter Two

Persistence Pays

One of the joys and challenges of teaching in a secondary school is the variety of demands posed by different age groups. A lively class of carefree thirteen-year-olds bursting to answer every question, Bear acknowledged as he drove into work the following morning after the visit to the Constable Centre, would stimulate his classroom management skills in a different way to an enquiring group of sixth-formers with designs on further study and the world of work. The unpredictability of diverse groups was at once refreshing, even rejuvenating, as well as occasionally unnerving. Whilst he enjoyed the reasonably adult conversation of the previous day's artists, he was not wholly sure whether their parting shot ('we look forward to learning more of your modelling career, sir') was to be pursued. Sometimes such comments were forgotten almost instantly; at other times apparent rumours concerning teachers were tenaciously grasped for weeks, even months, as if by a dog with a bone.

His main concern that morning was with pupils at the other end of the secondary school age spectrum. He was scheduled to conduct an assembly for the lower school in which selected members of his form, 8H, were recruited as participants to act out a presentation that he had prepared. At the time he received the programme of staff responsibilities he had not yet been asked to assist in the outing to Dedham Vale. Although he had ensured that his assistants had been briefed as to their responsibilities before his one-day absence, he was acutely aware of the average thirteen-year-old's ability to forget over a period as extended as twenty-four hours. He braced himself for a volley of panicked requests for clarification of individual roles, despite having conducted a rigorous rehearsal two days ago.

Bear resolved to arrive at his classroom in good time to be on hand for any last-minute queries from nervous performers. On this occasion, it transpired, his worries proved unfounded.

'Remember what you have to do, Claire?' he asked of one of the less alert members of the enlisted group of helpers.

'Oh, yes, sir,' replied Claire. 'Just dish out the cards in the right order.'

'Correct. They have been arranged, but they all have numbers in the top right-hand corner, so they don't go out of sequence.'

'Trust me, sir, got it all sorted.'

After similar utterances had been expressed by the other assistants, and Bear had registered his class, they made their way to the school hall where the assembly for the three youngest year groups was to take place.

As the remaining classes joined 8-H at the venue with their accompanying staff, Bear remained seated at the front along with his four helpers, who betrayed excitement at actually facing their contemporaries, trying to hide bashful grins. When all were assembled, Bear announced the hymn and the congregation rose and made a passable attempt at harmony in singing from their uniform red hymn books. Once all were seated, Scarlett needed no nudge from his form teacher to head to the lectern before reading the scripture passage for the day, stressing, as instructed, the key words, 'Seek and you will find.' Preliminaries over, Bear rose to introduce his topic.

'Today I would like to share with you the highlights of a great man's life,' he announced enigmatically. 'Listen to some of the most significant events in his life which 8-H will share with you.'

Claire stood with a pile of A4 sized yellow cards to Bear's left with Simon and Daniel behind, poised for action. As Claire handed the first card to Simon, the recipient strode forward and held it aloft momentarily for the audience to read the word in clear capitals, "FAILURE".

Bear announced:

'In 1831 the business he set up failed.'

Simon emphasised sombrely the word 'failure' before retreating to the back of the stage.

Claire then presented Daniel with a second card and he performed the identical routine as his predecessor, albeit with a touch more swagger. Daniel's card read, "DEFEAT", which he pronounced emphatically after his teacher's explanation:

'In 1832 he ran for the office of state legislator but was defeated.'

The pattern established, further cards were presented by the two boys indicating "BANKRUPTCY", "HEARTBREAK", "BREAKDOWN" and four further announcements of "DEFEAT", the final one for the office of Vice President of the United States. The highlights of this illustrious person's life and career seemed to be heading in one direction. The stage was set for some vintage Bear

24

oratory.

'How would you feel if you had so many setbacks? Would you feel you just wanted to give up?' he asked rhetorically of his audience of some two hundred captivated hearers. Those whom he taught were well acquainted with Bear's style of history teaching, which stressed the empathic, putting oneself in the shoes of those affected by the tide of events. His Head of Department, the more straight-laced Michael Streatham, felt his colleague strayed too far into the realms of the speculative and away from the hard facts of history, an assertion Bear rigorously refuted. There could be no denying that, on this occasion, Bear was drawing his assembly audience in by stirring their curiosity and sense of wonder.

Bear surveyed the audience deliberately for a few seconds to prolong a key dramatic pause, before continuing. 'There is one other highlight in this great man's life I need to mention…' – a shorter pause to extract maximum attention – 'In 1860 he was elected President of the United States. His name was Abraham Lincoln, and he is now known as one of the most famous presidents in US history. He is acclaimed for keeping the country together throughout the American Civil War. Even in the darkest days of the war, Lincoln never lost hope. He showed persistence and never gave up, no matter the odds against him nor what people said. He is widely credited for saving the United States as one nation during this tumultuous period.'

Bear's stirring words hung in the air as he wound up proceedings, stressing the virtue of persistence. As he left the auditorium and congratulated his helpers on their contributions to the morning's drama, he heaved a sigh of relief that the last of his major engagements for the academic year had been successfully delivered and he could look forward to the summer break a few days hence.

***

'Great assembly the other day, by the way, Bear,' complimented Head of Physics John Billington.

'Oh, right…, thanks, John,' was the history teacher's ponderous response as he struggled to recollect the events of five days ago. The usual end-of-term whirlwind had proceeded at its customary lightning speed and he, like his colleagues, was just starting to get his breath back. 'Glad you liked it,' he added as he took another sip of Italian white wine.

Bear noticed that his science colleague was in typical ebullient mood. Gregarious, larger than life, John had a reputation as a Mr Fix-it, with an engineer's confidence that no problem was too great to be unlocked for long. A gentle six-foot-four giant of a man, John had given Bear cause to wonder more than once if the historian's own first name would suit the physicist better. He was also aware that John's extrovert nature was such that he could stimulate conversation that could easily draw others in − a notable, if occasionally unwelcome, gift. Today was not untypical, as other colleagues standing nearby were attracted to the physics specialist's remark.

'What's zees?' asked Claudine Leblanc. 'Ees zees something I missed?'

'Just commenting on Bear's splendid thought-provoking junior assembly last week,' John explained. 'Life has been so busy since I've not had time to congratulate him.'

'Oh? Tell me more,' Claudine, who had not been present at the event, invited either of her two colleagues to elaborate, which Bear did.

'What a lovely idea!' gushed Claudine. The handsome woman from Bordeaux was often fulsome in her praise, a trait that had certainly endeared her to her pupils ever since starting at Princewood some dozen years ago. Her sincere but seemingly exaggerated interest could be felt to be disconcerting at times, particularly to single males such as Bear who had cause in the past to suspect the French teacher, now in her mid-forties, of having an interest in mothering them. Or even of pursuing a closer relationship. Neither assumption was true, however − it was just Claudine's way. She continued, 'lovely to get the children involved. You 'ave some great creative ideas, my Grizzly Bear.'

The relaxed atmosphere was almost tangible as the marquee had been cleared of parents and schoolchildren at the close of annual Prize giving, the event that marked the formal closure of the academic year at Princewood School. Now, at six on a warm July evening, the cares of teaching, marking, composing reports, administration, pastoral concerns were set aside for a few weeks with time to pause, reflect and recharge batteries. Most of the staff had stayed on for the barbecue for themselves and their families and several were enjoying a drink before the festivities began in earnest.

'So what are you doing in ze 'olidays, Grizzly?' enquired Claudine.

'I'm visiting a friend in Switzerland for a couple of weeks,' Bear replied casually.

'Yes, Bear's eying up a few Swiss beauties,' chipped in English teacher Rob McAllister.

27

'Well, you'd know about that sort of thing, Mac,' Bear retorted with a mischievous grin.

Anyone not picking up some very definite visual signals would have assumed a distinct tension between the pair, but Bear and Rob had been close friends for some years, and the latter's reputation had been long established. Rob had been known to start many a relationship, some of which had proved short lived. Impulsive, creative, he could be captivatingly charming, but many of his girlfriends had found him too intense. Bear, who had witnessed his friend at close quarters as co-coaches on the rugby field, could but agree.

'Who's this friend of yours, then, Bear?' asked geographer Rachel Rhodes.

'Just a friend from school. Tim works in a bank in Basel. He's been over there for a few years now and has always issued an open invitation. I've only got round to accepting it now. Haven't seen him for years.'

Like Rob, Rachel had been informed of Bear's holiday plans some weeks ago and Bear had confirmed he would endeavour to add to the geography teacher's photographic collection. For the past four years he had ensured he had some clear photographs to pass on to Rachel of the relevant border point in his travels. It had started with some spectacular images of the Pyrenees where France becomes Spain which were gratefully received and added to a display in the geographer's classroom. Pictures of rivers, mountains, paths and even just frontier posts had been helpful to Rachel in fixing an appreciation of the world's political and physical divisions in her pupils' consciousness.

For his forthcoming trip, Bear had made a mental note to add photos of the famous '*Dreiländereck*' to his itinerary, the buoy in the Rhine that marked the point where Germany, France and Switzerland converged. He acknowledged to himself that he already had photographic evidence of his one fleeting overnight visit to Basel as a student, when he had dived into the river fully clothed in response to a dare to be captured grasping the border marker in triumphant gladiatorial pose. Such a striking image from his dissolute youth, though doubtless amusing to onlookers from the student population, was probably not appropriate to the purposes of educational enlightenment and he resolved to find a contemporary alternative photo for Rachel, with himself out of the picture.

'*Hmm...* working for a Swiss bank,' Rob mused as though absorbing the news for the first time, although Bear had already told him of his holiday plans. 'I bet he's on a nice little earner there.'

'He's doing all right,' acknowledged Bear. 'Even given the higher cost of living in Switzerland. And he's not got a particular senior position, just a regular nine to five job, no overtime required.'

'You'll have to find out what the secret is, Bear, how we can earn a packet without stressing over children the whole time.'

'He'll probably say how lucky we are to have six weeks' holiday. I suspect I may gain some insight, but sympathy will be in very short supply.'

'So no female company planned?' Rob asked, feigning disappointment.

'It often pays not to plan too much, Mac. I will simply go with the flow.'

Bear reflected that relationships of sorts had developed more than once on visits abroad.

There had been Sophie, the extrovert saleswoman for a book publishers he had met on the Portuguese-Spanish border. Prior to her, just before embarking on a school trip to Germany, he was introduced to Laura, then training to be a vicar but a former teacher at Princewood School.

On both occasions a warm friendship had evolved, but no more than that. He was relieved that probing into his romantic prospects was curtailed as John changed the subject.

'Where exactly in Switzerland is Basel?' asked the Head of Physics.

As a geographer Rachel felt duty-bound to respond. 'The north-west corner, right on the border with both France and Germany.'

'I might 'ave known!' exclaimed Claudine with a wry grin at Bear as if the historian had been keeping a secret for ages that had finally been prised from his grasp. 'I knew my Grizzly Bear would be 'eading to some border or other! You are following your passion. I 'ope you 'ave a wonderful time, Borderer Bear,' she said, taking a swig of sparkling wine before gazing intently at him. 'Is that a real word, "borderer"?'

Bear confirmed the lexical validity of Claudine's remark and was amused at the label she used of him. Certainly, she was the member of staff who showed the keenest interest in what could justifiably be classified as a passion. Claudine was fascinated that most of Bear's holiday ventures involved a trip to one frontier or another, comparing life on different sides of the geographical divide, noting how not just language, but customs changed, often very subtly.

When he cheerfully stood in for an injured colleague to join the exchange trip to northern Bavaria, he was absorbed in the day visit to the former German Democratic Republic and fascinated to see how much and in some cases, how little had changed since reunification a few years previously. His journey to the far north of Portugal had left a profound impression on him as he noted the powerful fortifications on either side of the River Minho, an indication of more turbulent times, and he had crossed over into Spain by the iron bridge constructed by Gustave Eiffel.

He could naturally trace his fascination with borders to his upbringing. Although brought up in suburban Surrey, his parents hailed from the Anglo-Scottish border country. His father used to celebrate entering Carlisle, 'The Great Border City' he would announce as the road sign welcomed them each time the family headed north to visit relatives. No such visit was complete without a stroll along the famous Hadrian's Wall, the official frontier of the Roman Empire, usually on the windiest day possible, as Bear recalled. He could imagine himself as a Roman soldier on guard duty sent to the very edge of the world. On numerous occasions he found himself positioned atop the Roman Emperor's construction gazing out into the wilderness that would today represent the last remaining miles of English soil, perhaps a recruit from North Africa or one of Rome's other colonies, far from home and with years of arduous service stretching ahead of him in such unforgiving terrain.

He was brought out of his reverie back to the genteel surroundings of early evening drinks on a Suffolk lawn under the shadow of a marquee. John Billington had further comments to voice.

'Just as well you didn't tell them about how Lincoln met his end, Bear,' he remarked.

31

'Well, that's for another day, Billers. Political assassination didn't quite fit in with their words of persistence.'

'It's a great theme to do,' Billers observed. 'Although I'm not sure about the time of year. The ideal time would be about mid-October, when they've settled into the school routine, had a few knocks, failed a test or two, not been picked for a team. That's when learning to be persistent would have its optimum effect.'

'Oh, I don't know,' Rob interjected in support of his friend. 'A good assembly will be remembered whatever time of year it happens. Anyway, who knows whether children won't need persistence and perseverance over the holidays?'

'True,' John Billington conceded thoughtfully.

The evening followed an agreeable and convivial course as the Headmaster made a few informal concluding remarks as presentations were offered to two staff leaving for pastures new. Bear was happy to consume several glasses of wine before carefully heading homewards, grateful of the fact that his flat lay within walking distance at the edge of town. He had the weekend before him to recover from the rigours of term and prepare for his Swiss travels.

Chapter Three

Plans for a Soirée

There is something about the timing of an action, rather than the action itself, that can have the maximum impact on those affected, for good or ill. A compliment about one's appearance might be brushed off in some circumstances, but at the end of a tiring, demanding day, might be most gratefully received. A dismissive gesture to a sincere request might be resented as a personal slight or understood sympathetically as an indication of weariness and being overburdened with other priorities on the part of the one making the gesture. Our responses to others' deeds are determined largely by our moods. So might Ciara O'Malley have articulated her thoughts if she were feeling more charitably disposed toward her boss. Had she spoken her mind at that moment beyond a brief acknowledgement, however, a stream of harsh invective would have probably proceeded from her lips. She was not by nature an ungenerous person, but every now and then Ernst Schiffer could be relied upon to press, often unintentionally, just the wrong button. This extremely warm July lunchtime had been one of those presses.

'Oh, and this came this morning. Perhaps you can deal with it?' The section head of the Loans and Short-Term Exhibitions Department of the Neue Basler Kunstgalerie expressed his remark as a request but it was clear that he was unloading unwanted business on his assistant. Normally, Ciara would not resent the gesture; after all, that was her role, to assist in the correspondence concerning loans and temporary exhibitions with any administration that accompanied them. It was just that Ernst slipped the brown envelope into her in-tray at a minute to twelve just as he was heading off on his lunch break. It had to be a minute to twelve, of course. The rotund manager in his mid-fifties had been working at the gallery for over a dozen years and had cultivated a regular routine. Promptly at noon he would exit the office to amble to his flat just five minutes' walk from the gallery to be greeted by his wife who, in traditional Swiss fashion, would have a hot meal prepared for him. He would not be returning to his office until two o'clock, sometimes later. A very comfortable lifestyle, Ciara had remarked to herself on more than one occasion, wondering how his wife could tolerate what Ciara saw as a subservient role. She acknowledged that for many this was still the Swiss way even in the last decade of the twentieth century. Few women of her generation in Britain, or even her native Ireland would tolerate such submission.

There was, of course, nothing improper about Ernst passing the envelope on to his assistant. It was just that he waited until he passed her desk at a minute to noon as he was putting on his suit jacket before heading out the door for the next two hours. It was as if to say, 'I'm knocking off now. You keep cracking on.' The fact that Ciara was about to take a shorter lunch break was immaterial. It was the implication that she should not feel at liber ty to relax even as the clock was about to strike twelve. She did not actually *have to* deal with the item until after lunch. It was just the subtle emotional pressure placed on her to ensure she never felt too comfortable that annoyed her. Especially as she was often tempted to skim through the correspondence in question before beginning her break. That way she would be aware of weighty challenges ahead and she should not feel she could delay matters too long. Was this timing of delivering work into one's in-tray part of some agreed management tactic that her superiors learned about and were encouraged to deploy on their underlings?

If so, it worked. Ciara could not resist having a quick glance at the already opened envelope which had been stamped with the word 'bequests'. This was not unusual, as there were a number of wealthier citizens of Basel who were happy to pass on some of their collection of paintings to the gallery, having bequeathed other choice items to their offspring. Of course, not every component of a bequest could be displayed regularly, or even stored, and the family of the deceased had often to be informed that the item would be sent back to them or sold at auction within twelve months, whichever was their preference. Normally, the details of the bequest were a formal legal document, although on this occasion the envelope also contained a typed letter of four pages written by the deceased, underlining his wishes. Ciara's intended quick glance was extended to ten minutes as she scanned, then read the letter. She found herself surprisingly captivated by the contents but then cursed as she looked at her watch to note that she had squandered several minutes of her lunch break. She resolved to devote her attention to the document that afternoon along with a fair-sized pile of paperwork to attend to.

Ciara's usual half-hour escape to the Café Engelchen opposite the gallery was even shorter than usual and she returned to her labours with the aim to leave work at half-past four, unless Ernst found some other task that demanded her immediate attention. Unsurprisingly the Head of Loans and Short-Term Exhibitions sauntered back to the office at a few minutes past two after Ciara had been back at her desk beavering away for an hour and a half. In the three years she had worked at the gallery, Ernst's clockwork movements had caused her to emit a wry smile. Her Swiss colleague, Silke, a woman in her mid-forties with whom she shared an office, never seemed to bat an eyelid at Ernst's long lunch hours. It was just normal. But why should I even feel Ernst's extended lunch breaks to be worthy of observation, Ciara thought to herself.

Maybe others see her as just as much a creature of habit with her snatched thirty minutes in the café every day. Certainly, she had never adopted the orderly, measured Swiss routine in the seven years of living in Basel. She was always on the go, constantly seeking to complete the next task, determined to see it through to its conclusion. She never liked things left undone and had occasionally been known to stay on beyond office closing time to bring matters to a satisfactory fulfilment.

That afternoon proved to be gratifyingly productive with several matters resolved. The details for an incoming exhibition of a Norwegian landscape artist 'Scenes from the Fjords' had been finalised and the first stages of correspondence concerning the loan of portraits of Swiss reformers of the sixteenth century had been successfully administered prior to a planned six months' display in Edinburgh the following year. Normally, Ciara pondered as she boarded the tram on her return to her flat that afternoon, she would be feeling a deep sense of satisfaction.

The reason for the absence of such lightness of mood was easy to detect as it had returned to her throughout the afternoon. Why should a letter written by an old man virtually on his deathbed, possibly without his full mental faculties, be bugging her so much? The 'bequest' letter passed on to her by Ernst had been read and re-read and she was struggling to find an appropriate course of action in response. She berated herself at allowing the serenity of a fine summer evening to be disturbed as the tram wended its way into the western suburbs of the city. She resolved to devote more attention to the matter the following day.

After entering her flat and scanning her post over a cup of tea, she noticed her answerphone indicated a message. Pressing the relevant button indicated that the caller had just missed her by a matter of minutes. Sounds like someone acquainted with my movements and when I return to the flat, she assumed. Her instincts were validated when she heard a familiar voice, and she rang back immediately.

'Timbo, my old friend,' she announced cheerily. 'You rang?'

'Hi, Bee,' a jovial male voice responded. 'My timings are a bit out today. I was sure you'd be back home five minutes ago.'

'Not bad, though, you only just missed me.'

'Oh well, I obviously haven't been living in Switzerland long enough. Eight years and still my timing needs adjusting,' Tim gushed with a hearty chuckle. Ciara smiled at his remark; this was someone guaranteed to see the amusing side in the most mundane of situations.

Someone who could cheer you up no matter what sort of

day you've had. His laughter was infectious, and Ciara often shook her head in wonderment at how readily witticisms occurred to him.

'How's life back at the bank? Are they working you hard?' asked Ciara.

'Hard enough, Bee. We still miss you buzzing around keeping us on our toes.' Ciara smiled again as she was reminded of her nickname, one that she had inherited soon after she started working for the international bank, known in various guises according to the language deployed, but to an English speaker as the International Resettlement Bank, or simply IRB. Her four years in a largely clerical role had been financially rewarding, given generous Swiss salaries, but not providing the artistic and intellectual stimulation that she craved. She enjoyed the company of several colleagues of similar age, mostly expats from several European countries, and had found the experience of her first years in Switzerland culturally enriching.

Tim Sheldon had been one of those expats and one of the first, perhaps the originator, to use the sobriquet to describe his bustling Irish colleague with a no-nonsense approach to work, keen to complete tasks and sparing in her participation in office chatter. He had appreciated her company in lunch breaks and in social situations once working hours were concluded, but 'Bee' had been clear that she did not like to be distracted when her mind was on the job.

Tim enquired as to how she was enjoying life at the gallery, to which Ciara mentioned the current projects with which she was engaged.

'I can't say much as it's more than my job's worth, except to say that some lovely Scandinavian landscapes should be coming our way next spring if you care to drop in.'

'I'll bear that in mind, Bee,' he responded before changing tack. 'The reason I called…'

'Oh yes, you said something about next Tuesday?'

'I was wondering if you were free next Tuesday, as I am planning a little culinary soirée. Just having a few people round. Are you up for it?'

'That's very kind, Tim,' Ciara replied enthusiastically. A quick glimpse of her calendar carefully attached to the wall above the telephone confirmed that she was free that evening. She was genuinely appreciative of the invitation and knew that Tim was more than competent in the kitchen as well as being entertaining company. 'So who's coming? Any of the old gang showing up?'

'Well, there's Sarah, and Mark and Chantal—,' he began.

'That's lovely!' Ciara remarked. 'I haven't seen them for ages. I did bump into your lady recently, though, as I'm sure she told you.' Sarah had been going out with Tim for over a year. Mark and Chantal were an Anglo-French couple, recently married. All three prospective dinner guests worked for the bank. 'And let me guess, there must be another male involved to even up things. It wouldn't be a Sheldon soirée if he hadn't got everything perfectly balanced.'

'Well, it just so happens that I have someone coming to stay with me for a couple of weeks, someone I went to school with. I haven't seen him for a while.'

'I see. Someone to neutralise the bank-related conversation, eh?' Ciara queried playfully. 'He is single, I take it? Of course, the thought of matchmaking never entered your head…'

'Well, you never know. He's into history, so you might

have something in common.'

'So what's this young man's name?' she asked inquisitively, having deduced that Tim's friend was a similar age to her.

'Now that is the interesting part. His name is Bear.'

'Bear? As in the animal?' Ciara's response stemmed not just from natural curiosity as an instant recollection from her student days sprung to mind.

When Tim affirmed that she had heard correctly, Ciara asked light-heartedly how his friend had come to have such a name.

'If I remember rightly, he was named after some Swedish guitarist in a rock band in the sixties by the name of Björn, which we all know is Swedish for—'

'Bear,' Ciara completed crisply, momentarily unsettled as Tim had supplied precisely the information that she anticipated. She quickly recovered her composure and asked what prompted this Bear to visit.

'Just a simple tourist, wants to see a bit of Switzerland and no doubt share some schoolboy anecdotes with yours truly for old time's sake. He's a teacher in England and is about to break up for the summer.'

'The schools are already breaking up over there?' Ciara noted with astonishment.

'He's at a private school. They always break up a bit early and have a long summer break – seven or eight weeks, I believe.'

'All right for some, I suppose. Nice work if you can get it.'

'He'd probably say the same about us here in Switzerland, earning much more than we would for similar

40

jobs in the UK.'

The conversation continued amicably for a few moments as Tim related a few items of news concerning Ciara's former colleagues at the bank. She thanked him again for the kind invitation and said she looked forward to the evening immensely. After she hung up, she sat quietly on her sofa and stared at the wall vacantly before releasing a hearty laugh. Who would have thought it after all this time, she reflected, a real blast from the past? She congratulated herself at not reacting audibly when she learned the identity of Tim's visitor and eagerly anticipated the evening of five days' hence. Eight years had passed, and a lot of water had flowed under the bridge.

Ciara was not one given to intense soul-searching reflections and analysis of her life to date. She always believed in seizing the moment, although she was far from impulsive. She was astute in assessing situations whether regarding her career or particular operational tasks at work. Over the years she had gained a reputation as a diligent worker at the bank and in the last three years after she secured her current post at the gallery. Her nature was not to dwell on the past but every now and then little prompts in conversations led her to an emotional stock-take. It could hardly be otherwise with the imminent re-emergence of someone she had been close to during her student years. A calming influence, many had said of her new male friend when they started going out in their second year of university. Whatever his quirky ways, faults even, he was certainly that, calming.

Calm was definitely not a word associated with Ciara as she grew up in Limerick in the 1970s and '80s. As the youngest of five children, she had always had to fight her

41

corner.

Combative, determined, tenacious were adjectives most often applied to her as she observed her older siblings' successes and, in her eyes more often than not, struggles. She had a particular affection for her older brother Conor. He always referred to her as 'piglet' but had felt a definite protective responsibility to her, being some fourteen years her senior. Poor Conor. He had dropped out of university, struggling with drink and to maintain relationships and was only now putting his life together again. He always had helpful advice to impart; it was just a pity he had difficulties following it in his own life. Then there was her elder sister Roisin who had forged a successful career for herself in banking, seamlessly taking time out to have three children.

Wonder woman, Ciara had occasionally renamed her. Yet for all her sister's success Ciara could not help finding Roisin's path in life to be dull and functional. That didn't stop her soliciting her sister's advice and finding a route into banking which was to lead to her acquiring lucrative employment with the International Resettlement Bank in Basel. Middle child Padraig was safety-first personified; risk averse, careful to avoid the excesses of his older brother and settling for a safe, boring civil service post. And to complete the quartet of older siblings' life adventures that Ciara observed studiously, Siobhan had married young into what proved an abusive relationship from which she escaped after much suffering as a single mum, struggling to make ends meet. Their entrepreneur father with his flourishing haulage business in Limerick was able to help out those offspring in need, but Ciara was determined she would not be numbered amongst those needing handouts.

42

When she returned to work the following morning, her in-tray was relatively empty, although she knew the influx of postal items and doubtless, further requests from Ernst would ensue. She realised she would have to summon up resolve to make some decision on the unusual communication passed on to her under the banner of 'bequests'. Normally she would take the bull by the horns and wrestle with any issue that was hard to fathom out and not solicit help from colleagues. A rare independent streak that had been pointed out to her at the bank where the strong sense of teamwork prevailed. She was even tempted to engage Silke with chat and was about to utter a pleasantry about the warm weather and ask her colleague about any upcoming holidays, all as a prelude to soliciting advice. Then the phone rang on Silke's desk and Ciara heard her engage in what she recognised as a lengthy business conversation in Swiss German.

Over her period in Switzerland and in previous studies, she had acquired a fair grasp of the German language and could conduct formal discussions relatively comfortably with German or Austrian customers and associates. Like many expatriates living in the country, however, she found the range of variations in vowel sounds and vocabulary in 'Schwyzertütsch' beyond her. She frequently had to ask the person addressing her to revert to standard German. Her reading of German was sound and had enabled her to secure her current post, along with her earlier studies and knowledge of art. As she sensed that Silke's conversation was shaping to be quite a long one, she braced herself for making some formal notes on the letter of bequest she had already read the previous day.

The first few sentences were fairly standard, involving

43

details of items listed for members of the deceased's family. Being a widower, there was no wife to inherit the gentleman's not inconsiderable wealth, so two children were left with various assets and works of art as well as an equal share of the house that had recently been vacated. It was what Ciara read next that caused her to investigate with greater intensity:

'I need to inform the executors of the will that there are aspects of my past of which I am not proud. My love of painting, architecture and indeed all art forms has been sometimes expressed by greed and sadly, one as yet unresolved issue. I write to the Neue Basler Kunstgalerie as I trust this institution to carry out whatever research is necessary to bring the matter to a satisfactory conclusion. Through advancing age, declining health and ultimately my terminal condition and I confess, negligence in my earlier life I have left things undone...

Will you get to the point, man? Ciara thought to herself, and then realised how silly her reaction was, given that she had already digested the contents thoroughly the day before. She read on:

'Fifty years have passed, and it is my bitter regret that only now do I feel able to admit to what may be a grave crime against not only the laws of any decent society but also art in its purest sense. I would like to ask the Galerie to pursue what I will sadly no longer be able to...'

She paused to take notes and resolved to make the necessary enquiries. It was likely to be a wild goose chase at worst and a box-ticking exercise at best. After about half an hour's jotting down of details, punctuated by just one short phone call, she rose from her desk and headed to the archive department in the basement of the building. Franz Geissler,

44

the head archivist, was present as she presented her request.

'We don't often see you down here,' commented the studious fifty-year-old custodian of essential gallery documents. 'How can I help you?'

She explained that she wanted to check if a certain painting had ever been exhibited at the gallery, whether by being held in store for occasional exhibition or received on loan from another gallery. At least, if the painting was either held here in Basel, or was in circulation somewhere, that would solve the first mystery as to its whereabouts and verify that the old man had simply got his facts wrong or that his memory was fading in his later years.

'When you say "ever", do you mean literally since the gallery was founded?' queried Franz. The archivist was reluctant to undergo a thorough search without further clarification.

'Almost,' replied Ciara. She was aware that the so-called 'new' Basel art gallery had been founded in 1928. 'Can we go back to 1944? No, on second thoughts, to be on safe side, 1939?'

Franz cast a quizzical look, instantly recognising that the Second World War had some bearing on the Loans Assistant's search.

'I can let you pore through the files for the 1930s and 1940s. They are separate. Grab a seat at the spare desk, if you like and take your time,' he added amiably. 'If you need a longer look it'll have to be a photocopy with my authorisation.'

'I know,' Ciara replied, as she was familiar with the procedure. 'What letter is it?'

'D,' she answered as she followed the archivist along narrow aisles of shelving until they reached the box files marked 1930-39, from which Franz extracted the first file and handed it to her. A few seconds later he passed on a similar file labelled with the following decade. Ciara noted with curiosity that whereas for most countries, even her native Ireland which was neutral in the war, the years from 1939 to 1945 would constitute a section in themselves in any branch of administration, government or otherwise. For Switzerland, however, untouched by the ravages of the conflict raging around her, it seemed to have been business as usual. Ciara was unsure whether to feel comforted and assured or bewildered and bemused at that realisation. The same sized file, no bigger, no smaller, represented the decade that contained the conflict.

She thanked Franz and settled down to peruse the documents. The first file was something of a long shot and she was not surprised to find no clues in her search. It was very unlikely that the painting she was researching would have come to light in the first few months of the war, less still be transported over the border into Switzerland. Had she more time to study the data at leisure, she would have enjoyed piecing together the development of the gallery as various contacts were established with museums and galleries across Europe, partnerships forged and letters sent to the Neue Basler Kunstgalerie expressing heartfelt appreciation for their efforts to further Basel's reputation as a city of culture. She paused occasionally to scan the odd newspaper cutting that referred to an artist beginning with the letter 'D' but did not linger as the individual targeted was not mentioned. After discarding the 1930s file, she opened the one for the ensuing decade with eager curiosity. It was noticeable, though not unexpected, that the first half of the decade was relatively sparse with almost no communication regarding loans as the rest of the continent was in the throes of conflict. The file became much denser as the '40s came to an end but still no sign of any work by the painter in question being displayed in Basel, or any indication of the whereabouts of the painting.

Ciara puffed out her cheeks as she closed the second file. The fruitless quest for information was not unexpected, but frustrating, nonetheless. She realised that she would have to allot time to check the subsequent decades to rule out the possibility that the painting the old man wanted to track down had never passed through the gallery's hands. She glanced at her watch and noticed over an hour had passed. She would need to return to her desk. Normally she would be quite happy to relegate such an enquiry to the bottom of her work pile, to be resumed at a convenient moment. Yet the nagging feeling would not leave her that this was an issue that needed to be resolved without delay. She would need to exercise persistence to acquire the information.

Chapter Four

Calais-Bâle

As he entered the carriage at Calais-Maritime that lunchtime in mid-July, Bear was gratified to notice that he was its first occupant, a happy occurrence that afforded him the privilege of the prime position of a window seat, facing the direction of travel. He placed his rucksack on the overhead luggage shelf and inserted his holdall alongside after extracting his novel for later entertainment. The blue cagoul he had been wearing simply for pocket space to house peppermints, some loose change and most importantly, his passport, could now be discarded for a few hours. The warm temperatures meant that the extra layer was redundant, even with the freshening sea breezes on arrival at the port. He was pleased to place the coat next to his seat as a challenge to anyone contemplating sitting next to him. If possible, he would prefer the luxury of space for the hours ahead on the historic line across northern France and into Switzerland.

In fact, the train was barely a third full as the remaining passengers descended from the ferry and boarded the various carriages. School holidays had yet to begin for all except the independent schools in England and the annual rush of the first week of August in France was still a couple of weeks away. Hence, Bear was able to settle into the quaint 1930s-style carriage unhurried and take in the scenes around him.

His hope of a compartment to himself was dashed, however, as a thin, wiry man in his forties with a mop of untidy curly light brown hair entered and smiled in acknowledgement of his fellow passenger. The stranger stowed away his luggage in identical manner to Bear, although his baggage consisted of a suitcase and briefcase. From the latter he removed a newspaper which he proceeded to peruse once he had occupied the middle seat with his back to the direction of travel. He seemed perfectly happy to keep himself to himself, which, for the moment, suited Bear fine.

Bear was determined to savour what he could of the journey which had been recommended to him by his colleague in the history department, Peter Walton, a known railway enthusiast. The Calais-Bâle line, usually referring to the Swiss city by its French spelling, was renowned as one of the original lines to cross France in the heyday of passenger rail transportation, providing the well-to-do with access to the continent, and in particular, the Swiss ski resorts at a time when air travel was in its early, untried phase. It persisted with the enclosed compartments, limiting the number of occupants to six per compartment and thus enabling those seated within to be shielded from the noise in the rest of the train. Peter had warned him that the line was under threat as there were moves in French government circles to redirect all long-distance rail traffic from the UK to central Europe via Paris, as nowadays skiing enthusiasts flew to their destinations and eschewed the wearisome trek across northern France.

'It's now or never, if you want to try out this famous old line,' Peter had advised Bear ruefully when his fellow historian had mentioned he was considering the overland route.

'They can't do that!' Bear had reacted in mock horror. 'First Settle-Carlisle and now this. What is the world coming to?' he asked, as much to himself as to Peter, referring to the scenic, but uneconomic line across the moors of northern England that culminated in his parents' home city, a line that was threatened with closure. He had taken advantage of a visit to the border region the previous summer to sample the famous railway and savoured the captivating hillside landscape as the locomotive surged majestically through the Pennines. The flatlands of northern France, though less spectacular than his previous rail journey, had nevertheless been one of several motivators for Bear selecting the overland passage, given their proximity to the Belgian border. The historic nature of the line and the waning opportunities to experience it was a second. Cost was a third consideration, as the cheap airlines had yet to cover his required route. And a fourth attraction was simply to reactivate his carefree student days and transfer all the responsibility for getting to his destination on the SNCF instead of the stress of driving across swathes of French countryside.

He cast his gaze at a black and white photograph above the seating opposite. He could just about make out the title, 'La plage à Deauville, 1925' and smiled to himself as he took in the beach scene. A moustached gentleman relaxing on a deckchair, still wearing tie and breeches, the rolled-up sleeves his solitary concession to a warm summer's day, looked on as a lady with ankle-length skirt, long-sleeved blouse and bonnet, presumably his wife, directed their two equally well-dressed children in the art of sandcastle building. He reflected on what passed for relaxation back in the twenties. A quick twist of the neck enabled him to survey the corresponding picture above

50

the seating facing the direction of travel and notice similarly soberly attired couples taking the air in a park in Basel at a similar date in the past. Certainly, Bear could not complain about any lack of atmosphere engendered by his surroundings as the train finally moved off towards a short stop in Calais-Ville and into the countryside for the six-hour journey eastward.

After the suburbs of the channel port gave way to the flat landscape, not unfamiliar to Bear living as he did in East Anglia, he picked up his detective novel for some diversion. The coincidence of four murders with similar modus operandi in the heart of Paris had been noted and exercised the reasoning powers of the famous detective assigned to solve the crime and arrest the perpetrator. He discarded the novel as Maigret found himself, temporarily, of course, baffled by the motivation behind such heinous crimes. Bear profited from his prime window seat to survey the scenery, at the same time happy to let the experiences of the school year just completed ease into proper perspective and no longer exert the all-consuming pressure that was often felt in term-time. The daily grind of class management, preparation for appropriate delivery of lessons, the marking, advising, exhorting, writing of reports and regular dealings with parents demanded what felt like constant attention with minimal weekend pauses for breath. His mind turned to occasional brief escapes such as the recent visit to the Constable Centre as little oases in the desert of the educational treadmill and smiled as he recollected the banter that he had experienced with the sixth-formers that day. Not to mention the reference to the mysterious painting of Huguenots fleeing to Switzerland. It was not lost on him that he would be probably pursuing the same route as many of

51

those exiles in the course of the afternoon.

It was not all grind, of course. He could recall a number of humorous moments within the classroom and staffroom and enjoyed the company of most of the pupils and his colleagues. Yet he was always relieved when the school year came to an end; the opportunity to mark a firm conclusion and aim to be refreshed for a few weeks before September came around and the challenge of a new school year began. For that reason, he was always keen to depart on some holiday venture as soon as term finished, to draw a line in the sand immediately and experience an environment that had nothing to do with education – no class lists, no marks, no school rules, no talk of syllabi, exam requirements or targets.

Of course, he could never shut off his identity as a historian completely. He stared at the stark, unchanging countryside and inevitably started to recall topics he had delivered that concerned the regions he was passing through. The Western Front and its grinding, tortuous trench warfare as the competing armies in the First World War strove to drive the enemy back to another layer of trenches at huge cost to human lives and the gain of a few hundred metres of land. He marvelled at the dullness of the scenery that dominated for mile after mile and soon drifted into musing mode. Another 'what if' question came to mind. What if you were to be stationed on the front and saw comrades fall around you and survived in squalid conditions and your net gain (or even loss) was a few yards of terrain? How would you react if your commanding officer announced that for all your efforts for King, country and empire all you had achieved that term was a few measly yards?

Snap out of it, Bear, he told himself. He was well known

at school for his 'what if' questions as he deliberately tried to instil the element of empathy into any historical situation, encouraging his pupils to imagine they were experiencing the circumstances in question. His more conservative Head of Department Michael Streatham's concerns that Bear that was in danger of neglecting factual content at the expense of the imagination were, in Bear's mind at least, solidly rebutted by his students' impressive results in public examinations .

Bear was wont to soak in the atmosphere of any significant site and let his imagination have free rein, as now in northern France. However, that was enough reflection for now, he said to himself and returned to his detective novel, keen not to allow too may school reminiscences to dominate his thoughts. He looked forward to a dreamy few hours of escapism away from serious academic deliberations, giving his mind a rest from such weighty questions. He had a relatively quiet compartment with just the one other occupant who seemed absorbed in his newspaper and could switch off before enjoying the sights and sounds of Switzerland and meeting up with Tim that evening. The serenity of escapism did not last long.

'Ah, Maigret,' Bear heard from his travelling companion about an hour into the journey, '*Vous aimez les romans de…*?' The curly-haired individual spoke with a heavily anglicised accent as Bear instinctively raised his novel so that the full title was visible.

'Ah, you're English, I presume?' the stranger continued before completing his question in English, 'so you like Simenon's novels, then?'

'Well, I find they help pass the time,' Bear replied in non-committal fashion.

'They certainly do that,' acknowledged the other. 'More intricate than Christie's Poirot, I find. Retains a bit of subtlety in the plot. Keeps you on your toes more.' He spoke in an educated, almost upper-crust accent with clearly enunciated vowels, not speaking too quickly so that his hearer felt duty-bound to take in every syllable and accord him full attention. Yet even in imparting his words at a measured pace the enthusiasm for the subject came across immediately, so much so that Bear, although planning to consecrate the journey to his own thoughts and his novel entirely, found himself drawn into conversation against his will.

'Really? How do you notice that?' Bear asked.

For the next twenty minutes Bear was lured into a virtual monologue on literary techniques of the great thriller writers, their biographies, insights on life and respective merits as authors. Only then did the two travellers exchange personal details.

'I'm Charles Carraway, by the way, although friends call me Chas,' the loquacious one said, offering his hand, which Bear took and responded in kind.

'Bear Hoskins, good to meet you, Chas,' he said.

'A "Bear"? Now that *is* interesting, if not unique, at least in English. I've met four people called Lion, at least three Tigers and several Cats, but you're only the second Bear I've come across. How did you come to have such a name?'

Inevitably, Bear felt compelled to explain the origin of his being named after a 1960s Swedish drummer. 'So you're interested in animals?' he asked. He soon wished he hadn't.

'I have a professional interest. I teach philosophy at university and specialise in biosophism.' As Bear looked blank at the mention of the term, Chas proceeded with an explanation. 'It's still seen as a bit wacky by most of my colleagues, so it's relegated to a subsidiary subject, but we have a few takers and a growing fan base, as it were. Biosophism is the branch of philosophy that sees wisdom in all life forms, in the most obscure behaviours of any living being you come across. You can derive some fascinating life lessons from observing ants at work, the flight of geese or the antics of a squirrel.'

'Sounds intriguing,' commented Bear politely.

'Not intriguing enough for my colleagues yet, though,' lamented the philosopher. 'But it'll come. It will be a mainstream subject before long,' he added confidently. 'So what brings you on to this line heading out to Switzerland?'

Bear replied that he was visiting a friend in Basel on holiday and felt compelled to ask whether Chas was also in vacation mode.

'No, on professional business,' he responded. 'We have a conference in Zürich starting the day after tomorrow. Biosophists from all over Europe.'

'You didn't think of flying, then?' Bear queried.

'Good Lord, no! Always travel overland if I can. You always spot something of interest. I'm doing a seminar on garden birds' behaviour and how their occupation of certain favoured positions in the garden tells us about their perceived sense of hierarchy and desire to transmit this to all other occupants of the garden. Fascinating stuff. I don't suppose I'll see much garden life on this route, but there's always something to spot if you keep your eyes open.'

Chas gazed out of the window contentedly, seemingly someone in his element. Bear smiled cautiously and gradually returned to his novel, deeming the right amount of attention to have been given to satisfy the demands of politeness.

The train pulled in to the third stop along the journey somewhere in the Picardy region. As with its two predecessors, just a handful of passengers boarded the train, and Bear and Chas were spared further company. The train remained in the station for some five minutes, at the end of which what to Bear's ears came over as a muffled announcement was transmitted over the platform's loudspeakers. In response to Bear's puzzled look, Chas translated the gist of the information.

'Some blockage on the line just being cleared. We should be on our way in about ten minutes. Could be worse, I suppose... ooh, I say! This could be interesting,' he broke off suddenly, pointing to a rooftop of a house adjacent to the station. Again, Bear could only offer a bewildered expression as he looked at an unremarkable, functional edifice, until his companion directed his vision more precisely. 'Look at the roof and the television aerial.'

'Just a few birds,' muttered Bear.

'Watch them,' invited the philosopher. 'Watch how they change positions.'

So began Bear's unplanned initiation into the ways of the Biosophists. On the rooftop either side of a central chimney stood six or seven starlings in a row. A few feet above them on an aerial attached to the chimney were resting three others of their kind. After a few seconds one of the three highest birds flew off and its colleague positioned nearest to the chimney automatically assumed the first bird's place. Once that space had been vacated, the other starlings shuffled along to the middle and a newcomer adopted the outermost position to make up the numbers.

56

'And now watch the other side,' Chas alerted Bear eagerly. Sure enough, the innermost starling on the other side of the central chimney took over from another bird on the top, as if both realised that the time had come for a changeover.

'It's their innate sense of hierarchy,' explained the professor.

'Seems more like first come, first served,' observed Bear. 'Whoever arrives first gets the best view. Although I wonder why they don't stay on top long.'

'They don't want to overstay their welcome or feel too big for their boots. And they want to earn favour with the others next time they're on the bottom rung. Look at that gap created on the right.' In the middle of one of the lower groups a starling flew away, presumably bored with proceedings or pursuing a better option, but instead of its neighbour automatically shuffling to close the gap, it stayed in position, allowing the outermost bird to take off, flutter its wings and glide for a few feet before placing itself in the recently vacated space.

'Why aren't the others complaining about such queue-jumping?' asked Bear. 'If they've all patiently waited their turn to get to the highest perch, why do they all ow a newcomer to barge in?'

'The newbie was probably owed a favour because he gave way the other day, or shortened his time on the aerial, I would expect,' answered Chas confidently, not arrogantly or flippantly, but as one with a genuine interest in his subject and enjoying the confirmation of the theories he had formulated over many years. 'A huge sense of fair play and community spirit these starlings have, you know. Have you ever seen a murmuration in action?'

57

Bear's baffled look was answered by patient explanation as to how starlings gather and produce the most spectacular display of flying skills, often at twilight in late winter and early spring with the dexterity of a team of highly trained acrobats. The starlings, as conversation ensued for much of the remaining journey, proved but one example of philosophical principles derived from nature as Chas enlightened his fellow passenger with observations on the habits of a range of creatures and lessons to be drawn from them. As the flat scenery started to give way to the more hilly, wooded country of Alsace and the Swiss and German borders became nearer,

Bear was becoming surprisingly better informed and more stimulated than he had imagined at the beginning of the transit. He was in the role more of listener than speaker and his few comments about teaching history in Suffolk and a sprinkling of holiday reminiscences served as mere punctuation in the catalogue of observations on the animal kingdom.

When the train drew into the SNCF station at Basel, still officially part of France until passengers had shown their passports on alighting from the train, the philosopher, who was staying on to Zürich, wished Bear a happy stay in Basel. Bear thanked Chas for his company and wished him a successful conference. With his head in a spin from the ornithological stimulus, he stepped into the early evening sunshine for what he assumed to be a relaxing vacation.

Chapter Five

Rustic Retreat

Had the captain dwelt long enough on the fortunes of war and the irony of his unit's situation, he would have been unable to contain his mirth. A rueful smile did cross his lips occasionally as the military truck carrying a dozen men, fast dwindling supplies of munitions and a few chosen items of plunder tore through the Alsace countryside. Whilst still, officially, part of the Reich, the region had not been characterised by unfettered loyalty to a country it had only been reconnected to some four years earlier after an enforced separation of twenty-one years. The weary ambivalence of the populace was not lost on the combatants of the infantry division as black humour was the order of the day. Whilst Hauptmann Gerhard Schlessinger was not party to all the quips often expressed out of an officer's earshot, in lighter moments his lance corporal felt sharing some of the caustic remarks with the captain would do no harm and not incriminate anyone.

The pair shared the cab with the driver, Kraftfahrer Winkelmann who drove on impassively as Feldwebel Brandl passed on some of the comments he had heard the previous evening that would pass what he perceived to be the captain's censorship rules concerning maintenance of morale. Occasionally, Brandl opted for the cloak of anonymity to preserve the speaker's identity in case any gloomy thoughts be deemed treasonable.

'The Alsatians are a funny lot. You never know where you are with them. When we introduced conscription in '40, they weren't all champing at the bit. Someone suggested we get a megaphone when we enter the next village and do a recruitment drive for all able-bodied men under forty.'

'What, and ask them to join our merry band?' asked Schlessinger. 'I can't see that happening, *Feldwebel*. Let me guess, one of Baumann's quips?'

'I am sworn to secrecy. Have to protect my sources,' Brandl declared with a simulation of propriety before adding, 'besides, if I were to report everything being said, there aren't many who wouldn't be up for court martial.'

'True,' acknowledged the captain. 'At least they're having something to laugh about. God knows, there's been precious little of that these past few months.'

The tide of the war had turned, irrevocably as it was to transpire, against Germany. As mild October had given way to damp, dreary November, General Patton's Third Army had been making rapid progress towards the Rhine and with the limited, sparingly deployed radio contact the previous evening Schlessinger had been able to discern that Metz had fallen, with Strasbourg firmly in the Allies' sights. The proud assertion that Alsace still belonged to the Reich was being exposed as a vain hope. Schlessinger's unit, cut off from other vehicles heading east, was left with the solitary option of retreating beyond the Rhine and being available for a counter-offensive thought most likely to occur at the turn of the year. If they could reach the former border in time before being intercepted by Allied units. The French forces had liberated

Belfort and the window was closing fast.

If the Swabian unit of the Wiesbaden-based infantry division expected any sympathy from the Germanic province, it was at best restrained. Few ventured on to the streets as German military vehicles passed. A few brave, if foolhardy youths, brought up solely under French rule, ventured a few crude gestures as the truck hurtled by. Brandl had asked for directions and received a clear, confident reply from an older man in perfect German, only to discover that they had been misdirected to the tune of several kilometres. The ambivalence to the Nazi regime and belonging to the Reich was manifestly gripping the province.

'It looks like they are waiting to see who wins,' had been Schlessinger's observation. 'Can you blame them?' Brandl replied pointedly.

Schlessinger was minded to ask Winkelmann for an update on the fuel situation, but checked himself, having been informed an hour before that supplies were running low. If they couldn't get over the Rhine on what was in the tank, they would have to go foraging for any fuel that might still be available on farms, a very long shot indeed. They passed through a village with a few older inhabitants bothering to step outside to witness the depleted Swabian infantry's passage through a gloomy, featureless main street. The truck proceeded to meander through woodland as the road began to rise a couple of minutes after exiting the village. It was then that Winkelmann uttered a curse and the engine stuttered as if experiencing a coughing fit and cut out completely. The driver applied the handbrake, tried to restart the vehicle, but in vain. His look across to the captain said it all. The fuel had run out within a few kilometres of the Rhine crossing.

Schlessinger's barely functional watch confirmed that it was approaching four in the afternoon. Darkness would soon descend on the Alsace countryside. The options were limited. He considered sending some men into the village to find out if any diesel was available at any property but conceded that was an unlikely prospect. In any case, it would take at least a couple of hours to reach the village on foot. Brandl pointed out a track they had passed on the left as they had ascended the rise that had proved to mark the end of the truck's resistance. Perhaps that would lead to farm buildings, at the very least providing shelter for the night and giving them time to rethink before pushing across the river on the morrow. The lance corporal suggested taking a few men to investigate and reporting back in an hour.

'Good idea, *Feldwebel*,' Schlessinger assented. 'Take three with you and a jerry can. Who knows, you might even strike gold with fuel.'

Brandl had no difficulty finding volunteers as the weary band of infantrymen looked up as he called up to the occupants of the back of the truck. They were only too glad to stretch their legs and have some task to fulfil after the mind-sapping hours on the road. The selected detail duly trudged back towards the turning to begin their quest.

Their return some two hours later brought little positive news. There was a farm over a kilometre up a dirt track, but it had been scaled back considerably after the ravages of war. An elderly farmer with heavily accented German had bitterly announced that all his fuel had been commandeered and that he and his wife were left with poultry and a few pigs to eke out a meagre subsistence. Brandl had immediately recognised that the old man had no reason to lie and probably even had pro-German sympathies, having grown up in the region when it was still under Prussian control. As the lance corporal returned along the track, he directed his men into a small farm building, a barn capable of storing hay for regular disposal. Brandl had remarked to the farmer about the structure earlier, but the old man had shrugged his shoulders as if to say that he hardly used it these days, as the mechanical ability to tend his fields had been taken away from him. Brandl took that as assent to have a poke around the barn, and shortly afterwards reached the truck to report back to Schlessinger.

'Just various bales of hay, would make a relatively comfy bed for some of us, at least, if we don't mind the rats,' was the lance corporal's summary. His confirmation that the fuel supplies had not been forthcoming was no surprise.

With resignation Schlessinger announced to the men that they would be spending the night, possibly two, in the barn and making more extensive enquiries concerning fuel in the morning. In the meantime, the truck would be emptied of all content so that looters, even on this desolate landscape, would not have the opportunity to break in and help themselves to any weapons. They would have to make their rations stretch for a couple of days and adapt to their temporary quarters.

So it was that at half-past six on a damp, dreary late November evening, had there been any onlookers other than wildlife, they would have observed some twenty German infantrymen transporting various items of weaponry, food supplies and a few curious looking objects not apparently serving any practical purpose. If suspicions that a bizarre midnight picnic was being prepared had arisen, they would not have been entirely fanciful. Two of the more junior privates were tasked with carrying three almost square, but

63

relatively flat items, each protected with strong cardboard and sealed in string. Schlessinger instructed them to be placed in a pile and transported with a carrier at either end. Whilst not the heaviest of items, they were cumbersome in the extreme and placed demands of teamwork between the two assigned transporters to walk in time with each other.

When out of earshot of the captain, the inevitable groans and grumbles were exchanged between privates Piehler and Klammt.

'So, these are Schlessinger's souvenirs from his time in Champagne,' muttered Piehler from behind.

Klammt barely turned his head in reply, eager to complete the uncomfortable mission with maximum expediency. 'I can't see much sign of Champagne here. I don't know what is so important that it needs to be kept from looters.'

'Not exactly perfume from Paris for his lady friend, is it?'

Piehler's comments were cut short by Brandl exhorting them to keep quiet and get a move on. Half an hour later they had reached the sanctuary of the little-used barn. Judicious use of torchlight indicate d several surprisingly neatly stacked bundles of hay which could serve as bedding for perhaps half the contingent. Schlessinger decided on a sleeping rota so that they would all have the benefit of at least a few hours on the softer surface while the rest had to make do with the dusty stone barn floor. Rations were restricted to biscuits and acorn coffee as the company tried to settle down for an early night with the intention of an early start the next day to forage in earnest. The late evening card games that had been a feature of the unit's entertainment in the summer months had long since been discarded through insufficient daylight.

Schlessinger was not prepared to allow precious torchlight to be sacrificed on such trivia, no matter his concerns for the men's morale in experiencing some form of diversion. Before turning in he instructed radio operator Vering to contact what passed for their mobile HQ. He was gratified that Vering was able to get through without undue delay. The reply from the operator at the end of the line required the original plan to speak to a more senior officer to go out the window, and radically altered Schlessinger's plans for the night.

'Where are you, Gamma?' Gamma was the name assigned to the set attached to their vehicle. On hearing Schlessinger's imprecise description of their location, the voice at the end of the line became more urgent. 'You need to get the hell out of there now, Gamma. Have you heard about Strasbourg…?'

Once the news of the chaotic, rapid abandonment of Strasbourg filtered through and the proximity of French and American forces became clear, the sleeping arrangements for the Swabian infantry were abruptly torn up. The few who had dozed off were rudely awaken, instructions were issued for the transport of the realistically portable supplies and the troop prepared to leave the barn and head towards the Rhine as fast as possible, on foot, on largely empty stomachs. Most of the heavy weaponry was abandoned and anything too bulky or burdensome was also left in the barn. Once the men had exited, Schlessinger asked Brandl to have them all wait outside while he re-entered for a 'final check'. He hesitated as he spotted the three cardboard cladded objects that Piehler and Klammt had so valiantly transported earlier that evening. Extracting the largest of the three, he heaved it free and slid it across the barn floor to a corner of the barn where some disused wardrobes were being stored next to some farm tools. He quickly dismissed the initial hiding place as impractical and was about to abandon his project when he spotted a viable alternative. He took a couple of minutes to insert the chosen item into a secure position, long enough for Brandl to feel obliged to call out.

'You all right in there, sir? Need any assistance?'

'No, all sorted out now, Brandl. Time to move off.'

And they did just that, covering the remaining, as it turned out, eight kilometres to the Rhine and crossing just after four the following morning. The province of Alsace was shortly liberated from German control and none of the infantry troop returned even after the war. The aborted night in the barn proved a little-told story of minimal significance in the years that followed amongst those who survived the conflict, although few could have anticipated the building's significance that was to emerge come the end of the century.

Chapter Six

A Blast from the Past

If the unorthodox nature of the one-sided conversation with Professor Charles Carraway had left Bear feeling he had been drawn into a parallel universe, there was a comforting antidote as his friend greeted him at the entrance hall of the SNCF station.

'Bear Hoskins! You survived the Calais-Bâle line and lived to tell the tale!' Tim Sheldon exclaimed warmly. 'How are you, my friend?' he asked as he enveloped the weary traveller with an appropriate bear hug.

Bear grinned as he responded to the greeting of his old school friend he had not seen for four years. The inviting, almost provocative tone of voice with which Tim referred to the rail journey just completed suggested he had some knowledge of the curious encounter Bear had had with his fellow passenger. Bear felt noticeably relaxed, despite his fatigue, and encouraged to enlighten his host with his experience of sharing a compartment with such an expert in the field of biosophism. He decided to save the details for later, once more conventional topics had been discussed. He was unaware that he was not the first person to benefit from Tim's engaging humour that week, although it would not have surprised him had he known.

Tim directed his guest along a short ten-minute walk in

the early evening sunshine towards his flat. Turning into a narrow pedestrian street, they entered an imposing block of solid 1920s stone adjacent to a convenience store. After stepping out of the lift to alight on the third floor, they entered Tim's flat, far removed from the model of bachelor decadence of Bear's own abode in Suffolk. It seemed the Swiss neatness and efficiency had left its mark on Tim as there was scarcely an item out of place. Newspapers and magazines were neatly stacked away, an attractive three-piece suite and coffee table dominated the spacious living room and a separate dining area adorned one corner of the same room. He had assembled several ornaments of pottery to decorate a sideboard and a few prints of presumably Swiss mountain scenes hung on the walls. The sideboard also housed several framed photographs mainly of people of similar age to Tim and Bear, enjoying skiing, camping, rambling and other outdoor activities. A very comfortable existence, thought Bear, he has obviously done well for himself.

While Tim changed out of his work clothes, Bear gazed at one of the photos which showed Tim with his arm around a smiling young woman in some woodland setting, both equipped in walking gear for the great outdoors. As Tim returned from his bedroom, he noticed Bear's gaze and remarked cheerfully,

'Ah, I see you have met Sarah! You will get the opportunity to be properly acquainted with my young lady tomorrow.'

'Sounds good,' replied Bear. 'I'll look forward to it.'

'She thought it prudent not to appear tonight so as to let us have a boys' night in, as she put it. Or as I put it, a boys' night out. Your choice?'

On Bear asking what the options for the evening were, Tim suggested heading to a popular bistro around the corner, his 'go-to' solution if Sarah wasn't around and he didn't feel like cooking. Decent food, reasonable prices for Switzerland, was the reinforcement that was required to entice Bear out for the evening.

After they had chatted concerning respective employment, social life and relationships on the way to the bistro, it seemed natural for Bear to enquire as to his host's relationship with Sarah. Tim revealed that she was an accountant at the bank and that they had been going out for just over a year. While they surveyed the menu and after toasting each other's success on receiving two glasses of beer, Tim was happy to supply a description of his lady's qualities. 'Pragmatic, not the most creative individual in the world on her own admission, but great at spotting problems. And pretty stunning, of course, don't you think, but I would say that, wouldn't I? You'll see for yourself tomorrow evening.'

As Tim had paused for dramatic effect, Bear gazed at his friend inquisitively to assure him of his full attention and allow him to maximise the impact of the announcement. Bear guessed that Tim was about to declare, given his flamboyant use of language, that he was planning a culinary soirée.

'I'm holding a little, shall we say, culinary soirée, in which my cooking talents will be laid on the line.'

'Sounds exciting, and very brave,' observed Bear.

'It's not my first effort by a long chalk. I have developed my wizardry in the kitchen since I've been in Basel. Mind you, I'm glad you weren't subjected to some of my earlier efforts. The gang have been very tolerant of my faltering attempts at haute cuisine. You'll meet some of them tomorrow.'

'Sounds intriguing. So who are the members of this gang?' Bear asked, suddenly becoming aware that he was responding to Tim's pronouncements with 'sounds' followed by a supportive adjective and resolved to vary his manner of complimentary observations.

'There's Sarah, of course, Mark and Chantal – they both work at the bank in an adjacent office to me, and Bee – she used to work with us but left to work in a gallery a few years ago. It should be—'

'Bee?' Bear interrupted.

'Well, Ciara, to give her real name,' clarified Tim, emphasising the middle syllable. 'We always called her "Bee", as in busy bee, as she was always buzzing around, getting things done. Always on the go.'

'Ciara?' Bear repeated Tim's pronunciation. 'Must be of Italian origin,' he mused.

'Hardly,' Tim answered, but did not elaborate as the waiter appeared to take their order.

No sooner had the order been received than Tim was bursting with news. 'Have you heard about Jimmy Watkins?'

'Can't say I have,' Bear replied. 'What's he been up to?'

'He's just become national ballroom dancing champion, him and his partner! I never knew he was into that sort of thing.'

'Can't remember him volunteering for the Tango Experience,' Bear remarked, recalling the name of the sixth-form ballroom dance club that was set up during their schooldays. 'Mind you, he could have done no worse than the pair of us, with our two left feet!'

'Well, my two left feet for sure. You seem to get the hang

of the Latin steps after a while. I'm no better, alas, as Sarah will gladly testify.'

'Well, as they say, it's the taking part that counts.'

'Just as well in my case. You could say the same about my skiing, two left feet. Took me ages to master after moving here. At least now I can get down the mountain without falling over all the time. I'm not going to break any Olympic records, though...'

And so the evening continued with a flow of merry reminiscences from schooldays, recent challenges at work and interesting holidays and visits they had undergone. After the memories had been concluded for the evening, Bear had little difficulty drifting to sleep in Tim's spare room and was woken by his host who was about to leave for work. Cheerful but rushed instructions were issued about Bear helping himself to breakfast, how to operate the keys to the flat and building and where to go to amuse himself in getting his bearings on his first day in the city. Bear thanked Tim with the parting words of his host to pace himself to be on fine form for the culinary extravaganza that evening, for which Bear's assistance would be appreciated.

The rest of the day saw Bear gradually get a feel of the city with a stroll through the Old Town, exploration of the historical museum and a couple of significant churches, and a gentle amble through a park. He wandered into a few shops and a quick calculation confirmed what he had heard about Swiss prices being on the steep side, so he refrained from making any purchases. He was equally frugal as he stumbled upon the Marktplatz, the vast piazza with the imposing Town Hall looking on in distinctive red stone splendour. The ubiquitous pigeons scattered as he cast his eyes at various market stalls, his thoughts periodically interrupted with the planned evening ahead. He looked forward to being acquainted with Tim's 'gang' and imagined that the pragmatic Sarah might just be the perfect complement to his flamboyant host. He wondered how Mark and Chantal had got together, whether Switzerland was as much a draw for a French person as a Brit, and why this Ciara whose name sounded Italian but apparently wasn't had moved on from the bank to work in an art gallery. Some obvious questions to pose to his fellow diners that evening.

As indicated by Tim, Bear had returned to the flat after a day's exploration in time for his host's return at 5.30. After the briefest exchange as to how the day went, Tim had changed and donned an apron with the menu plans at the ready – prawn cocktails, lamb ragout and Eton Mess with coffee and liqueurs to finish. Bear's assistance in chopping vegetables was sought and willingly supplied. Shortly after seven o'clock Tim's intercom buzzed and from his amorous response it was clear that Sarah was the first to arrive. After warmly embracing her and enquiring how her day had gone, he introduced his friend.

'I've heard a lot about you,' declared Sarah with a challenging smile. She was a strikingly attractive young woman with long, chestnut hair and prominent earrings in the shape of shells. It was as if they demanded attention of the person's face between them and communicated the message that this was someone efficient, to be listened to, pragmatic, full of sensible financial advice. Bear formed such an impression in a matter of seconds and wondered if he was letting his imagination run away with itself.

'Some, at least, good, I hope,' replied Bear modestly.

72

'Oh, all good,' confirmed Sarah as she took a seat at one of the sofas. 'I hear you are a historian.'

'That's right.'

'There should be plenty to keep you amused in Basel. Or perhaps you want a break from historical sights while you're on holiday?'

'I suppose in my line of work there's always something to spot. The past is always making itself known, some would say rearing its ugly head.' Was that a quote from some sage in a bygone era, Bear wondered? He hoped it didn't sound too much like a hackneyed cliché.

'Well, let's hope if it does, it proves stimulating for you,' commented Sarah enigmatically. Bear wondered whether such comments were to be proved prophetic. He didn't have long to wait for confirmation.

A few minutes later, Tim responded to his intercom again to let in Mark and Chantal. The former, a stocky individual with the build of a prop forward, grasped Bear's hand heartily and welcomed him to Basel, saying how the place grows on you, but that he had been living there six years and still felt a stranger. Mind you, it had supplied a wife. The lady in question, taller than her partner and slim, exchanged kisses on both cheeks with both Sarah and Tim, and as Bear was standing next to his host, he surprisingly naturally partook of the same salute. As Tim poured various cocktails as the opening to his soirée, Bear found Chantal a particularly good listener with a couple of interesting questions as to Bear's teaching endeavours, although she had to reprimand her husband mildly for throwing in a quip about privilege and long holidays into the mix.

Some ten minutes had elapsed when the intercom

sounded for the final time.

'That must be Bee,' reacted Tim and on hearing a couple of words of greeting, granted his final guest access to the building.

Bear's response to the new arrival was instantaneous. He paused abruptly when responding to Chantal's genuine interest in the rigours of the private school system in England and the demands on teachers' time; his delay in delivering his thoughts elicited amused glances between Chantal and her husband.

The accent was slightly refined but the intonation and sing-song harmony were just the same, even after all this time. It was a voice that still caused a tingling of excitement inside him, heightened by its unexpected appearance. He listened in disbelief as the final guest was ushered into Tim's flat and came into view.

'Bee! Lovely to see you. It's been too long!' exclaimed Tim, who initiated the two-cheek kiss. Bear later speculated whether Chantal's Gallic origins had been the source of that greeting, as Sarah, Mark and Chantal all greeted their former colleague warmly, all commenting on how well she was looking and how they hadn't seen her for ages. 'Ages' meant about six weeks, as Bear later discovered. He watched as an open-mouthed onlooker as the newcomer, with her singing Irish lilt and familiar, ready laugh responded to the embrace of the 'gang'. Then she turned in Bear's direction and before Tim had a chance to make an introduction, smiled inquisitively at Bear and remarked:

'So my hunch wasn't wrong. I knew there couldn't be that many Bears in the woods. Had to be your good self!'

'Hello, Ciara,' mumbled Bear with the emphasis on the

first syllable of her name.

'Is that all you've got to say after all this time? Come on, give us a hug at least.' She enveloped him in a firm embrace to which he responded equally firmly, though in a self-conscious manner.

'You two know each other! I had no—', uttered Tim, momentarily lost for words, and then felt a touch uneasy, as he realised that the pair's relationship had been at one time especially close. He was afraid that Bear or Ciara, or both, might suspect a set-up which could make for uneasy conversation, but Ciara quickly defused the situation.

'It's all right, Timbo, we go back a long way. From your description I had a feeling I had come across your house guest before.'

'I didn't. I had no idea,' declared Bear sheepishly.

The rest of the evening passed as something of a blur for Bear. A brief exchange of details of their respective career histories passed between him and Ciara. She had heard from Tim that Bear had gone into teaching and had not been surprised, although Bear had not expressed any such desire while they knew each other at university. She could imagine him inspiring pupils with hypotheses as to how history could have turned out differently but for certain protagonists' decisions. Bear in turn was not at all surprised to note that Ciara had found a niche in the art world. It was not until well into the meal that conversation turned to their common experiences.

'So am I correct in assuming that you two went out with each other at one time?' Sarah, ever the pragmatist, was keen not to beat about the bush.

'For five, perhaps six months,' Ciara affirmed, turning

towards Bear for confirmation of the time span, to which Bear assented with a nod. 'It was while I was studying history of art at Manchester, and Bear was studying history.'

'An old flame!' Tim responded. 'Who would have thought it? I honestly had no idea,' he added, clearly still wishing to add weight to his earlier apology.

'I see,' declared Chantal, sensing the need to move the conversation on. 'I knew you had some background in art and that's why you left IRB for the gallery.'

'Quite a prestigious background, even,' Bear felt compelled to add. 'Ciara was an EU-funded scholar with Brussels paying for her tuition. No ordinary student.'

'Well, strictly speaking, it was the European Community in those days,' Ciara answered by way of clarification. 'They were kind enough to give grants to people wishing to study history of art and wanted all member states included. I was chosen as Ireland's representative.'

'Ireland's representative, eh? Sounds a bit like Eurovision,' Mark quipped.

'It was a bit like that, with one of the local papers in Limerick making a big deal of it and showing off a photo of me in front of some painting in the local gallery. Our local girl representing Ireland abroad and all that! Of course, the trouble was, even with the expansion in the European Union, I couldn't find any jobs in the field, so went into banking instead, deciding that the path my sister took was worth pursuing. That's how I ended up in Basel with the IRB. The irony was, when I did finally find a job in a gallery, starting to put my degree to good use, it was in a country outside the EU!' Ciara held the attention of the company without difficulty, as they enjoyed the flowing rhythm of her melodious Irish diction. They were reminded of her eloquence when able to relax that contrasted with her occasionally fiery, business-like approach to work they had experienced when she was never to be distracted from the demands of the day's work.

Bear found himself in the unusual position of honoured guest as the evening progressed.

The assembled company seemed only too pleased to hear from a world outside their banking bubble and as the Eton Mess gave way to coffee and they withdrew to more comfortable seats, Bear was prompted to share a few anecdotes of amusing incidents in the classroom and observations of staffroom characters past and present. He was curious to piece together Ciara's movements over the past eight years; she had supplied the headlines in terms of professional advancement, but her emotional development since they last met was still unknown to him. One brief conversation towards the end of the evening indicated that she desired to fill similar gaps in Bear's life history, possibly with the same motive. Her proposal to meet up the following day, if he was free, seemed more of a summons than a request, but nonetheless compelling. The soirée drifted towards its conclusion at half-past eleven and the guests thanked Tim for a successful culinary and social experience with an agreement to 'do this again sometime'. Ciara gave Bear a challenging smile to confirm their arrangement and the guests left together.

'Phew!' exhaled Tim, slumping on the armchair. 'That was the evening that was!'

'Quite a night,' commented Bear. 'A masterpiece of hospitality. If you ever get tired of the banking world, Timbo,

I can see a second career looming. You should keep up these cooking skills.'

'Just a bit of fun, though it can be hard work at times. But what a jolly evening! They certainly seemed to enjoy your schoolmaster tales. Maybe you should write a book one day? It would be amusing if nothing else.' Tim paused, musing and reflecting on the few hours that had passed before continuing. 'One of your old flames, eh? Who would have thought it? You are a man of dark secrets, Bear Hoskins.'

'I wasn't exactly concealing anything,' Bear protested. 'I didn't even know who Ciara, or Bee, was until I heard her accent in the corridor.'

'Mind you, she kept it dark as well. Must have guessed it was you staying with me when I said I had a history teacher called Bear with me. It's almost as though you were plotting something, the pair of you.'

As Bear did not respond other than with a wry grin, Tim continued, 'couldn't help noticing Bee writing something on a card and handing it to you. None of my business, mind you. Say if I'm intruding. Does that mean you two are meeting up this week?'

'Tomorrow lunchtime, at some café near her work. Just to reminisce a bit and talk about a few mutual friends and faces from the past.'

'I knew it! Old flames are the best. Somehow, the fire never quite goes out. But you want to tread carefully. You never know where the flames might lead you.'

Chapter Seven

Fanning the Flame

The following morning provided the last in a sequence of frustrating visits to the archives for Ciara. She had decided her search for details in her 'bequest' enquiry required thorough verification that the painting in question had never passed through the portals of the Neue Basler Kunstgalerie. Having been satisfied that the gallery had no such connection, she thanked Franz for his trouble and said she wouldn't be bothering him further. He expressed regret, saying how he would miss her visits, a declaration which was not issued merely out of politeness but from appreciation for something to engage his mind and keep him on his toes. After her latest investigation in the archives had confirmed that the 1990s had seen no exhibits from Jean Duclos, let alone the relevant painting, she concluded her trail had gone cold and wider enquiries might be called for.

She glanced at the clock and noted half an hour before lunch break, resolving not to consult any missives from Ernst that should appear on the cusp of noon. Her morning, apart from her trip to the archives, had been punctuated by recollections of Bear's appearance the previous evening. She looked forward to their lunch date, curious as she was to find out more of his career and personal history over the past eight years. Inevitably, her thoughts drifted to their university days, of coming across the thoughtful history student who was not afraid of an argument but prepared to conduct it with gentle humour, always ready to put himself in the shoes of the relevant protagonist in history and empathise with his or her dilemmas. She smiled as she recalled how they had been left in the Arts Faculty coffee bar towards the end of their first year after it was announced that a lecture was cancelled through lecturer sickness; the pair of them had continued what had started as a group discussion as the rest of their group dispersed. Up to that point she knew Bear just as a face in the one lecture they had in common. He had been freed to pursue the topic being debated further and Ciara was willing to extend what had become a tête à tête, the first of many.

So had begun a relationship that had lasted a term and a half with numerous outings to cultural events, cafés, pubs, art galleries and parks in and around Manchester. She had warmed to his sensitive speculation on current as well as historical events, and he had enthused at her eye for detail that was a key attribute of a history of art student. When Bear had asked why she hadn't considered becoming an artist, she had responded by assuring him that she wouldn't inflict her efforts at drawing or painting on anybody. It had been a carefree time for those few months as they pursued their studies while living in student halls of residence.

Bear, meanwhile, was relieved to escape from Tim's profuse apologies that morning. He was up and dressed and able to accompany his host at breakfast where Tim still dwelt on the evening before.

'I honestly had no idea I was reigniting an old flame,' he said for the third or fourth time. 'If I'd known…'

His guest strove to conceal a mild irritation at being

reminded of the strange turn of events. 'It's no problem. I'm glad you invited her. It gives us a chance to catch up.'

'Unfinished business, eh?' Tim replied warily, aware that Bear had arranged to meet Ciara for lunch. 'You want to be careful. You never know what embers are still burning.'

'Maybe,' acknowledged Bear. 'But having shared a large chunk of our student life, we could hardly ignore each other. She was asking about several people and I couldn't fill her in on every detail last night. And vice-versa.'

As he wandered the streets of Basel later that morning, having donned baseball cap and sunglasses to shield himself from the fierce central European midsummer sunshine, he grimaced at the thought that conversation might dry up after their initial exchange of details the night before. At least Ciara will have the excuse to return to work after lunch and if discussion descends into a perfunctory box-ticking exercise of finding out about fellow alumni's whereabouts since graduating, they would be able to part naturally without recourse to mumbled embarrassed tones. Yet Bear could not dispel a strong sense that the lunchtime encounter would not be their last of his stay in Switzerland.

He arrived outside the Café Engelchen, having studiously followed his city map, purchased the previous day. He noticed the red and white striped awnings and was gratified to find a vacant table amongst several in a row outside that was comfortably shielded from the sun's rays. He consulted his watch for the umpteenth time to note that at five to twelve he could now occupy a seat and await his companion. In doing so, he gaze d across the street at a modern white stone building with welcoming glass doors and detected that it was indeed the Neue Basler Kunstgalerie. Bold posters advertising current and forthcoming exhibitions adorned either side of the entrance. He was drawn out of his stare by a waitress wanting to take his order and was able to mumble a pre-rehearsed German phrase to indicate he was waiting for someone. No sooner had he done so than a familiar figure appeared across the street.

Dressed in a cream blouse, smart lime green skirt and sandals and carrying a patterned shoulder bag, Ciara emitted a confident, business-like appearance that exuded her femininity and self-assurance that had only been intermittently apparent in the prosaic jeans and sweaters of their shared student years. As she noticed Bear and acknowledged him with a cheerful wave, he took a sharp intake of breath. Here was someone who had grown into her surroundings, he sensed, who was confident in the value and purpose of her position in life. Her wavy light brown hair shone in the midday sunshine, almost adding extra sparkle to her appearance and encouraging Bear to take full advantage of this unexpected opportunity to deepen their acquaintance. Tim's cautionary words about reigniting flames crossed his mind momentarily; he was swift to dismiss them and assure himself that the next hour was all about catching up. They could enjoy a pleasant exchange so long as he steered clear of the issues that had caused them to go their separate ways all those years ago.

After they had greeted each other and Ciara had congratulated Bear on his choice of a shady table just before the lunchtime rush, he was strangely heartened that she seemed so relaxed in the company of one with shared history and tensions. I t was soon apparent that she was eager to share any news that hadn't been included in their initial conversation the previous evening.

'Fancy you showing up in Basel!' she exclaimed. Bear steered a safe course, underlining how Tim and he went back a long way and mentioning the journey from Calais, drawing a laugh from Ciara as he regaled her with the encounter with Chas and the university don's observations on starlings' hierarchical tendencies. She ordered a usual sandwich lunch with iced coffee, which Bear duplicated, and was happy to ask him about his job in Suffolk, an area with which she was not familiar.

'Sounds a bit sleepy to me, you know, out of the way, a bit like the west of Ireland,' she surmised.

'Certainly not as lively as Manchester,' Bear acknowledged.

'So are you involved in a church there?' she enquired. That enquiry did strike him as somewhat direct, especially as she had tended to favour the verb 'involve' concerning his attachment to an evangelical church during much of his student years. He referred to his current membership of Grove Street Baptist Church in Princewood, and added that whilst he attended regularly, he wasn't that 'involved' in term-time, although he had helped out in holiday activities and other projects. It seemed natural, however, to share his participation as a wise man in the nativity production the previous Christmas directed by drama specialist Cynthia Standish, the pastor's wife.

'Ha! A wise man!' Ciara laughed at the thought. 'I can just see you pontificating and predicting the future, or whatever the wise men did. Tailor made for Bear that part, I'd say.'

Brief complimentary notes on Cynthia and her husband Michael elicited a nod from Ciara and an observation that they sounded 'pretty normal'. Bear had the impression that she was holding back from a reference to those evangelical 'extremists' that she had encountered when attending a couple of meetings in Manchester on Bear's suggestion. His retort at the time that anyone with passion was bound to come across as extreme to others hadn't gone down well at the time, and he was wary of reigniting sources of disagreement unnecessarily. For now, such issues were steered clear of as Bear asked Ciara what drew her to Basel in particular and about her experience of the city.

'What drew me?' she retorted with feigned astonishment and a cheeky grin. 'I am genuinely amazed that you can ask such a question.' Bear savoured her harmonious Irish lilt as she emphasised her affected shock by pronouncing each syllable of the adverb distinctly, with the trademark Irish pronunciation of the 'I' as in 'eye'; it had been one of the favourite words Bear liked to hear from the lips of his erstwhile partner. Her reaction raised a knowing smile from Bear; if Ciara identified the source of his amusement, she did not show it as she continued, 'how can you say such a thing? Basel is the cultural capital of Switzerland, I'll have you know. Famous for its museums and galleries, so it is!'

'Well, some would say "you would say that", given your position,' Bear responded.

'But it's true, Bear. I shouldn't say it as a competitor, sorry partner in Basel's cultural experience, but the Stadtgalerie, the main gallery, our big sister, is well worth a visit. Although they tend to go in for more traditional exhibitions than we do. You know, they stick to established schools of painting and are a lot less adventurous than we are. I suppose they don't need to be. Seriously, there is much to explore. Holbein lived here, you know.'

84

'Really?' Bear did not need an introduction to the famous sixteenth-century portrait painter to royalty whose depiction of Henry VIII had been a notable project.

'And Basel is a major heartland of democracy. In 1967, Mister Historian, so I hope you're listening, the population of this fair city of Basel voted in favour of buying three works of art by Picasso that would otherwise have been sold when there was some financial crisis in the owner's family. That means Basel became the first city in the world where the population of a political community democratically voted to acquire works of art for a public institution. Impressive, eh? Quite a "first", isn't it?'

'Very commendable,' commented Bear taking a sip of his iced coffee.

'Apparently, Picasso was so moved by the generosity of spirit that he later gifted the city three additional paintings,' Ciara continued, 'anyway, that's my ambassadorial work for the Basel Tourist Board complete for today. Make sure you visit our gallery during your stay.'

'Oh, I will for sure, Ciara,' Bear assured her, genuinely, at least because she had stirred his curiosity. 'Actually, I thought of you a couple of weeks ago...'

'Oh really?' Ciara asked.

Bear was thus encouraged to share his experience of the trip to the Constable Centre and recollections of conversations with Ciara on art history. He announced that she would have been most proud of him when he supplied the answer to Gisele's teaser by declaring the prominence of the Barbizon School. Ciara affirmed how impressed she was that the knowledge she passed on to him those years ago had not gone to waste and asked what Barbizon paintings or prints had been on display. Bear referred to them as best he could remember, adding that Gisele had made mention of a missing painting concerning travel to Switzerland to add a touch of mystery to her talk. He was about to describe the remainder of that day and the humorous banter with the students on the riverbank when he was sharply interrupted.

'Wait a moment,' Ciara said, raising a palm to persuade her companion to pause. 'Do you remember the name of that painting?'

Bear's knowledge of European history was such that he did not even need to consider before answering. '*The Flight of the Huguenots*,' he said simply. He could not have anticipated the reaction from across the table.

'I don't believe it!' Ciara drew both hands to her mouth in astonishment, not before her louder than intended exclamation had been heard by diners at the neighbouring outdoor table who turned their heads momentarily in amusement. It was a few seconds before she elaborated. 'I need to tell you about something that came up recently.' She paused, searching for the right words with which to launch her revelation. 'A letter that was passed on to me along with a bequest to the gallery,' she explained. 'Are you in a hurry to get anywhere?'

'No, just going with the flow,' Bear replied amiably.

'I'll be right back.'

She rose and headed back into the gallery, returning with a brown envelope in her hand two minutes later. Bear noticed that as she approached the carefree smile of the earlier sighting of her crossing the same road had been replaced by a pensive, almost anxious frown. She resumed her seat and showed him Gerhard Schlessinger's letter. She explained that the former captain in the Wehrmacht had recently died and bequeathed several paintings from his collection to the Neue Basler Kunstgalerie for exhibition or auction, as the gallery saw fit. He added a confession and hoped the gallery could take steps to address an issue that had plagued him and

86

remained unresolved in his lifetime.

'Listen to this bit,' Ciara continued excitedly, translating Schlessinger's epistle as she went, 'he goes on to say,'

"I would like to ask the Galerie to pursue what I will sadly no longer be able to and track down a painting. During the German Army's retreat through north-eastern France in November 1944, our unit stayed a night in a barn outside a village in Alsace. We were short of fuel and planned to commandeer some the next day before crossing back over the Rhine. As senior officer in charge of the unit I took the precaution of having some valuables from our truck moved into the barn for the night. That included, I am ashamed to say, three paintings I stole from our temporary headquarters in Champagne. Two are just charming little landscapes by local artists, but the largest of the three is of more significant provenance. It is a scene depicting the flight of Huguenot believers leaving France for the safety of Switzerland in 1685. I understand it to be a missing painting by Jean Duclos, but I have never been able to verify that.

"Unfortunately, we learned from radio contact of the advancing Allied armies that night and realised we had to leave immediately, so we did; we abandoned the barn, the truck and what we could not carry, including the paintings. I hid them as best I could, hoping one day to return but I never did. Throughout my long, and in many people's eyes, successful life, I have occasionally checked to see if the Duclos painting had been sold or exhibited anywhere, but it has never come to light. If the gallery is able to conduct some research and the painting can be secured, I would like any proceeds to go towards repairing the damage caused by the devastation of the war in which I was a participant..."

Ciara relayed specific wishes of the deceased and explained her dilemma. She felt duty-bound to pursue

87

enquiries as far as they could reasonably be extended. Bear raised an obvious objection.

'Surely it is up to his family to carry out any such investigation on his behalf?' he pondered. 'If he was so wracked with guilt for war crimes, can't his offspring deal with it?'

'That's just it,' Ciara clarified. 'He specifically asks that his son Paul is not informed of the contents of this letter. It seems the family knows only about the actual will, which leaves various paintings and other works of art to his grandchildren.'

'Grandchildren? So, skipping a generation? Sounds like there's not much love lost between father and son. Do we know why?' He was immediately conscious of the inadvertent use of the first-person pronoun and felt uncomfortably drawn into an issue not of his making.

'No idea,' replied Ciara with a shrug. 'Some long-standing family feud, I suppose.'

'No other children to pass his stuff on to?'

'A daughter living in the States, married to an American and very comfortable, thank you, with whom Gerhard hadn't had much contact for years before he died.'

'And this Schlessinger claims to have been successful in his life. In what way?'

'"Schlessinger Glas". It's a well-known manufacturer of ornamental glassware in the Black Forest, not far across the border. Appears he did very well for himself and appreciated the finer things in life. His son Paul took over the reins when Gerhard retired. I don't know why they fell out.'

'Perhaps Paul didn't like the way Daddy ran the business and made sweeping changes,' Bear speculated.

There was a lull in conversation as Bear gazed into the street absently while Ciara studied the closing lines of the letter for the umpteenth time. Slowly she looked up and engaged her companion's attention.

'Are you particularly busy this afternoon?' she asked, offering the sweetest of smiles. Bear braced himself for the inevitable request he knew he would find hard to refuse. It was as though they were frozen in time and the typical conversations of their courting days at university were resurfacing.

***

Less than an hour later Bear had to exercise restraint to avoid muttering to himself, asking how he had been persuaded into the action he was about to take. He had taken a quarter of an hour to cross town and approach the imposing Stadtgalerie, a massive four-storey structure in solid mid-nineteenth-century stone. It specialised in detailed, thorough representations of particular schools of art and eschewed what it deemed trivia. The alternative angles on art movements such as studies in treachery, psychological crises in famous artists and various themed exhibitions were considered beneath the remit of a 'serious' player like the Stadtgalerie. All the above exhibitions had been presented by the Neue Basler Kunstgalerie in recent years and received enthusiastic reviews in the specialist press. Even the NBK's less successful offerings such as the history and evolution of skiing attire in artwork were nevertheless complimented for their originality, boldness and willingness to explore new angles. Such frivolity was not for the oldest and most prestigious gallery in the city. As Bear climbed the dozen steps and entered the building, he perceived that the principal exhibitions involved the works of a French impressionist and the Dutch masters of the eighteenth century. Safe and reliable, he thought to himself, echoing Ciara's earlier somewhat disparaging words.

He noticed a dazzling chandelier dangling from a pristine white ceiling and a solid mahogany enquiry desk to the left of a smaller cash desk. A young woman dressed smartly in a navy-blue suit and striped necktie was finishing dealing with a customer's enquiry. Bear ascertained from prominently displayed badges depicting national flags on her uniform that she was conversant in English and French, as Ciara had anticipated, and communication would not be an issue. As his predecessor in the queue moved away expressing his thanks, Bear braced himself for the unusual request with which Ciara had entrusted him. She had warded off his suggestion that she should make the approach herself by protesting that her face was too well known in the larger gallery from various conferences and cultural events she had attended. Thus, Bear had to bite the bullet and deliver the request as pre-rehearsed in the café an hour ago.

'Good afternoon. I wonder if you can help me…?' he began.

'Yes, sir,' the young woman replied with a warm smile and in immaculate English. 'We will try our best.'

'This is an unusual query, but I'm particularly interested in some painters in the Barbizon School in the nineteenth century. I'm trying to track down some work by Jean Duclos, in particular…'

'Ah yes, sir, you will find work from that period on the second floor. We have a few paintings by Duclos on display at the moment, I believe.'

'I wondered if you have one particular painting, *The Flight of the Huguenots*?' Bear tried hard to disguise his uneasy breathing as he knew full well the answer to that question. If the painting were on display, it would have been common knowledge by now. It was the possible past movements of the work that concerned him. He was relieved, and amused, to note that the gallery employee's response was just as Ciara had predicted.

'One moment, please, I'll see if I can find out for you.' She picked up her internal telephone and dialled. She conducted a conversation in Swiss-German with a colleague in which Bear understood very little except the name of the painting in English. Two minutes later, a grey-haired, bespectacled man in his late fifties approached the desk. The young woman indicated the customer with the query and introduced her colleague as Max.

'I'm very interested in your enquiry, Mr...?' he prompted. 'Hoskins,' Bear supplied.

'Mr Hoskins. We do have an extensive collection from the Barbizon School,' he continued in clear English, delivered with traditionally measured Swiss German diction, 'and a few of Duclos' works, but perhaps you are unaware that this particular painting has been lost for at least fifty years?'

'Oh,' Bear responded with feigned surprise. 'I didn't know that,' he added, trying not to wince at his falsehood. 'Has it never been displayed in this gallery? I mean, with the Swiss theme and the prominence of Basel, I would have thought your gallery might have exhibited it at one time.'

'If we had had the opportunity, sir, we would gladly have done so. Sadly, the painting has not passed these doors in the gallery's history, I can assure you of that. I gather there is some correspondence by the painter that indicates he did construct such a piece, but it has never come to light. I would love to see it if it does!' he concluded with a knowing smile.

'Oh, what a pity!' Bear offered a pained smile to express his fake disappointment that merely confirmed what his café companion had predicted.

'If you come across it on your travels, please let us

know!' Max jested.

Some amiable conversation ensued, at the end of which Bear promised to take Max up on the offer to see the Barbizon School's works on the second floor another time and the former wished him an enjoyable remainder of his stay in Basel. He thanked Max and the employee behind the desk for their help and said he would schedule a gallery visit another day. He turned to exit the building and was about to head into the sunshine when he was approached by a burly gentleman in his late forties dressed in smart shirt and tie but carrying a jacket over his shoulder. Bear felt a little uneasy at this pose as it almost seemed as if the individual was hiding a weapon underneath the jacket.

In impeccable English, if in a less melodic and more prosaic tone than Max moments earlier, he addressed the British historian.

'Excuse me, sir,' he began with rigid Germanic formality, pronouncing each word carefully. 'I am sorry to trouble you, but I could not help hearing part of your conversation. It seems we have a common interest.'

'Oh, really?' Bear asked warily.

'Allow me to explain,' the stranger continued and offered his hand which Bear gingerly accepted, 'my name is Paul Schlessinger.'

Chapter Eight

A Family Business Diverges

'Industrial espionage, eh? At least that's what it sounds like, Bear. You want to be careful.'

Bear absorbed the counsel of his host with a weary smile. If he had heard the excited observation from anyone other than Tim Sheldon, he might have been at best mildly irritated or suspecting the self-appointed counsellor to be stirring matters up for his own diversion. He knew, however, that Tim had the endearing habit of detecting excitement and wonder in the most mundane of situations, a boyish trait he had retained since their schooldays. He was also acutely aware that this was not the first time in the past few days that Tim had advised him to be careful. The admonition concerning stoking up fires engendered by 'old flames', whilst partly motivated by amusement and intrigue, nevertheless transmitted his friend's concern for him. As he gratefully accepted Tim's offer of a cool pre-dinner beer, he decided to clarify the nature of his earlier errand on Ciara's behalf.

'It was hardly espionage. I was asking a question about a painting, and the expert informed me that it was not being exhibited. End of story.'

'All the same, if this Max gets wind that Ciara put you up to it, it could cause a stir in the Basel artistic community,' Tim responded, still in counselling mode. 'You know, using a third

93

party to ferret out information to gain an advantage. You want to be careful he doesn't see you two together and work out you've been plotting something.' Despite having known Tim for so many years, Bear was struggling to determine whether his host was offering his thoughts as an amused observer or a genuinely concerned friend. The suggestion of cultural wars engendered by underhand enquiries would have seemed preposterous from the lips of anyone else; Bear marvelled at how convincing and apparently guileless Tim presented.

'I'm more worried about this Schlessinger chap than what Max whatever his name is might do,' Bear continued. He elaborated on the incident he had just alluded to and how the glass manufacturing executive had declared a common interest in the works of Jean Duclos and presented him with his business card. The German manager seemed put out that as a humble teacher, Bear had been unable to reciprocate. Schlessinger's parting words had been amicable but not without an undercurrent of menace, it seemed to Bear. 'He said, "If you come across any of his paintings, I would be really grateful if you could let me know. It is good to meet someone who appreciates Duclos' works." And then he shook hands with me a second time, nodded respectfully, turned and left the building.'

'Sounds as if he reckons there are things his dad should have left to him, or knew about their whereabouts but didn't let on,' concluded Tim, taking a thoughtful swig of beer. As Bear did not reply other than with a shrug, Tim continued, 'so you reported these findings back to Bee… Ciara?' He made a conscious effort to add the correct pronunciation of her name now that Bear had supplied it the previous evening.

Bear explained that he had called in at the NBK later that

94

afternoon and been informed that Ciara was at a meeting; he had left a message to ring him back at the number where he was staying. He suspected she would do so anyway. As if on cue, the telephone rang in Tim's flat and his reversion to Ciara's nickname immediately identified the speaker. A few pleasantries were exchanged in which she repeated her thanks for Tim's hospitality and compliments on his culinary talents before the phone was handed to Bear to continue the conversation.

Ciara began by apologising for not being available when Bear had enquired late that afternoon to report on his encounter at the Stadtgalerie. She had been summoned by Ernst to go through some proposed exhibits for a forthcoming exhibition, to check they were 'singing from the same hymn sheet', as she put it. She asked initially whether any light had been shed on the missing painting but was not surprised that the answer was in the negative.

She probed further. 'Who did you speak to there? Was it Max?'

'It was,' he confirmed. 'And he was absolutely confident the painting had never been displayed there.'

'Then it hasn't. No question about it. Max is an encyclopaedia. He would know instinctively if a work had ever been on display at the Stadtgalerie. And he's met me before, so I couldn't really ask him directly. So you see why I needed to pass the buck? Sorry if it was a burden.'

'No, it was an interesting little outing, but made more interesting as I was about to leave ...' Bear paused deliberately, so as not to diminish the drama of his encounter with the German glass manufacturer, and also to prepare Ciara for an uncomfortable revelation. He proceeded to recount the

95

details of the conversation, including the hope expressed by Paul that he be kept informed of any developments.

'Sounds a bit creepy to me, this Paul Schlessinger,' Ciara responded warily.

'He seems quite well connected, and not short of funds,' Bear observed. 'I got the impression that he may have suspected the painting is out there somewhere and his late father might be the key to discovering where.'

'Well, it doesn't look as if it's in Basel anywhere. I *am* grateful for your research, Bear, especially while you're on holiday.'

The customary response of acknowledging the gratitude would normally have drawn a line under the enquiry. Bear surprised even himself by his question, directed as much at himself as at Ciara.

'Where else could the painting be?' The historian in Bear struggled to let go of unresolved issues that a bit of investigating could resolve.

'I suppose it may be in France somewhere,' Ciara replied hesitantly. 'Although why it hasn't been publicised, I can't imagine.'

As the conversation descended from the summit of such earnest enquiries to more gentle chatter as to how Bear was planning to spend his holiday in Switzerland, the unspoken speculation in both of them cast a troubling shadow. With vague promises to keep in touch and meet up at least once before Bear returned home, the conversation was concluded amicably. In his case Bear was conscious of Tim's discreet but visible presence in the background. He was wary of conveying anything that could reignite his friend's perception that past passions had not been entirely doused. As he replaced the receiver and remained in thoughtful mode for a few seconds, as did Ciara in another part of the city, he was beset with another pressing thought: after all this time, it surely couldn't be… could it?

**

It was a seemingly throwaway remark by Ernst that provided Ciara with an unexpected opportunity to pursue her apparently stillborn enquiries into Duclos' missing work. Normally, she would discuss bequests to the gallery with her boss at the beginning of each month, first Thursday being the traditional slot, where Ciara would outline proposals for administering such gifts. Ernst would either rubber-stamp his approval, or occasionally, veto her plans and decree that certain items need to be submitted for auction subject to the deceased's family's agreement, on the grounds that exhibition in the foreseeable future was most unlikely. The morning after meeting Bear at the café and his subsequent errand to the Stadtgalerie, Ciara seized the moment when Ernst stepped into her office to talk to Silke, confirming briefly that he had agreed to the latter's holiday request for September. As Ernst turned to leave, Ciara asked to run something by him, wondering if he had been acquainted with the late Gerhard Schlessinger. His reply was illuminating.

'Gerhard? Oh yes, I knew him,' her boss replied, seemingly grateful to be able to expound on a subject of interest long dormant. 'A great supporter of the gallery, he was. I met him at functions a few times, before the cancer got a grip on him, poor chap. I gather he didn't get out much at all in his last years.'

97

'Support? As in, financially?'

'Oh, yes. Regularly responded to appeals and gave generously. He attended a few launch parties for new exhibitions over the years, although quite a few were before my time. I was sad to hear of his passing.'

Ciara's curiosity was stirred. 'Why was he so keen to support a Swiss gallery?'

Ernst, who had been standing, perched his backside on a spare corner of Ciara's desk as he realised a lengthier explanation was in order. 'Well, thereby hangs a tale. It seems Gerhard particularly wanted to favour neutral Switzerland lest Europe be beset by war again. His wartime experiences profoundly affected him, so I hear. He favoured Swiss ideals of liberalism and neutrality.'

'Do you know anything of his wartime experiences?' Ciara queried carefully, wary of overstepping the mark. When Ernst revealed that he could supply no further knowledge, she extracted Gerhard's bequest letter from her in-tray and showed it to him. 'What do you make of this?'

He took the proffered document and began reading. As he did so, his lips pursed as he absorbed the account of the seminal night spent in an Alsace barn in 1944.

'Well I never!' he exclaimed. 'I never knew he was an art thief! Self-confessed, albeit from beyond the grave. Although... I do recall there was a newspaper article years ago insinuating that he may have stolen treasures from France, but it was just a local hack trying to make a fast buck with some overblown story. Or so it appeared at the time, nothing proven. No, old Gerhard always had a reputation for appreciating the fine arts for their own sake and built his business on those lines.'

'Have you ever met his son, Paul?' Ciara could not resist asking the obvious question. The frown appearing on Ernst's brow was revealing, as though he had just bitten on something sour.

'A different character altogether. If, and I would say it's a big if, Gerhard was involved in art theft, it was out of a love of art. You could see it in how his firm was run with the most exquisite glassware and beautiful subtle designs. Since Paul took over, Schlessinger Glas have diversified, and not for the better, in my opinion. They have gone in for crude cartoon designs and much more downmarket stuff in a big way, appealing to mankind's cruder instincts.' As Ciara did not respond, Ernst felt entitled to elaborate in a sort of homily denouncing the woes of poor artistic taste. 'No, for Schlessinger junior art is simply a way to self-aggrandisement. Whereas for Gerhard, art had intrinsic value, to be appreciated for its own sake, for Paul it has merely extrinsic value, a means to an end. If it makes money for Paul Schlessinger, go for it. If not, ditch it. That's his philosophy of art in a nutshell.'

'But he's a businessman,' argued Ciara, making a token effort to present the opposite view. 'He would say the proof of the pudding is whether the glassware makes money.'

'I can't argue with that,' Ernst said with a resigned sigh. 'Call me a snob if you like, but I know I'm not alone. Schlessinger Glas used to be a byword for elegance and quality with intricate designs of classical images on a whole host of items. Now it appeals to the mass market with crude representations of Japanese comic characters and frankly kitsch depictions of tourist sites which for some reason retailers are happy to purchase.'

'But has it worked for the company? Surely that's the bottom line.'

'Well, that's the interesting thing. In the seven years since Paul has had sole charge and introduced these changes, profits seem to have stagnated, and some of the traditional customers have reined in their orders or even cancelled altogether. The loss has been partially offset with new customers, of course, but you could hardly say the diversification has been a roaring success. Now Paul has said that was down to increased manufacturing costs and that the long-term results will justify his change of course, but... well, let's just say the jury is still out.'

Ernst made as though to return to his office, but Ciara delayed him with a final question. 'What would you advise me do in trying to locate this missing painting?'

'If it hasn't shown up anywhere obvious, it's almost certainly lost forever or else never existed in the first place. Don't forget that Gerhard, God rest his soul, was well into his eighties when he wrote that bequest, and I'm not sure he had all his mental faculties. His recollection of those paintings in some barn may be pretty hazy.'

'So, what could I do?'

'There's not much you can do,' Ernst replied with a shrug. 'Maybe check if a similar painting has been recovered in France, but it's unlikely to be a Duclos, or we'd have heard of it by now. I wouldn't waste much time on it if I were you.'

Logically, Ernst was right, Ciara told herself, and a brief word to the executors of Gerhard's will should indicate that the gallery had been unable to carry out the request as the missing painting had not come to light, and probably did not come under its jurisdiction anyway. Yet this was a matter that she could not relinquish and her concentration throughout the rest of the day was fitful. She was not alone in this condition.

**

A rare quiet moment allowed the Chief Executive to gaze out of his first-floor window on to the picture postcard scene of the town of Hirschingen in the Black Forest just to the south of Freiburg. The July heat was inviting as he took in the familiar scene of church spires, narrow medieval streets and beautifully arranged avenues, and he wished he could declare the rest of the day '*hitzefrei* '. Now that *would* be an idea, he said to himself. The joyful experience of his childhood had occurred on perhaps two of three occasions in mid-summer when the mercury hit over 35 degrees Celsius and the rest of the school day was cancelled, 'free through the heat', as German federal law allowed in such rare circumstances. He pondered about making a similar discretionary edict in his position of authority. Just let the whole workforce have the rest of the day off. Why not? Despite air conditioning the working conditions in his office were becoming oppressive as the clock ticked around to his scheduled eleven o'clock meeting. He knew perfectly well why not. First, he himself had meetings to attend with senior managers and suppliers who had travelled from a distance. Secondly, such a move would set a dangerous precedent and be a gift to the unions. He was not obliged to declare work conditions unsustainable in a heatwave, and as long as adequate provision for drinking water and rest breaks was afforded, there was no reason for production to be halted. The machine that was Schlessinger Glas would go rumbling on.

Paul Schlessinger scanned once more the brief for his meeting with senior managers, the weekly gathering to discuss sales, production, marketing and finance. He had a few comments to make on the slow uptake of sales in Italy for certain lines and was curious to know whether the intended slogan applied via transfer to a set of whisky glasses destined for the English-speaking market might include a level of irony beyond the targeted consumer. He was interested to hear his head of marketing's remarks on the subject. He appended a written note to himself to ask.

Wolfgang for any examples of similar irony having been successful in the Anglo-Saxon arena but was convinced the latter would have done his research. Wolfgang was meticulous in his marketing campaigns and even the seemingly wackiest scheme was not the product of a whim. There would be solid reasoning behind the slogan. That was reassuring, Paul told himself, although faintly disconcerting to acknowledge that the most light-hearted of messages could be the source of such thorough discussion.

The Chief Executive was braced for a demanding meeting and wondered when he would have time to consecrate to the extracurricular project that had attracted his attention in recent weeks. His mind returned to the conversation with his wife the previous evening as he was snarled up in traffic returning from his incursion into Switzerland. He had extracted his bulky mobile phone to inform her of his likely delayed arrival for dinner. While stationary in the queue on the autobahn heading north, he was acutely conscious of the faces either side of him gazing at this flamboyant executive with this unusual heavy object glued to his ear. He had deduced their likely thoughts, that he was showing off with his privileged access to new technology for the sole purpose of saying he was going to be late, nothing more profound. And they would be right, of course; the new status symbol was used predominantly to state that he was delayed on the way to or from a meeting. On this occasion, he reflected, Monika Schlessinger's reply had been more probing than usual.

'Where are you? I didn't know you were on the road today,' she had queried.

He knew he couldn't conceal his whereabouts from her. That was one of the drawbacks of a wife working for the firm. Her position as assistant manager of human resources meant that she was acquainted with any planned visits off-site that day. He affirmed that he had popped over the border to see a few contacts.

'Why did you need to go to Switzerland? You met up with the Rheinfelden crew only a couple of weeks ago.' Schlessinger Glas had a distribution outlet in Rheinfelden, just outside Basel, that served the whole of western Switzerland. 'Don't tell me you weren't... oh, please don't say you were asking about this painting, Paul...'

His hesitation was all the confirmation she needed. He had covered his tracks with a half-lie. 'I did manage to make some enquiries as part of my visit, yes, but—'

'It's not worth it, Paul. Even if your dad did have the painting at one time, it's very unlikely he knew where it was when he died. There's no sense in dragging up the past, but I might as well talk to myself about this. When you've set your mind on something...'

'Look, Monika, it might, just might be something of value that could be a major find. No harm in checking.'

'Well, I hope you are not going to be obsessed with

hopping over the border in the next few weeks. Don't forget we're going out with the boys on Tuesday. You haven't forgotten, have you? Celebrating Kai's exam results. Just the sort of thing you'd forget.'

He had sighed and promised he wouldn't forget. He had uttered a brief calculation of his arrival time with the white lie that the traffic was on the move and demanded his full attention, so as not to prolong the exchange.

Paul was brought out of his reverie by his secretary asking if he had time to sign a document before the meeting. He asked her to put it in his in-tray as he gathered his papers before facing his managerial team. As he headed towards the meeting room, thoughts of how to quiz the mercurial Wolfgang Singer with an appropriate witticism proved elusive. 'What is one over the eight, anyway?' he asked himself.

Chapter Nine

Cross-Border Curry

The next few days left Bear in something of a quandary. On the one hand he was keen to optimise the opportunity to discover as much of the country as he could and profit from the freedom of an independent traveller, afforded as he knew in advance that Tim would be unable to secure time off work during the week. However, he was acutely aware that an issue had been sparked by his and Ciara's interest in a particular work of art that seemed to be shared with a glassware executive. He was eager to meet up with Ciara again and at least discover how she was progressing in her enquiries, if any more were to be pursued. He was unwilling, however, to give the impression of wanting to revive former passions from their student days and deemed it wise to leave a few days before re-establishing contact, perhaps for another casual coffee and chat at her favoured café, unless she approached him first. Of course, both had moved on since studying in Manchester and there was no question of restoring any intimate relationship, he told himself. Neither of them had shown any inclination in that direction. Although they had by no means exhausted the topics of conversation to fill in the blanks of the past eight years.

Thoughts of Ciara, the Huguenots and Paul Schlessinger were never far from his mind as he took advantage of the efficient Swiss railway system for a day trip to Zürich. It did not escape his notice that he was heading in the same direction as his erstwhile railway acquaintance Chas and speculated at the remote possibility of encountering the professor in biosophism in that city, if his conference had not concluded by now. He wondered whether a further lecture on starlings or other creatures would almost come as a light relief after the curious developments concerning a search for a lost painting. The sights of Zürich were explored, boxes ticked and his apparent limited enthusiasm for exploration, unusual for Bear, was not lost on Tim over the next couple of days as Bear strolled in the environs of Basel and took in further sights.

Even the weekend's activities, carefully planned by Tim, seemed only partially successful in lifting his guest out of his deep introspective mood. Bear joined Tim and Sarah in a trip to Lucerne on Saturday and was suitably impressed by the breath-taking scenery around the lake and enjoyed an hour-long boat trip. His concentration wavered more than once over mealtimes, as it did the following day as they took him to the bank's social club in the country for Sunday lunch and a lazy afternoon by the pool. Tim even got to the stage of apologising for not being available to his guest more, an apology which Bear quickly countered.

With over five hundred people employed at the bank, the club was always well patronised at the weekends and Bear was introduced to a few of Tim and Sarah's colleagues who were eager to engage Bear in discussion of matters relating to Basel and Suffolk. Much of the afternoon was spent under the protection of parasols amid searing heat by the poolside enjoying cooling drinks, and the atmosphere could hardly have been more relaxed. The light-hearted conversation proved just a temporary stemming of the flow of apparent unease that Tim detected, and he took advantage of Bear's occupation in a monologue from a particularly garrulous colleague on the virtues of liberalism to excuse himself. When Sarah whispered to ask what had taken up his time after Tim returned several minutes later, he explained that he had made a phone call concerning Tuesday night. On receiving clarification, Sarah nodded and added that she thought that was an excellent idea.

The new working week saw further city exploration by Bear by day and a visit to the cinema with his host on Monday evening. Bear was informed in the interval that they would be joined by 'Bee', as well as Sarah, for the unofficial office night out the following evening.

'You'll enjoy this. A rare cross-border sortie, into Germany.' He felt like adding that Bear would enjoy the occasion much more now that Ciara had agreed to come. He would not have been wrong in his estimation, although not because of any renascent romantic inclinations. Bear was anxious to learn how much progress, if any, the gallery employee had made in her enquiries concerning a certain potential masterpiece. He was unwilling to be seen to be pestering Ciara and arranging another lunchtime date at the café which might be interpreted as a pretext for deepening their relationship. Now he was grateful to Tim for providing a natural opportunity to enquire further on Ciara's research. He asked what the occasion was for heading over the border on Tuesday.

'As I say, you'll like this, judging from your years in Manchester, although this might feel a bit like taking coals to Newcastle,' Tim prefaced, leaving Bear momentarily puzzled

107

how northern English cities fitted into the scenario of an evening visit to the Black Forest. 'We, that is some workmates and you and I, are going for a curry.'

'A curry?' Bear looked askance at his friend. He had not anticipated such a culinary experience that was so familiar to him so deep into the European continent.

'Yes, a curry,' continued Tim, 'there's a decent Indian restaurant in a place called Bad Bremsingen about ten miles or so into Germany. Easy to reach on the train. Lovely quaint little spa town. We've ordered a table for ten. Sarah's going, as are Mark and Chantal, and a few others, some Brits, a couple of French and one or two Swiss. I anticipated you'd be up for it after your experience in showing me the gastronomic delights of Rusholme, was it?'

Bear confirmed that Tim was correct in his recollection of the district of Manchester where they had shared a Vindaloo during Tim's visit while Bear was studying in the city. He also enthusiastically voiced his approval for the plan but expressed surprise that such eating establishments existed in Germany, or Switzerland for that matter.

'Oh, there are a few, not as many as in Britain. The thing is, I have to warn you, that Germans are not used to very spicy flavours, so the curries tend to be a good deal milder than you might be used to. They have toned down the Vindaloos and Madrases for the targeted clientele. But it's a popular restaurant; we had to book a couple of weeks in advance.' Tim did not add that it was highly convenient that someone had been obliged to drop out a few days ago, enabling him to include Ciara as a late replacement.

Tuesday duly came round and Bear, as instructed, walked briskly to meet his host outside the Badischer Bahnhof at a

108

quarter to six prior to the short train journey over the border. He was forewarned and forearmed with both a passport and some Deutschmarks, insisting that he would pay at least his share of the bill, after Tim had kindly treated him on the first night of his stay. He had, in any case, retained over twenty Marks from his previous visit to Germany on school business a couple of years ago and never got round to changing them back into Sterling, but had supplemented them with some additional Marks as well as Swiss and French Francs, anticipating the possibility of using a variety of currencies on his trip. The plans afoot to establish a single European currency throughout the European Union had stirred in him more than a passing interest, although such a move would not affect Switzerland, nor, he suspected, the United Kingdom, which would stick doggedly to its pound as a symbol of independence.

On approaching the station building, he immediately recognised Tim who was engaged in conversation with two young men, presumably colleagues who were to be part of the outing. He was cheerfully greeted by Tim and introduced to co-workers Christophe and Karl, French and Swiss respectively, who drew Bear into conversation about his stay in Basel to date. Bear was able to relate his boat trip along the Rhine that day and being able to enjoy some of the scenery outside town. He mentioned photographing the spot on the water where the three countries converged without elaborating that he was fulfilling a regular request for his colleague Rachel.

He also refrained from reference to his exuberant entry into the water some years earlier. Tim might have been tempted to intervene but did not react to Bear's mention of the river, presumably, thought Bear, because he had already supplied the anecdote to his colleagues.

The group swelled in numbers as first Mark and Chantal joined them, then Ciara appeared. She needed to be introduced to Christophe, who had joined the bank since her departure, and to two others who completed the group, save for the last member of the company. With her usual pragmatic efficiency, Sarah timed her appearance to perfection, enabling them enough time to secure day return tickets to Bad Bremsingen.

'No significant progress, before you ask,' Ciara informed Bear as they queued for tickets. 'I'll let you know what I do know later.' She was right in anticipating that now was not the time to unload any developments on Duclos as the group of young people were in festive mood, as befitted a warm summer evening on what promised to be a pleasant evening out with the train taking the strain. A cheerful bubble of conversation was maintained in the railway carriage as the train slid out of Basel into the Baden-Württemberg region of Germany with Bear registering another crossing of borders and looking forward to savouring any of the contrasts he might experience. He was curious to know of any findings Ciara had gleaned in her research, however limited, even to learn about the reason for 'no news', but he was frustrated as Chantal, in particular, was keen to find out how he had been enjoying his trip. He was happy to oblige and converse during the fifteen-minute transit as the Black Forest's conifers started to loom in the distance. The question occurred to him as to how effective this natural cover might have been to any political refugees on the run trying to escape the Nazi regime for the freedom of liberal Switzerland. Yet now the contrast with fifty years previous could not be more pronounced, as a group of young urban office workers enjoyed the freedom from the city's stifling summer heat for the balm of a delightful German spa town.

The sense of wellbeing continued as the group left the station concourse and descended half a dozen steps on to the pavement outside. Immediately a panoramic view of the wooded valley made itself known. Bad Bremsingen station was located on the top of the hill and a turning area enabled passengers to be dropped off after ascending the lengthy rise from the main road. A few of the party instinctively directed their steps to descend along the road, but Tim swiftly alerted them to a short cut. To the right of the station on exiting, a paved path headed part way through the woods and alighted at a meadow where the path continued diagonally downhill to the centre of town. Tim and Sarah had visited the chosen restaurant a couple of times before and were confident of the menu's quality, but most of the group seemed unfamiliar with the setting. Ciara confirmed she had visited the town before, but by road, and was as charmed as Bear by the gentle rambling route they were able to exploit. A pastoral idyll was the label Bear instinctively attached to the scene as they passed an elderly gentleman on a bench and exchanged greetings in the early evening sunshine.

The ten-minute amble took the visitors through a gate on to one of the main thoroughfares of the town. Bad Bremsingen's streets were busy with a fair sprinkling of tourists ambling to savour the early evening air. The bank employees and friends were obliged to dodge and weave their way through the throng. The imposing thermal baths, mainstay of the tourist trade, were immediately visible in late nineteenth century architectural splendour. A passing admiring gaze was all that could be afforded on this occasion as the group sauntered into the pedestrian zone and were able to acknowledge the fine presentation of hanging flower baskets adorning much of the route.

The unmistakable smell of rich spices greeted them as they shortly found themselves at their destination and Tim led them into the Taj Mahal, where they were directed to their reserved table. Tim asked if there were any significant wishes as to seating arrangements, subtly asking Ciara if she wanted to sit opposite Bear and 'reminisce on old times', a remark that stimulated conversation involving the pair and their neighbours. Bear and four others had their backs against the wall of the restaurant and could observe the comings and goings as three other tables were occupied on their arrival.

As they clarified to Christophe and Helen the surprise nature of their reunion the week before, much to the amusement of their hearers, Bear and Ciara were temporarily prevented from discussing painting matters. While Bear naturally asked his table companions how they had come to work in Basel and how they took to life in Switzerland, he was only vaguely aware of the table behind Ciara and those others facing the wall being occupied. A family of four settled into their seats which were at right angles to the longer table of ten that accommodated the bank party. At this point Bear noticed two young men in their late teens or early twenties conversing in German and expressing enthusiasm for something, perhaps the menu, or the setting, or for all he knew, the latest motorbike on the market or sports news.

As poppadoms and drinks arrived and orders were taken with Tim repeating his advice for all not to expect the dishes to be ultra-spicy, conversation proceeded merrily. Helen

112

worked in a different department to Christophe, so they spent the next few minutes being acquainted as the latter explained how he had applied for the position in Basel after a dull spell in a clerical role in Lyon. Helen, who hailed from Dundee, had visited that city a few times as a friend had spent a year abroad there as a foreign language assistant and returned to work there, so she was naturally curious. This exchange gave Bear the opportunity to ask about Ciara's findings.

'Don't get your hopes up,' she said, cracking a piece of poppadom as if to emphasise the crushing of hopes. 'I took the liberty of ringing an organisation in France that is a register of art works. I didn't know this, but there is such a thing, a national register. Anything that is displayed in a gallery or any building that receives visitors, say an old stately home or historic site or whatever... they all have to be registered.'

Bear listened eagerly as she paused. She decided to spare him the details of a protracted exchange that was exacerbated by her limited command of French. 'They put me through to someone who knows his stuff who assured me categorically that no such painting was on the register... "*Je vous assure, mademoiselle*",' she mimicked with a severity of tone. 'So if it's out there, it can only be in private hands. Anyway, I gave the name of the Neue Basler Kunstgalerie and said we would be interested in learning of any further developments.' A further pause prompted Bear to gesture that there must be more to the story. He was disappointed. 'And that was about it. Except this chap said something like, "Wouldn't we all, mademoiselle?" or words to that effect.'

Conversation continued with Ciara mentioning a couple of incidents at the gallery and the NBK was referred to more than once. It was at this point that Bear became conscious that the man sitting behind Christophe at right angles was catching a sight of Ciara and showing an interest in her account. A quick glance confirmed his suspicions. His heart started to beat faster as he felt the need to hide his face momentarily to give himself time to think. The words that came out were largely instinctive.

'I just need to note something down,' he said, reaching for his rucksack that was stashed underneath his chair, 'something you just said rang a bell.'

Ciara shot a puzzled look as Bear extracted a biro and tore off a page from his diary, an unremarkable week in March punctuated by a parents' evening and a History Department meeting. In a blank space he wrote two letters of the alphabet, followed by an instruction.

' "P.S."?' she mouthed quietly in response to Bear's signal to keep her voice down. 'What do you mean by "listening behind you"?'

At this point Bear suddenly realised he need not revert to scrawl and produced a card from his wallet that he had received a few days earlier with the name and professional contact details of Paul Schlessinger. He showed her the card. Instinctively, she made as to turn round but checked herself. Bear confirmed at low voice that the glassware executive seemed to be out for a family meal with his wife, he presumed, and two sons. He determined not to look directly at the family group so as not to attract Schlessinger's attention and be compelled to engage in conversation. Had he done so he would have noticed a spirited disagreement between siblings on an issue of national politics with their mother acting as peacemaker and encouraging them to moderate their volume and nudging her husband for support. The latter's gaze was already drawn to

114

the references to galleries and paintings made by the young lady on the next table. She was speaking English with a rhythmical, musical tone, quite harmonious and pleasant on the ear, although difficult for Paul to decipher in a crowded restaurant. He was curious to learn what her connection with a gallery might be. Once he noticed that the conversation that she was having with the young man opposite her had subsided, he returned his attention to clarifying areas of the political arena that his sons were debating, thereby cooling their youthful ardour, much to Monika's relief.

It was not long, however, before Paul's attention was again diverted to the adjacent table and this time Bear's guard had dropped. He had answered a question from Helen about whether he had been to Lucerne yet, and as he looked up to recall what he had seen that Saturday, his gaze met that of Paul. The executive smiled benevolently in Bear's direction and raised a glass of white wine in recognition of their common outing. The history teacher nodded and returned the smile cordially.

Bear was intermittently engaged in conversation with his neighbours, for which he was grateful as he noted with even sparing glances in Paul Schlessinger's direction that the latter was struggling to concentrate on dialogue at his own table. Monika had to reprimand him on more than one occasion for allowing his eyes to drift to the larger gathering. His excuse that he was intrigued at hearing some unusual accents cut little ice with his spouse. He was straining for any detail, any morsel of information, that might re direct him on the trail of his much sought-after potential masterpiece. Didn't the young woman with the Irish accent say something about every work of art being registered in France? Did that confirm the likelihood that the *Flight of the Huguenots* never left French soil? Perhaps somewhere in the Paris region, or Champagne, where he understood his father to have been based during the Occupation.

'I need to get a closer look at this Paul Schlessinger,' Ciara said in hushed tones, reaching across to Bear. 'I won't be a moment.' With that she rose and headed past the family of four in direction of the toilets. Her movements were followed with interest by Paul, and Monika was not insensitive to her husband's head being turned. Two minutes later Ciara slowly reappeared and was able to take in Paul's features, especially as he was distracted yet again on her return. 'I've seen him at the NBK,' she announced softly. 'Asking questions at reception just the other day. He's definitely up to something.'

Her suspicions, shared by Bear, were confirmed ten minutes later when Paul casually rose from his seat and strolled over to a poster on the wall at the end of the row of seats where Ciara was positioned. Further along a yet unoccupied table of four was set, enabling Paul to reach across and consult the poster. A map of regions of India with their culinary specialities adorned much of the wall as Paul feigned interest, tracing a 'curry route' across that vast country with his fingers with childlike fascination. This manoeuvre gave him the opportunity to turn his head slightly and study Ciara's features briefly. Bear observed the ardent student of Indian cuisine and recognised that Ciara could be the next target of the glassware executive's investigations.

When Paul had sat down again, Bear gestured to Ciara to play along with his ruse as he raised his voice slightly. 'So you're out of the gallery for the next few days, then?'

116

Her puzzled response was momentary before she replied complicitly, 'That's right. I've been due some leave for a while. Taking myself off for the rest of the week.'

'Where to?' Bear felt compelled to ask.

'Now that would be telling,' Ciara answered enigmatically. 'I'll have to wait and see.' Christophe almost derailed Bear's plan by asking where Ciara was heading on holiday, but she quickly countered and drew him into revealing his own plans for the rest of the summer.

Conversation then turned to places of interest, some of which were known to several on the table and references to galleries and artwork remained unspoken throughout the rest of the evening.

An hour and a quarter later the party paid their bill, rose and left the Taj Mahal for the gentle saunter back through town and up the hill for the return train back over the border. Contrasting emotions were evident among several diners after their curry experience. Paul Schlessinger was left clenching his fist in frustration at realising that there was not one, but two individuals who seemed to have a vested interest in locating Duclos' missing work, yet he was no closer to establishing a strategy for finding it. Tim Sheldon, meanwhile, witnessed the playful banter of his house guest and former colleague in celebration at their ruse to indicate Ciara was not apparently contactable for the next few days. He congratulated himself on the inspired late decision to invite Ciara to join the outing.

Chapter Ten

Alsace Expedition

As the white Fiat Panda gathered speed in direction of Mulhouse early that Friday morning, its occupants reflected on the brisk pace of events of the past few days. The earnest discussions they had shared and the sense of both urgency and absurdity in their proposed mission, in roughly equal measure, came to mind. The passenger had puffed out his cheeks on leaving Basel at dawn and cast a wary, semi-nervous smile at the driver. She in turn had smiled back uneasily but without concealing her excitement at the possibilities the day might bring. Once they had crossed into France and tracked the Rhine initially towards Mulhouse, their conversation became more animated and businesslike as their quest grew more focused.

'Right, in the next couple of minutes we should see a sign for the first on the shortlist,' announced the driver.

The passenger supplied the name from the list they had drawn up the previous day. He pronounced the syllables of the Germanic-sounding village with precision that he was aware implied a conviction that he was struggling to muster. The apparent futility of the day's venture struck him for the umpteenth time since his companion had suggested the outing two days previously. The chances of success were minimal; still, at least the day would be a memorable, possibly unique, experience.

Bear momentarily recalled the lunchtime rendezvous the day following their visit to the Indian restaurant. He had been happy to meet up again as he had planned to stay in Basel that day with a view to accompanying Tim on further exploration of the country at the weekend before returning home on Monday. When Ciara appeared shortly after noon that Wednesday, the resolute look that spelt purpose indicated that she had made a significant decision. He knew from their student years that she had an idea formulated that would need a strong argument to dislodge. Bear was not wrong in his perception and could find no such reasoning to dissuade her. He remembered their exchange as he kept his eyes open for the first village on their list.

'So let me get this straight,' he had said deliberately once they had placed their order at the Café Engelchen. 'You are proposing to go over into Alsace to look for a painting that may or may not still be in a barn a few miles from the border after a gap of fifty years. It *may not* even be a genuine Duclos. It *may* no longer be in any condition to recognise, let alone display. The barn *may not* even exist anymore. And you are planning to ask your boss for a day off to look for this potential masterpiece.'

'Correct,' Ciara had replied crisply. 'Except for the last point...' She paused for effect. 'I have already taken the day off and Ernst has agreed. We are going to spend Friday looking.'

As bemused as Bear was at Ciara's decision to initiate the search, he had to acknowledge that he was enticed by the venture. If it did prove a wild goose chase, at least they will have seen some pleasant countryside together. He was also more than intrigued at the prospect, however remote, of uncovering an artwork that had been missing for so long, especially given the interest stirred a few weeks ago in Dedham Vale and the forthcoming Barbizon School anniversary. It would be quite a find, he had to concede, and worth a day or two looking, if only to say they had tried and failed. The subtle enquiries of Paul Schlessinger motivated him to make the effort to track down the painting, if only to ensure the *Flight of the Huguenots* did not fall into the wrong hands. The lunchtime café conversation with Ciara proved more focused than their previous encounters. It was agreed to identify a shortlist of possible villages, outside which the barn might conceivably be located.

So, it was that they were travelling north along the route départementale 468 through the plain of the Haut-Rhin département, with the Vosges mountains to the west and the Rhine and German border to the east. They made significant progress through the early morning rush hour, as most of the traffic was travelling in the opposite direction. Numerous Alsatians were heading to work in Switzerland where the wages were higher but returning in the evening to spend them freely in France. A sign off to the left indicated the name of the first candidate. Ciara turned off and after a few minutes negotiating the minor roads, they came upon the first village. She parked on the main street within sight of what seemed like a war memorial and slowly reminded them both of the pre-established signs to identify.

'Some sort of memorial in the centre, yes. Tick the box,' she directed. 'But no sign of a statue of a warrior. No tick there.'

'A statue that may have been removed,' Bear reminded

120

her as they both knew that they had to hold the distant recollections of Gerhard Schlessinger lightly.

'Right size of village, just a couple of streets, although the village we're looking for may have grown since 1944, so a tentative tick,' Ciara instructed. 'What about the exit routes?'

The next quarter of an hour was spent driving a mile or so out of the village, firstly continuing the road by which they had entered, then returning to the centre to explore the other road crossing the central square. The sought-after elevation after an extended mass of conifers did not materialise, and it was clear that the topographical description passed on by the former captain in the Swabian Infantry did not match the area around the village; nor was there a sign of any barn within sight of the main road. After checking the exit routes carefully, it was agreed that Bear should cross the first village off their list. Hauptmann Schlessinger had definitely not aborted the planned night's rest anywhere nearby.

The procedure was repeated some fifteen minutes later at a neighbouring village. The agreed tactic: head to the centre, identify any possible monument with a warrior's statue, check all exit routes for two miles, look for conifers and side roads, and barns. Village number two was soon dismissed as there were no such roads or farm tracks leading off at the top of any incline.

Three more candidates were surveyed by mid-morning without the remotest indication that the retreating German unit had passed their way half a century ago.

'Oh well, at least it's a nice day, gorgeous scenery,' Bear commented on the continuing heatwave with manufactured optimism as they paused to contemplate their next move. 'Nice place to stop for an evening.'

'In late November, in war-ravaged Europe?' questioned Ciara. 'I'm not surprised they didn't hang around.'

The sixth village promised more as the obligatory statue occupied the main square with some sort of monument to the war dead, although the figure was clearly in civilian dress. Both travellers conceded that Gerhard's fading memory or limited time to observe his surroundings might have led to a misperception of a warrior being represented. The road out of the village rose noticeably and after flattening out, did provide a turn-off to the left along a farm road. Some sort of farm building could be seen in the distance, clearly separate from the rest of the farm. Bear remarked that it seemed much further than the hundred and fifty metres indicated in Gerhard's bequest instructions, but they decided to investigate, nevertheless, and headed down the lane in direction of the barn. A sturdy structure with a corrugated iron roof was open, with bales of hay stored within. They stepped out of the car, approached the building across a tarmac surface and looked inside.

Dressed as they both were in t-shirt, shorts and trainers, their appearance could hardly have been more incongruous in that agricultural environment. There was little room for storage of any artwork, or anything of substance, for that matter, which they were able to ascertain in the few seconds that were afforded them. They were about to turn and resume their journey when they were confronted with two Alsatians, one human, one canine. The latter, unleashed but obedient to the restraining commands of his master, had started to bark vociferously. The farmer, in cloth cap, coarse checked shirt, thick trousers and Wellington boots, called out to them menacingly.

'Oh… *Entschuldigung*,' was the first thing that entered Ciara's head to say as her partner in crime remained speechless, rooted to the spot. Although addressed in French, her instinctive reply in German was how she had grown used to responding to strangers over her years in Basel.

'*Sie haben hier nichts verloren*,' emphasised the farmer menacingly.

Ciara smiled sweetly and simulated pathetic feminine helplessness with a sentence that Bear did not understand. A brusque response from the local pointed back to the main road and a couple of sentences of explanation ensured the travellers had no further reason to admire his property.

'*Danke sehr*… er, *merci Monsieur*,' uttered Ciara gratefully with a smile of enlightenment as if the farmer had made her day by unlocking a mystery as to how to find an elusive location. Bear followed suit with a mumbled 'merci' and a sheepish grin as they rejoined the car hastily and returned to the main road with a few sharp valedictory barks from the canine guard in their wake.

'What did he say to us?' asked Bear when they were clear of the site.

'He said we hadn't lost anything there. Meaning, what the heck were we doing on his land,' Ciara replied. 'I suspect even if they knew no other German, all farmers in this area would know it as a phrase to come in handy in case interfering tourists overstep the mark. I pretended we needed to get to the village we'd just visited.'

'I bet that convinced him,' Bear observed ironically. 'I'm sure it didn't. He looked at us as if we were mad.'

'I'm not sure his view would have changed if we'd told him what we were really looking for.'

The seventh village on the list was just a kilometre up the road and the flat landscape and lack of any clear memorial markers in the centre quickly ruled it out of contention. They drove further into the country and decided to pause in a secluded woodland layby that seemed a starting point for rambles. The summary of the morning's endeavours was brief. Seven down, at least five to go, and possibly a few others. Vital not to be put off by irate, protective farmers, and important to keep looking.

'Persistence is what is called for,' announced Ciara. 'No stone unturned.'

'Funny you should mention persistence,' Bear noted. 'I'm going to have to practise what I preached a few weeks ago.' He then relayed the details of the much-acclaimed assembly on Abraham Lincoln's life, in between swigs of water that they both partook of liberally in the midday heat. 'Everything seemed to be doomed to failure, yet he ends up not just President, but a very successful one at that.'

'So we must keep on looking,' agreed Ciara. 'Even if it takes all day.'

'That's what we agreed. "Seek and you will find",' he quoted dreamily. '"Knock and the door will be opened to you."'

'Don't get all biblical on me now, that's all we need,' Ciara responded wearily.

'Sorry, can't help it, it's just what springs to mind.'

'I suppose if you're immersed in that stuff week after week it becomes second nature to quote scripture. Well, fair play to you, if you find it helps ...' She paused, surveyed the peaceful shaded woodland scene and her unusually contemplative manner conveyed a reluctance to press on immediately with their search. She turned to her passenger and remarked, 'You never came out with any of these confident pronouncements back in the good old days, you know. Before you got in with the God Squad, I mean. It was always lots of speculation about what if this hadn't happened and wondering how things might have turned out differently. It was like living in a... I don't know, I suppose a fairy-tale land. You were fun to be with...'

'And I'm not fun to be with anymore?' Bear pulled a downcast face in mock-disappointment.'

'I'm not saying that,' affirmed Ciara. 'It's just different. For months while we were going out it was all asking questions and enjoying the power of the imagination, then it was all absolutes. You were convinced of what you believed and that was that, at least that's how it seemed at the time...' Her voice trailed away, wistfully, it appeared to Bear.

He did recall their many dates in that period at university. The initial conversation after the unexpected cancellation of the lecture had been followed by four or five chance encounters at the students' union building, in the Arts Faculty café and once in the main university library, where it transpired that their studies on the aftermath of the French Revolution and the Reign of Terror coincided. One was studying the apparent dearth of artistic output in that period, the other the main political events. They had met in an aisle between bookshelves and found they were pursuing the same material. A decision to share one book and even discuss the findings together proved the launch-pad of a close relationship. He remembered how Ciara had often taken the lead in suggesting outings, using her degree subject as an excuse to visit the environs of Manchester, not just the city's galleries but stately homes in Cheshire and the Peak District, exploiting any information gleaned from paintings viewed to inform her studies and enjoy a good day out into the bargain. Bear was happy to be dragged to places to keep her company and play a largely supportive role, challenging his friend with speculative comments on the way history turned on the whims of a politician or a general's tactical decision and could have been much different. He had amused Ciara the other night by confirming that his pupils were continually entertained by his trademark 'What if...' and 'Put yourself in the shoes of...' challenges.

His recollections were curtailed as Ciara was the first to emerge from their reminiscences and waved a hand across his face. He was obliged to ask for the question to be repeated. The suggestion of pausing for lunch was warmly received and Bear as map-reader was tasked with locating the nearest available settlement. He selected a village about ten miles south-east of Colmar and within a few minutes, they had alighted on the central square. Noticing a number of more modern buildings, they quickly concluded that this large village had grown significantly in recent years and probably served as a commuter village for Colmar. Having parked on one of the side roads, they located a table outside a café near the centre. The decision not to take a packed lunch, taken partly to avoid Swiss prices, allowed them time to enjoy the surroundings and take stock of the morning's efforts.

'Not a roaring success so far,' ventured Bear, once their orders of ham salads had been taken.

'True, but we knew it was always going to be tough, especially with fifty years of natural and man-made growth to factor in,' was Ciara's assessment.

'Don't get me wrong, it's nice to be out and about and it's an area of France I've never visited, but it does seem like looking for a needle in a haystack.' Bear instinctively smiled at the expression, which prompted Ciara to press for an explanation. 'My esteemed head of department, Michael – that's one of his pet phrases. "Never mind looking for a needle in a haystack," he says, "You've got to find the right haystack first." He says it about all problems, not just in history classes, but any issues in department meetings that are hard to resolve. Very old school is our Michael. He has a particular way of doing things.'

'Is that a bad thing?'

'No, except that we have had our differences. He sees me as too dreamy, relying on conjecture and empathy too much instead of good old factual evidence. A charge I refute, by the way.'

Ciara retorted knowingly, 'I can see where he's coming from. You do like to speculate, let your imagination take you to places. You wouldn't be Bear Hoskins if you didn't.' She paused before adding, 'In some ways you haven't changed one iota.'

Nor have you, Bear thought. Still the same Ciara, eager to take the lead and full of ideas for excursions. Still the same pugnacious spirit of a youngest child. Not put off by the apparent hurdles in tracking down Duclos' masterpiece, feeding off my dreamy comments.

'But you were right to mention persistence,' Bear acknowledged. 'Who knows what we might discover after lunch? We have to dream, at least.'

'Who knows what might happen if we do find the hidden

127

treasure? You know, we might even be invited on to The Double F Show. Now wouldn't that be something?'

'The Double F Show?' Bear stared back at his companion. 'What is that when it's at home?'

Ciara returned an even more pronounced stare at Bear's query. 'Don't tell me you haven't heard of The Double F Show. Bear Hoskins, I am genuinely shocked! I live in Switzerland and I don't have access to British television, and even I know what The Double F Show is. Have you really not seen it?' As Bear could do no more than shake his head apologetically, Ciara was pleased to launch into a tirade of mock-horror. 'A man of your education, I am genuinely shocked! What an uncultured lot you must be in Suffolk. I would have thought The Double F Show would be the talk of the staff room every Wednesday break time!'

'Can't say it's ever come up. Sounds a bit rude to me, must be a late-night show, after the nine o'clock watershed. You know, when all the bad language comes on.'

'Eight o'clock on Tuesday evenings,' she corrected him. 'If I remember what my sister told me. She has recorded all the shows of the recent series and sent the videotapes over to me. That's why I said I'm surprised you teachers aren't talking about it on Wednesday mornings.'

'Ah, well, I have the excuse of my midweek church group that meets on a Tuesday night. So what am I missing out on?'

She paused as the salads arrived, allowing her more time to prepare her dramatic proclamation of the programme. 'The Double F Show, I will have you know, is the nickname of *Fame or Forgery*, featuring the inimitable Finola Flowers, in which members of the general public produce works of art that they have come across or have noticed gathering dust in their attic and reckon they might have a masterpiece.'

Bear nodded. He vaguely recalled the name of the television celebrity being mentioned in the staff room, but it had never registered any interest in him. Until now.

'You won't forget Finola once you've seen her,' continued Ciara, 'vibrant Scottish woman with a squeaky voice, can be quite friendly, even jokey with the guests, makes them feel really important and really at home on the show, although more often than not she has to disappoint them. Each week a panel of experts assess the item in question for authenticity, and she usually has to say it's a fake. Very occasionally, the piece will be genuine, and lead to fame and fortune. Who knows, that could be us!'

Bear commented that there were a few television programmes emerging that involved valuation of antiques. He assumed The Double F Show to be in this category. Ciara disabused him of this notion.

'Different set up entirely. It's a curious mixture. Finola sells it as art for the masses, and it's not just your average suburban middle classes who get to go on the show. There are some winners from quite humble backgrounds. And she flirts outrageously with all the men on the show, makes it clear that there are no pretences. Yet the experts are top notch, and the final verdict is very formal. It's quite an awe-inspiring moment when she opens the envelope.'

'Envelope?'

'At the end of the show, they gather around a round table and she opens an envelope with the official verdict of the assessing authority. That is always the final word on whether the work is a forgery or leads to lasting fame. I'm really surprised you've never seen it; it's been on for a few series now.'

'I will look out for it in future,' he promised vaguely as they gratefully turned their attention to the salads that had appeared.

Conversation revolved around the proximity of Colmar. 'Pretty little city, very historic,' commented Ciara. 'Venice of the North, some say, because of its urban waterways. Pity we don't have more time to pay a visit.'

Venice of the North, mused Bear. Everything needs a nickname, as if the actual name can't stand alone. Like The Double F Show, or whatever it is. I suppose every place, every institution needs a secondary phrase, some motto or sub-title to give it emphasis. He remembered Princewood School's Latin motto *per aspera ad astra*. The sky is the limit, in modern parlance, or reaching the stars through hard work. He wondered what sort of motto or watchword Gerhard Schlessinger's unit had marched, or wearily trudged under as they beat a hasty retreat and how incongruous it must have felt. On an impulse, he put down his cutlery and reached into his rucksack to extract his notebook on which various thoughts had been recorded in readiness for the day's search.

'What did we say about downing tools for an hour?' Ciara reprimanded him. 'You can look at our notes after lunch.'

'Just checking something,' Bear explained, and having surveyed the desired reference, hastily returned the pad to his rucksack.

After conversation meandered around Ciara's previous visits to Colmar (just two in eight years) and other occasional ventures into Alsace, the resolve to avoid returning prematurely to the task in hand proved irresistible. Rule nothing out and nothing in had been a much-expressed principle. The inevitable questions were exchanged as the pair considered the unresolved challenge before them. Had the barn long since been demolished? If still in existence, was it locked, and could they somehow ask the farmer permission to look inside with their scrawled explanation in very patchy French of why they needed to snoop around agricultural property?

They agreed that a return to work in the neighbouring villages was called for. As they rose from their seats, Bear suggested a brief circuit of the main square, he reasoned, just to sample the atmosphere and make use of the remaining minutes of their agreed hour's rest. A fountain had been tastefully erected in the middle of the square and attracted a handful of visitors happy to partake of their lunch amid the midday warmth. There were several shops, some selling tourist wares, exploiting the proximity of a stately home and a fifteenth- century church near the town centre. Other businesses were closed for the lunch hour, but there was one establishment that caught Bear's eye.

'A museum?' remarked Ciara. 'I wouldn't have thought this place big enough to boast one.'

It was, indeed, a small enterprise, consisting of just two rooms. It was open throughout the lunch period to catch whatever tourist trade came its way. Since entry was free, Ciara was prepared to agree to Bear's suggestion to take a quick look. They were greeted by an elderly custodian who smiled as he looked up from his newspaper and exchanged greetings. Their brief wander through the compact exhibition would have been more absorbing if they had allowed themselves more time. In the first room, displays covered the history of the area, details of the lives of prominent local dignitaries and key events in centuries gone by included, notably, the passage of Huguenots escaping France under Louis XIV, the Revolution, of course, the coming of the railways and the development of educational establishments. The second room comprised the Prussian invasion of 1870 and the return of Alsace to German rule, subsequent restoration to France from 1918 and a prominent glass case on the Occupation from 1940.

It was at that point that Bear's eye was drawn to a display of several regimental crests.

One in particular arrested him. When questioned by Ciara as to what had caught his attention, he pointed to the relevant insignia.

'*Kraft durch Treue,*' she read out, 'strength through loyalty. So what?' she started to ask, but immediately answered her own question. 'So this is Gerhard's regiment!'

Bear confirmed the detail he had checked in the notebook minutes earlier. He looked up at a map of the area with a series of arrows. The headings were all in French, with smaller subtitles in German. He asked Ciara what the arrows referred to, although he had an inkling already. She was able to confirm his hunch.

'It's the routes taken in the retreat of the German forces in 1944.'

'And where does the Swabian Infantry fit in?' Bear pondered and followed the arrow's colour that corresponded to that regiment. 'That takes us roughly to…'

'About ten miles north of Colmar!' Ciara finished his sentence. 'I know it's not an exact calculation, but that's much further north than we've been looking.'

Bear paused to consider his response as if weighing the logic of the moves of the German forces fifty years previously in his mind. 'We naturally assumed they would have been well away from Strasbourg to have a chance of getting across the Rhine after that city fell. We've been looking too far south. I reckon we could tear up our shortlist and look at villages near to the next border crossing north of here.'

'But we don't have a list of villages north of Colmar. It would be starting from scratch,' protested Ciara.

'I reckon it's our best bet,' Bear pronounced.

They managed respectful smiles and expressions of thanks to the elderly custodian and walked briskly back to the car. A brief survey of the map and they headed off in a north-easterly direction as Bear hastily scribbled down a revised shortlist.

If they thought that the sudden change of direction would instantly breathe new life into their flagging quest, the next three hours exposed the fallacy of such a notion. As map-reader Bear was no longer relying on a pre-selected list of targeted sites but responding off the cuff to the nearest village in the vicinity. Six more locations in a thirty-kilometre radius were explored with not the slightest sign of a farm building that might have sheltered the Swabian Infantry unit for a few hours that November evening. As the time approached five o'clock and the limited daylight available became a factor, conversation started to become fractious. Ciara, weary at having to respond to unconvincing directions from her passenger, expressed a couple of barbed remarks at the indecisiveness of Bear's instructions, especially pointing out that it was his decision to explore villages further north before their initial list had been exhausted. He plaintively responded

133

that she had agreed to the readjustment and asserted that the revised plan was as good as any. They both had half a mind to complete the villages on the list and were aware that they were getting closer to Strasbourg. Any further north would see them into territory that Schlessinger's unit could almost certainly never have entered without being captured, given the transport difficulties that beset them.

'Last one, then we retrace our steps,' Ciara announced adamantly as they entered a well-kept but otherwise not especially attractive village. They were vaguely aware of some form of war memorial in the centre as they drove through, but the sought-after incline on exiting did not materialise. After driving for over two kilometres along a deserted country road, Ciara slid to a halt and switched off the engine with a sigh. The farm track off to the left was conspicuous by its absence, although a faint turning to the right was visible some fifty yards ahead of them. She let out an exasperated sigh and Bear was on the point of suggesting they find the départementale again to revisit the area south of Colmar when he caught sight of some dark shapes moving across the sky just to their right. The tight concentration of such forms inevitably triggered an amusing recent memory in the history teacher, one that had seemed inconsequential at the time but was now about to prove enticing.

Chapter Eleven

Discovery

'I cannot for the life of me see what holds your fascination,' Ciara pronounced, shaking her head as if to say that her passenger had taken leave of his senses. Yet at his request she started the engine and slowly headed forward in low gear in pursuit of the sight that had gripped his attention.

Bear had enough time to explain quickly the source of his curiosity, reminding her of the encounter on the train from Calais he had related the previous week.

'I'm just curious to see where they land,' he offered. His companion's manufactured smile indicated that she was willing to humour him but only as a momentary diversion.

They followed the mass of dark shapes that swarmed across the sky, apparently coming to rest some thirty feet above ground to the right of the road. At this point the shapes disappeared from view as they were obscured by a thick blanket of fir trees. Ciara drove purposefully into the turning and about fifty yards along a rugged track, whose use had been clearly reserved for agricultural vehicles, they alighted upon a substantial farm building in a clearing some twenty yards back from the track. There was room for vehicles to turn and it was obvious that the building was in use. She put on the brakes and drew to a halt just as Bear spotted the aerial phenomenon.

'There they are!' he exclaimed rather more triumphantly than he intended, and more in relief that his hunch had been borne out and they had not wasted several minutes of their search with this distraction.

'Okay, so there are a few starlings, God bless them,' Ciara noted. 'And what great pearl of wisdom would your friend Charles have to impart if he were here?'

'Chas,' Bear corrected. 'He would probably say something about hierarchy and the starlings' innate sense of their place.'

'You mean in the general pecking order? Surely that's true of any species?'

'Ah, but this is more to do with their sense of justice and fair play and whose turn it is to be in the centre.' He wondered why he had allowed his voice to drop to a whisper as if they were observing a rare species that they dared not disturb.

Ciara switched off the engine as Bear directed his gaze to the roof of the building. He noted with fascination that a dozen starlings had congregated along the edge with a raised platform, presumably a chimney as far as they could discern from a distance, occupied by two of the group. After staring upwards for half a minute, Bear observed a repetition in smaller scale of the phenomenon he had experienced during the extended halt on the Calais-Bâle line and encouraged his reluctant companion to take in the spectacle.

'Watch how they change places,' he suggested.

It was almost on cue that one of the two starlings on the chimney flew off to be replaced by the innermost colleague from the roof edge. Another bird decided to fly off, and instead of shuffling on to claim the vacated spot nearer the centre, the nearest starling held its position, allowing the outermost fellow to flutter its wings, take off and glide into position and assume the space liberated by the departed one. A virtual replica of the enactment witnessed days ago at the station buildings under Chas's expert guidance. Bear marvelled at this confirmation of the wonders of biosophism and noticed that Ciara was captivated, staring intently at the sight.

After exchanging amused comments as the starlings respectfully acknowledged the positional rights of one another, the onlookers realised they had been distracted for some five minutes. It was Bear who suggested that they should perhaps be moving on, only for his companion to check such thoughts.

'You don't suppose this could be the barn we're looking for?' Ciara offered.

'Unlikely, as we came at it from the wrong side,' Bear replied confidently. 'We turned right out of the village, remember.'

'And what is there to prevent another village being ahead of us, and if we approached from the opposite direction, we would have retraced Gerhard Schlessinger's route?'

The answer seemed so obvious that Bear had to concede that a long day had taken its toll on his powers of logic. A quick examination of the map confirmed that the nearest settlement was a mere three kilometres along the road, so Ciara's supposition was credible. It took a tilt of her head in the direction of the building, responded to in kind, for the two to step out of the vehicle and stride towards the barn. Bear reflected instantaneously on facial signals that had characterised their earlier courtship being alive and well and easily read even after such time had elapsed.

137

As they approached the building, it became clear that the point of access was a wide sliding metal door. Gingerly Bear grasped the handle and emitted a startled gasp that the door gave way and could be rolled across. His companion nodded faintly, her eyes lighting up as he hesitated, indicating for him to complete opening up. The door slid across a rail and within a few seconds the interior was visible, still giving sufficient light at five o'clock on a summer afternoon to enable the visitors to survey the contents.

The pair's first impressions were that the scene was timeless and featureless. In a surface area of some twenty metres by ten, the left-hand side was bare, with a grey stone floor undisturbed by any sign of activity. At the back a few tools had been assembled, leaning against the wall, not in any obvious permanent resting place, as if the owner was undecided where to store them. To the visitors' right, however, a mass of hay had been stacked, mounting up to ten feet high. Instinctively Bear advanced for no other reason than to ensure they had not left unexplored any possibility of locating their quarry. The sight was characterless except for one feature that left him puzzled.

'What is it?' enquired Ciara.

'Nothing, really,' replied Bear. 'I'm just curious as to why underneath all this hay this half of the barn has an uneven cobbled floor, while the other half which is apparently not being used, has a nice flat stone surface.'

'Maybe the farmer couldn't afford to pave the whole floor,' suggested Ciara half-heartedly.

'Or he hadn't got round to finishing the job yet,' added Bear. 'It's as if the flooring is from two separate eras. *Hmm...* I wonder...?' he continued in contemplative mood.

Bear took a closer look at the surface at the edge of the bundles of hay. Ciara strove to suppress a sigh, and then conceded with a smile of recognition that her erstwhile partner's penchant for spotting details of interest, often of a historical nature, had not deserted him. She recalled instances years ago of being obliged to stop and follow the historian's stare as something had caught his eye. Occasional moments of enlightenment had added a sparkle to their courtship. Now, as he patrolled the borders of the hay pile, her initial exasperation gave way to eagerness to find out if her companion had located anything of interest, whether relevant to their quest or not. His attention seemed drawn to something on the cobbled surface adjacent to the hay.

'Anything of interest?' she asked from a guarded distance, keeping a lookout for any comings and goings by the owner of the property.

'I'm not sure,' he replied. 'Looks like some sort of board. Some wooden frame that I can only see a part of because the hay is in the way.'

Ciara was sufficiently curious to approach and it require d merely an exchange of knowing smiles for them to agree to shift the hay piles between them. Fortunately, they were not stacked too high to make the clearance of the board prohibitive. With careful application of body weight, they were able to push the obstruction away from the wooden board. Bear was tempted to remind Ciara of his colleague's remark about finding the correct haystack, and how amusing it might be if he could report as much on his return to the Princewood staffroom but thought better of it. Levity would have to wait, and time was of the essence, not just with limited daylight hours to play with, but more probably, the likely

139

return of the farmer no doubt demanding an explanation for their intrusion.

They were able to nudge the pile obscuring the board sufficiently to see exactly what was beneath. The cobbled stones gave way to a square opening, bordered by dusty, rotting woodwork. Initially, Bear had to manoeuvre sharply as he realised that the solid surface was replaced by a group of less secure metal rings, all of them rusting badly. Once they had cleared the area sufficiently, they were able to examine the metalwork more closely. Eight rods covered the space, perhaps four feet by three to form a grill, through which a darkened recess was barely visible. As far as they could discern, it extended perhaps six feet underground.

'I wonder…?' Bear asked himself again as he knelt down and gripped one of the outer rods. A few vigorous pulls and the grill came loose, allowing access below.

'Should we be doing this?' Ciara asked nervously. After showing so much initiative and vision over the past few days, she seemed to be faltering as their investigation was deepening and potentially reaching a conclusion.

'We can't back out now, surely,' Bear appealed. 'Anyway,' he added, aware of his companion's anxiety about being caught in the act, 'you have the full authority of the Neuer Basler Kunstgalerie.'

'Hardly. I just have permission to have the day off. I don't think our jurisdiction extends this far.'

'Torch?' Bear asked Ciara to shine the instrument that they had agreed would be necessary once inside any of the candidate buildings.

She duly shone down into the space. As anticipated, about six feet extended towards the bottom. There seemed to be no

140

distinguishing features with a surface of straw, dust and a combination of mud and manure. Little to retain the travellers' attention other than a disused underground storage space for some long-discontinued agricultural activity. However, to cover all the possible options, she directed the beam to the left, where the stone walls of the passage indicated the same width as at its opening, and then to the right. It was at that point that Bear abruptly instructed Ciara to hold the torch at that angle.

'What do we have here?' he asked as much to himself as to her. On the right side of the underground storage space, instead of the solid walls a hollow recess was visible. He noticed also a series of metal rungs that facilitated descent. One had rusted away and fallen from its perch, but the rest were intact. He did not wait to ask for advice on whether to descend. A few seconds later he was scrambling in the darkness to see if anything of significance lay beyond.

He did not have to look far. Less than two feet away he espied a rectangular, cardboard package, apparently flat, covered in dust, thick cobwebs and at least one dead spider, which he brushed off swiftly. Carefully, he pulled the object towards himself, ignoring in his fascination the anxious enquiries of his partner at the surface. Once the entire package was in his grasp, he was able to appreciate the dimensions. The cardboard packaging was intact, still secured by string that was presumably originally white but now greyed through the years of being shielded from the light.

'Bear? What is it? Have you found something?' Ciara called out, her voice exhibiting the tension of the moment.

Bear assured her that he was ascending and asked for her assistance as he hauled himself up to the top. As he reached the final rung, he handed her the package to enable himself to complete the exit. He dusted himself off as she examined the object. It was heavy, four feet long and two feet high, with a depth of perhaps six to nine inches. That the package contained a work of art of some kind, whatever its quality, was now no longer in dispute.

'It couldn't be, could it?' she asked, turning to Bear in astonishment.

Bear did not answer for a few seconds but when he did, decided that covering their tracks was the priority. 'I suggest we cover up the hole and make a swift exit.'

The replacement of the hay to its original position was performed quicker than the earlier manoeuvre. Ciara slid the barn door shut as Bear carried the package to the Fiat Panda. The first thing they noticed was that the object could not fit into the boot of the compact little automobile and had to rest on the back seat for the moment. Hearing the sound of a tractor in the distance, they decided to leave nothing to chance, returned to the main road and continued for perhaps two kilometres before finding a secluded spot amidst some trees that filtered the early evening sunshine. They had agreed to inspect their prize at the first available opportunity, but Bear's hesitation in leaving his seat prompted Ciara to encourage him to attend to the job in hand.

'Wait a moment,' he said, raising a cautionary hand. 'I've had a sudden thought.'

He was oblivious to Ciara's frown as he took a few seconds to articulate this thought. 'Didn't Gerhard mention three paintings he left in the barn? The Huguenots, and two landscapes by local artists?'

Ciara winced as she realised that in their haste to depart

from the scene, they had committed the elementary error they had each warned the other not to make. They had no way of knowing which of the three paintings, assuming a painting it was, they had extracted from the underground passage. 'Only one way to find out,' she said resolutely as they both stepped out of the vehicle to pull out the package. 'If it's one of the lesser ones, that means a return visit is required.'

'That is, of course,' Bear said. 'If it is one of the paintings from 1944 at all.'

'I can answer that question,' Ciara replied decisively. She pointed to a scrawl on the back of the packaging in faded ballpoint pen. 'There… "Hpt Schlessinger", as in Hauptmann Schlessinger. It's definitely one belonging to Captain Schlessinger.'

Bear drew a sharp intake of breath at this confirmation. 'Belonging, I would say, is a very loose term,' he commented as he proceeded to untie the package. Four lengths of string were released, after which the cardboard covering that had been hastily applied some fifty years previously came loose and the contents were gently pulled aside.

It took them a few moments to take in the scene. The landscape was clearly meant to predominate with the mountains in the distance and a rugged, stony road in the foreground with an overloaded makeshift cart carrying the occupants' entire goods and chattels. A late afternoon scene was being enacted outside a wayside cottage where a farmworker was in earnest conversation with another man, presumably the head of the travelling family. A woman and at least three children were seated in the cart with a solitary grey horse waiting patiently for instructions to proceed. None of the actors' faces were discernible, a deliberate ploy on the part

143

of the painter so as not to distract from the natural elements. The cottage was simply built, unpretentious, designed for practical use rather than any aesthetic value. In the distance another labourer had briefly paused to follow the scene being enacted, curious to ascertain why this family had stopped on their travels, or indeed, why they should be on the move at all. The dress of all participants very clearly dated them in the late seventeenth or early eighteenth century. The colours were dark, communicating a harshness in the environment and the season, judging from the colouring of the leaves, was decidedly autumn. From the dress of the travelling group, it could be deduced that they were of fair social standing, middle classes who could afford transportation but had fallen on hard times to the extent that they were being driven into exile.

Bear turned to Ciara for confirmation. 'Could it possibly be…?' he asked hesitantly.

The art historian was in no doubt. 'Unless it's a very elaborate forgery, which is most unlikely,' she said with a confidence that could not diminish the awe with which she absorbed the images before her. 'Everything in the description in Duclos' correspondence is there. He mentions the scene in detail – the travellers looking for lodging, Swiss mountains in the distance, curious, half-hearted, puzzled locals not sure whether they should help them out with lodging. A whole family reduced to transporting their whole world in a cart. And notice what is stashed behind the woman…'

'Ah, I see,' Bear acknowledged immediately. He needed no further convincing.

The prominent, albeit faded white cross adorning the Bible confirmed that these were Protestant refugees being depicted. Ciara looked then at the inscription in the bottom right-hand corner. 'That clinches it,' she said, pointing at the lettering.

' "T.D."? And a few squiggles?' Bear was doubtful.

'Jean Duclos always wrote his capital "j" more like a "t". Either he painted this picture, or someone very familiar with his style did,' Ciara pronounced assuredly.

'So what happens now?' he posed warily but excited. He turned to the art expert for how to handle such cases. Ciara was aware of the responsibility thrust upon her but had to confess that she had not encountered such a case before, certainly not in comparable circumstances.

'Shouldn't we inform the farmer that we have found something of value on his land?' Bear suggested.

'And admit to trespassing?' Ciara retorted. 'I reckon we need to get this painting checked out properly and we can let the landowner know we have "borrowed" it as part of an investigation into a legacy.'

'That sounds as if we're on very thin ice legally,' Bear commented.

'True, but the farmer didn't know of the painting in the first place. It has sat there for fifty years! He wouldn't know it's missing. And he almost certainly wasn't the landowner when these Germans stopped by back in 1944. He has no claim to it.'

'All the same, we can't *not* let him know.'

'Which we will. In any case, this won't mean a thing if it's not genuine. We have to find out if it is a Duclos first, although the signs are good.'

Bear reluctantly agreed that they should transport the painting, wrapped up again in its original packaging, back across the border. It was now past seven o'clock and they were not likely to reach Basel before nine. They decided to return home with their prize and sleep on the issue of what to do next. Not that the matter was laid to rest as they headed back along the *départementale*. Who had rights of ownership in such cases, Bear wanted to know? It depended on from whom Schlessinger had stolen the painting, assuming he had done so, answered Ciara. If an owner could not be traced, she added, the issue gets more complicated. Alsace was officially part of Germany at the time, although it had now ceased to be. French authorities could possibly take possession of any unclaimed work of art found on French soil.

'Surely, the German government had just as much a claim,' Bear suggested.

'Maybe a third party needs to adjudicate,' Ciara replied. 'What better than a respected Swiss gallery, with access to laws pertaining to ownership of works of art?'

It was a discussion that was maintained off and on throughout their return journey until they reached the border crossing. Ciara instructed her passenger to offer a polite smile and let her provide an explanation for the unusual package on the back seat, only partially obscured by a tartan picnic rug, should it be required. Fortunately, the border officials, late on a Friday evening, were not in the mood for confrontation with a youngish couple clearly returning from a summer's day out and waved them through.

Chapter Twelve

Initiation into the Double F World

The lack of reaction from within the flat was disconcerting. It was shortly before ten when Tim re-entered his property to check on his house guest. No stirring in response to the turning of the key, nor even to his announcement that he had returned from spending the night at Sarah's on the other side of the city. In fact, there had been no contact since Thursday evening when Bear revealed his arrangement to meet up with Ciara at dawn the following day in pursuit of their improbable quest. Tim's advice about the value of prudence and taking care had been met with a weary smile. Whilst Bear had raised the possibility of a late return to Basel from their expedition, Tim was still concerned that his attempt to ring from his girlfriend's residence close to midnight had met with silence. The scenario that he had envisaged of the pair of them falling foul of the law on their cross-border incursion and being apprehended for trespassing in the name of art hung uneasily in the air until he knocked on the guest room door.

It was with some relief that a muffled grunt confirmed that his guest was stirring. Tim's offer to prepare some coffee was met with a shade more coherence, and some ten minutes later the dishevelled figure of Bear emerged into the lounge in t-shirt and pyjama shorts, uttering a sleepy greeting in response to his host's breezy salutation. Wary of expressing more concern of the historian's risky adventures, for which he would receive at best a patronising grin and a half-hearted promise to comply, Tim refrained from passing judgement on the outing which had clearly taken its toll on Bear.

'I don't know, about three, I suppose,' the history teacher replied in response to his host's predictable opening question. It was often Bear's deliberate choice while on holiday not to look at his watch, spending as he did most of the year checking the time to ensure each lesson was carefully divided into appropriate chunks. On this occasion, however, he genuinely could not recall the time he returned from depositing the previous day's trophy at Ciara's flat.

'I hadn't put you and Bee down as heavy drinkers,' noted Tim. 'I suppose you must have had a few, though, recalling old times…?'

Bear confirmed that they had indulged in the contents of a bottle of red wine, although more as a reward for their exertions than from any desire to celebrate, exhilarating though their find had been. The overriding emotion had been one of bewilderment and speculation as to what to do next. Despite the intense discussions on the subject on their return journey from Alsace, no firm conclusion had been reached. Bear was still in deep introspection as he wearily asked his host to repeat his second question while he gingerly sipped the proffered cup of black coffee. His reply prompted open-mouthed amazement.

'You mean you actually discovered this painting in some barn? Exactly as you planned?'

Bear nodded and added that he could not be sure of the artwork's authenticity, but Ciara sounded optimistic. He supplied a compressed version of their find, omitting the role

148

played by the starlings for simplicity's sake.

'And I thought you two were up late just drowning your sorrows at a fruitless search... or reminiscing again on old times... or even reigniting old flames, you know,' Tim remarked, supplying the last possibility with a degree of hesitation.

'It was more like a council of war, part one, as to decide what we do next,' Bear replied. 'We agreed to meet up again this afternoon to come to a definite decision.'

That labelling of their late-night conversation was a slight exaggeration; Bear immediately realised but did not correct himself. He was still coming to terms with the new day and was not about to divulge the contents of his evening with Ciara. Tim sagely refrained from prying as his guest gradually sipped his coffee. Bear had discussed the likely next moves with his fellow 'barnstormer', an expression Ciara stumbled upon around midnight with a giggle, but much of the time was spent in further reminiscences from university days, remembering characters long since forgotten and a few that one of them was in touch with. Bear's mind drifted to amusing moments of their months of courtship.

'Remember the wild flowers?' Ciara reminded him over their third glass of Merlot. 'How could I forget?' Bear responded. He settled back into the easy chair he was occupying and revelled in recollecting the incident. He had, on impulse, picked a cluster of wildflowers from parkland one afternoon while venturing to visit Ciara at her hall of residence. When she thanked him for such a spontaneous romantic gesture, he revealed where he had gathered them. She had replied in convincing but simulated horror at Bear having removed plants from protected council land, an offence that could incur a fine at best, or even a custodial sentence.

Ancient medieval by-laws, she insisted, challenging the historian's grasp of jurisprudence. It was a few days before she owned up that she was joking. Would you have really gone to prison, she challenged him. For you, anything, had been his simple reply, a phrase that had remained a watchword between the pair of them for some months. Until they broke up, of course.

'What happened with us, Bear?' she asked half-rhetorically. He did not need her to clarify that she meant: why did they go their separate ways?

'Well, I suppose one explanation might be that you found my Christianity too hot to handle,' Bear mused before quickly adding by way of concession, 'or I got a bit too fiery and insensitive.'

'Your form of Christianity,' Ciara corrected. 'You've got to agree you were a bit intense.'

As Bear did not immediately respond, she expanded, 'I'm all for finding the good in every religion, but that doesn't mean you have to join some... brotherhood, or some weird sect that whips everyone up into a frenzy.'

'Do you think I'm frenzied?'

'Not now, as far as I can tell. You seem to have calmed down. Matured with age, I suppose, like a good wine. Talking of which...' she reached for the bottle and topped them both up.

'Finding the good?' Bear belatedly addressed her last remark. 'Where would you find the best concentration of goodness in one person in history? Surely, it's a simple matter of faith in following him. '

'I don't know, I think you're oversimplifying matters. Life is full of complex issues, and yours is just one path of many.'

'And what's your path?'

'I suppose I'm still working it out,' she said with a shrug.

'Well, maybe you might find the solutions if you looked in the right place.'

'What, all in the good book, you mean?'

Bear did not pursue the subject, other than to say his faith worked for him. He was aware that she had experienced a semi-religious upbringing in Ireland characterised by social occasions, rituals and church attendance, but where personal spiritual experience was meant to be kept private. His gentle probing seemed to indicate that her adherence to such practices had waned significantly since starting to live in Switzerland, and her description of herself as a non-practising Catholic had elicited a knee-jerk response in the past. How can you improve at anything if you don't practise, he had asked. She had responded rather enigmatically that there were different aspects of life that she was practising and being better acquainted with, without elaborating which aspects.

He had felt it prudent to change the subject. Their shared adventure seemed to justify broaching a potentially sore topic.

'So what happened with Steve?' He remembered in their final weeks of study meeting her in the students' union building and being introduced to her new beau, a finance and accountancy student. She had confirmed that they had been seeing each other for a few weeks.

'In the end, not a lot,' she recalled ruefully. 'He found a job in the US, got snarled up in corporate finance, seemed to be loving it, asked if I wanted to move to the States. He came over to Ireland when I was still working for a bank in Limerick. All he talked of was money. Left me cold. Any desire for learning, improving himself culturally was totally destroyed, or at least heavily suppressed.' Her telegram form of delivery suggested she had rattled off the sequence of details on multiple occasions.

'No one since?'

'Just someone from the IRB here in Basel who left a few years ago. He was dishonest, cheated on me and confessed when I confronted him. You won't have heard his name uttered at Timbo's soirée. The gang all know not to ever mention him in my presence. What about you? Any further flames, as Timbo would say?'

'Some very close female companions, but no, no "re-ignition", if that's the right word.'

'You must be dedicated to your job. Or your church, I suppose. No time for romance,' she speculated.

He was tempted to add that in his job children were forever starting rumours about staff, usually quite innocently through misunderstanding. The first time he presented Rachel Rhodes with her photos of borders had been in the presence of two fifth-formers who deduced that the content of the envelopes delivered was of a personal, rather than professional nature. It had taken the best part of an academic year for the rumours of the historian dating the geographer to subside. He decided to refrain from further comment on his limited romantic ventures to date.

Conversation had returned to the prospects of their find being recognised as a genuine Duclos. Ciara reprised her reference of the previous lunchtime and suggested an obvious avenue to pursue.

'Would this F Show really be interested in the likes of us?' he asked. 'For a start, you don't even live in the UK and the painting would have to stay in Switzerland.'

'It's got to be worth a try,' she urged with increasing passion. Then on an impulse, she asked, 'You've never seen the show, have you? Why don't we watch an episode and you can see for yourself?'

Before he could reply, Ciara had walked smartly to a cupboard behind her television where a pack of videotapes was located. She selected one, inserted it into the recorder and invited her guest to sit back and enjoy the show as the clock showed half-past one in the morning.

The next forty-five minutes proved to be something of an education for the history teacher. He winced at the glitzy, showy introduction as a male announcer with what appeared a provocatively seductive tone proclaimed: 'Welcome to the show that might make you a fortune or may turn out be a big let-down. Either way we will learn a lot about two sets of people who think they may have uncovered a great masterpiece. Bringing art to the people, it's... *Fame or Forgery*!' he exclaimed, his voice going up an octave. Applause and a few catcalls resounded from a studio. 'Yes, it's The Double F Show!' Cue for further sustained applause. Ciara chortled at the formulaic presentation that barely varied from week to week, even though she had seen it many times. 'And here's your hostess, Finola Flowers!'

A beaming petite middle-aged woman bestrode the centre of the studio to yet more claps and a clearly choreographed chant of 'Fi-no-la!' She smiled at the camera, feigned embarrassment at the warmth of reception and winked at someone in the studio audience, making it evident that she

153

was interacting with her followers. Bear prepared to endure a painful three quarters of an hour of superficial, fake emotion when he was curiously stirred by the voice that addressed the viewers once the applause had died down. In rich, soothing Glaswegian tones Finola invited her audience to share in the stories of two participants. At that point a clip was shown of the two featured stories and Bear's cynical pre-judgement started to subside. Retired army officer Michael and his wife Marjorie from north Devon had discovered a portrait in their loft that they had been unaware was in their possession. They had helped clear his aunt's house when she died and never got round to removing excess baggage from the attic. One rainy afternoon, they had gritted their teeth and noticed a rather impressive depiction of a famous nineteenth-century politician. Michael and Marjorie both spoke eloquently in precise, military diction, not wanting to waste words, expressing the desire to see if there was anything that they could pass on to the grandchildren. They had been advised by their son to verify 'the lie of the land' with '*Fame or Forgery*' and once he had assured them to 'back them up to the hilt', they had elected to make further enquiries which led to them being accepted as participants on the show.

Next, Barry and Maureen, a couple in their late twenties from Tyneside, talked about being 'gobsmacked' when they bought a landscape of the Lake District at a bring-and-buy sale a year ago. Money was tight and they had just saved enough to buy their own home, but with a baby on the way, they had to make savings, and holidays for the next year would have to be put on hold. What had 'gobsmacked' them was a friend who spotted the painting in their lounge and reckoned it might be worth a few bob. "'Why don't you check

154

it out with The Double F Show, man?" one of me marrers said. So we did, and here we are,' proclaimed Barry triumphantly.

'Two contrasting stories from different ends of the country,' Finola summed up, as she addressed the camera once more at the end of the clip. 'But are these works the genuine article?' She named the artists whose work was thought to be represented after initial views by amateurs. 'It could make a huge difference to the lives of our two couples. What will it be? Will it be fame... or forgery?' She paused to add provocatively, 'We'll find out more after the break. Don't go anywhere!'

Ciara wound the tape forward and they resumed watching. Her earlier description of the proceedings and of Finola herself proved accurate. The presenter was especially flirtatious with the male guests but read all the invitees astutely. She was cheeky with Michael, throwing in military puns, hoping they wouldn't be missing the target that night, but knew when to rein herself in and after the initial banter engaged in serious discussion with the couple as to the likely provenance and value of their painting. She was more matey with Barry and Maureen, maintaining more relaxed conversation and using more gambling terminology with references to 'striking it rich' and playing their cards right. Bear had to acknowledge that the show had been skilfully produced, thoughtfully edited and put together. It was certainly succeeding in bringing art to the masses, but not so dumbed down as to deter the art aficionados.

Occasionally, Ciara looked across to see Bear's reactions and was gratified to notice that he was more engrossed than she thought possible. After Finola had sought out some

155

experts in the relevant fields to get an idea as to the probable hurdles the work of art had to overcome to be recognised as genuine, the paintings were presented before a panel who gave their verdict in a sealed envelope. Each couple in turn was asked for their immediate reaction once Finola carefully read the considered verdict of the panel.

On this occasion, it was the wealthier ex-military man and his wife who were disappointed when told that the work was an adroit but fraudulent attempt to imitate a major nineteenth-century portraitist. Their quest was dubbed 'forgery' and they reacted with good grace, saying how much they had enjoyed the experience. Two minutes later the atmosphere in the studio was very different as Barry and Maureen were informed that the considered, yet unanimous verdict of the experts was that they had unearthed a rare gem, an authentic landscape from one of Lakeland's finest artists. The work would fetch a tidy sum at auction. When the estimated price was communicated, the couple embraced excitedly and were hugged warmly by the hostess while cheers reverberated around the studio. 'Fame' was the result that was emphasised by Finola, at which the grateful beneficiaries of such fortune could barely articulate their joy. The programme concluded with Finola facing the camera to challenge her televisual audience to chance their arm and see if they had any valuable works hidden in their attic that they could submit.

Bear did not go as far as to declare himself a convert to 'The Double F Show' but affirmed that the programme was not without its artistic merits when Ciara asked him for his opinions on the proceedings. She hurled a cushion at him in playful disdain at his faint praise but recognised that watching at such an unholy hour might have impeded his judgement and suggested it was time for her to drive him back to Tim's flat.

That morning, being Saturday, Tim announced that he had one or two ideas for an outing involving Bear and Sarah but wondered whether Bear had some unfinished business at Ciara's end of town. Bear apologised profusely that there were a few loose ends to tie up and could not guarantee when he would be free. Tim was accommodating and an agreement was made to meet up in time for dinner. When Bear sloped off shortly before midday to meet Ciara for lunch, he felt more than a pang of guilt at exploiting his host's hospitality and spending yet more time with what Tim would call an 'old flame'. Well, hardly my fault, Bear thought to himself as he boarded the tram to Ciara's flat, none of this would ever have happened if Tim hadn't invited her to his soirée, although Bear was glad his friend had done so.

***

The remainder of that Saturday had an unreal feel about it. It would be his last meeting with Ciara before returning home. Whilst certainly not experiencing any romantic reawakening, the adventure of Friday and the preparation for it in the days preceding, had stirred the adrenaline. The conclusion of business would leave him feeling somewhat flat. As arranged, Ciara led Bear to a different café from their earlier encounters, this time well away from the gallery and any prying eyes or over-sensitive ears. Ciara had already disclosed that she would not be available the following day as she had agreed to attend the christening of a colleague's baby on Sunday morning followed by an extended celebratory lunch. Duty calls, she had announced ruefully, indicating that the social occasion was one to be endured with a smile rather than relished.

Though disappointed that Saturday would be the last day they would meet on this trip, Bear was strangely relieved as he could devote his attention to his host without being distracted.

In the event, their last meeting proved surprisingly ordered and straightforward following the jovial viewing of Finola and company the night before and the celebration and bewilderment of their find. Ciara was able to allay Bear's anxiety over the illegality of lifting a potentially valuable work of art from a farmer's property. She was confident she could handle that side of the affair and assured him also that she could contact the company that produced the show with a request to appear on it. She would use her contacts in the field to ensure the painting was properly valued. All Bear needed to do for the moment was to sit tight and wait for developments.

And that was that. In the cold light of day, there was not much more to be said. Ciara had obviously thought things through and having slept on the matter, had come up with her master plan. In comparison to the banter and recollections over past romance and deep spiritual matters of the night before, the conversation was muted and perfunctory. They parted in good time for Bear to join Tim and Sarah for the evening, hugging each other warmly and promised to keep in touch. Bear said he looked forward to hearing of further developments.

His stay in Switzerland came to a slightly anti-climactic end. He was determined not to appear as distant as he had allowed himself to be the previous weekend and strove to participate fully in conversation both that evening and the following day when a short walk was followed by another visit to the bank's social club. On Monday morning, mutual apologies as well as thanks were exchanged between host and guest as each declared that he did not spend as much time with the other. Tim expressed pleasure that Bear had met up with an 'old flame', with another friendly warning to proceed with caution. Tim summed up the events of the fortnight by saying there was a lot that Bear 'wanted to be careful about': old flames, industrial espionage, potential art theft, antagonising a prominent German entrepreneur, the list goes on. You're better off out of the way, had been Tim's cheery conclusion.

Bear rejoined the Calais-Bâle line later that Monday morning, following Tim's tip to take advantage of experiencing the 1920s atmosphere of the dining car preserved from that era. Bear was happy to stare out of the window of the carriage in its splendid décor as he reflected on the past fortnight. Was the involvement with Ciara worth it, especially as there were potentially some loose ends to address? A long shot, surely, he concluded without any great conviction. Art being brought to the masses offering potential fortune, sounded laudable, so long as you are prepared for the disappointment of forgery. But surely, they wouldn't even consider a history teacher at an independent school, the height of privilege, and someone who handles artwork for a living, for goodness' sake? Hardly the most enticing of participants. He was somewhat disquieted how frequently these thoughts returned to him despite the distractions of Maigret over the next six hours as the train surged through the French countryside.

Chapter Thirteen

Change of Course for Millennium Pathway

Not for the first time in the past three years, Mike Devenish turned away from the letterhead he had just discarded and rolled his eyes. The Production Manager of Creative Arts Programmes, to give him his full title, had never taken to the name Millennium Pathway Productions, but he had been obliged to concede that, as the last decade of the twentieth century progressed, the label had acquired a certain resonance. It had been the idea of CEO Walter Williamson, not one known for creative inspiration. Walter's talents lay in spotting the opportunity for new business, maximising the financial benefits from any fresh venture. A dynamic name for a television production company for the new millennium, Walter had declared with confidence. No one at that board meeting had dared voice dissent. Certainly, the previous name for the company, Valiant Productions was universally considered worthy, respectable but rather dull, evoking knights of old or heroes struggling against insuperable odds, the idea of trying your best but possibly coming up short. Millennium Pathway was the bold name to face the new millennium, conjuring up notions of discovery, new conquests and innovation. Mike recalled one or two puzzled looks at that first meeting at the dawn of the 1990s, as it was evident that not everyone present was familiar with the term 'millennium'.

They soon learned and were active promoting the renamed brand.

Mike had to acknowledge that Walter had unexpectedly struck gold with his rebranding of the firm. Since the Salford-based company had seized the opportunity early to commandeer the crucial 'm' word, many in the industry, and not a few in the general public naturally referred to Millennium Pathway when conversation turned to the approaching close of the century, although still a few years away. A masterstroke, Mike had to admit. Walter was more than just a money-making machine; he had his moments of inspiration.

It was with his own potential stroke of genius that Mike concerned himself that morning in late August. To have called a meeting , but three days after the pre-series get together had finalised details for the show, had stirred murmurings of concern amongst the attendees, not least because two of the principal players were on leave and would have to accept decisions being made in their absence. Mike knew that his credibility was on the line by making the propos al that he was about to deliver at short notice. A brief emergency meeting at ten o'clock had been communicated to all concerned. Seven staff agreed to drop everything, or at least postpone other activities, to attend. Mike hardly needed to remind himself that his idea had better be good. He knew it was; convincing the rest of the team was another matter.

He looked at his watch for the third time in as many minutes and gathered his papers, rose from his desk, left his office and headed towards the boardroom.

The seven summoned members of the team were already assembled, seated at the long table. Mike had readily joked that no one should 'stand on ceremony' waiting for a meeting to begin. They should take their seats in advance and be ready to commence proceedings promptly. Whereas the usual relaxed but professional feel to the gathering had been present the last time they had gathered just three days ago, on this occasion there was tension in the air. At the previous pre-series meeting there had been considerable banter prior to Mike calling proceedings to order, himself supplying a wisecrack that was well received; on this occasion conversation did not have to be broken up as faces turned eagerly but warily in his direction. There was an impatience, in some even an irritation, in wanting to know why they had been summoned unexpectedly.

As he took his seat at the head of the table, Mike distributed two printed sheets to each person present.

'Thank you all for coming,' he began. 'I know how busy you all are, so I trust I won't need to keep you for long. There is just one item on the agenda, and it is the contents of these two sheets which I would like you to peruse for a few moments.'

The layout of the pages was quite familiar to all present. They had seen numerous similar documents at previous meetings. Indeed, Raj Chopra identified the information immediately. As programme researcher he had been occupied assembling the dossier on potential contestants and recognised the two people profiled. His colleagues took a little longer to assimilate the information. Mike checked they had had enough time to digest the details and was about to begin his explanation when Jim Spencer spoke first.

'So why do we need to know about these two now?' Jim questioned in his piercing Liverpudlian tone. The sound engineer was nothing if not blunt and could be relied upon to get to the point. 'Why didn't we discuss them on Thursday?'

'For the simple reason that we didn't know about them until Friday,' Mike explained. 'The application reached me on Friday morning, and Raj worked tirelessly assembling the profiles.'

The energetic researcher in his late twenties nodded and smiled quietly to confirm his clandestine involvement.

'Well, it's all very well put together, Raj, given the short turnaround,' acknowledged production designer Charis Forbes. 'But I don't see why we need to discuss them today... unless, that is...?' Her question was effectively completed by her choleric Scouser colleague, whose tone verged on the belligerent.

'Are you saying we should fit them in the next series?' Jim challenged Mike. 'After we decided on the order on Thursday?'

'That is what I am saying, Jim, yes,' the production director replied calmly.

'I thought this was going to be some sort of an emergency meeting,' confessed film editor Martin Beckworth, his relief palpable. 'I thought you were going to announce drastic cuts, or that the show was being pulled from ITV.'

'It did sound a bit dramatic when we got the call,' added Charis.

If the team thought Mike had taken leave of his senses, it was fortunate that he quickly elucidated. 'I want us to find a slot for them in this coming series, probably not the first couple of programmes, but probably week six or seven. This is an opportunity too good to miss if you look at the profiles closely. The invitations won't be sent until this afternoon, so we still have time to make a late change.'

The production director was being deliberately guarded in his comments. As far as possible, he wanted the team to work things out for themselves.

'Well, it's an interesting couple, I grant you that,' press officer Brian Stapleton mused. 'But I don't see...'

'It's more than interesting, Brian,' Mike affirmed, eager to direct the attendees' attention to the specifics of the couple in question. 'Look at the openings we can create. Look at where he works, and the connections he might have. More importantly, notice where *she* works. This is an opportunity that is too good to overlook.'

'Is it a potential winner?' asked Martin.

All eyes turned to Samantha Higgins. The artistic director had been silent to that point.

Finally, she spoke up. 'Judging from what Raj has been able to dig up, she certainly knows her art, so there is a chance they could hit the jackpot. Even if they don't win, they have the potential to lose well and be very interesting contestants into the bargain.'

Jim struggled to restrain himself. His socialist instincts kicked in as he saw the programme being hijacked by elitism. 'Hang on a second, what do you mean, *interesting*? He teaches in some poncy private school, and she is a professional, for God's sake! She works in a gallery. This is supposed to be The Double F Show! What happened to art for the people?'

While the sound engineer's face turned earnestly around the table in search of support, or at least some response, Mike simply replied, 'They are just as much people as other participants. And if you look at question four, you'll see that

164

this is a very unique story.'

A pause broke the tension temporarily as the attendees scanned the relevant section carefully. A few smiles broke out as they did so.

'You've got to admit, Jim, it's pretty unusual,' declared Martin. 'What with the painting being lost in the war and this couple meeting up after several years apart. Whether they win or not, it has got some potential. It's not as if she came across the painting in the normal course of her work. I mean, finding the painting in a barn…'

'Aye, aye,' continued Jim with a mischievous wink, 'and what were they planning to get up to in a barn on a hot summer's day? Better not answer that one, folks, let's just say they were wanting to cool off from the heat. Certainly not looking for artwork.'

'But they were, Jim,' affirmed Samantha emphatically. 'If you look carefully at the girl's testimony. They were specifically looking for a Duclos painting.'

'Hardly a girl,' commented Brian. 'Getting on for thirty.'

Jim waved his hand in a dismissive gesture as if to say he was not impressed with the account of the find by the would-be participant Miss Ciara O'Malley, never mind her credentials as a faithful follower of The Double F Show, even while exiled in Switzerland. His scepticism was not broadly shared, but Martin did supply a caveat.

'I think we can safely assume she knows her art, given her background and her work, but isn't there the tiniest danger that she is looking for some cheap publicity for her gallery and that she could be taking us for a ride?'

'You could suspect ulterior motives in any participant,' Mike stated. 'That's a risk we always take. But what's different about this couple is the timing of the thing.'

Several puzzled looks were exchanged across the table until it became clear that Samantha perceived exactly to what Mike was referring. She volunteered an explanation. 'If you look at the last paragraph, where she says how thrilled she would be to take part, "especially given that next year will be such a special one in the memory of the great Barbizon school artists".' The artistic director patiently outlined the significance of the anniversary and the plans for exhibitions in London and elsewhere.

'If we get in there first with a programme aired in the early part of next year, and do it well,' she stressed. 'We would be way ahead of the game. Millennium Pathway would be seen as the pioneers, the innovators, leaders in the field of spotting quality artwork and unearthing hidden gems.'

'Which is why Walter came up with the name for MP in the first place,' Mike said, dextrously picking up the baton. 'Boldly facing the challenges of the new millennium.'

'Huh,' Jim snorted. 'I'm not sure the challenges will be any different from now when we hear Big Ben chime on the first of January 2000. Millennium or no millennium, it's always going to be art for the people, not for the professionals. I think it's a bad move. I think we should—'

'Actually,' interrupted Raj with the quiet enthusiasm of one delighted to throw in a pearl of wisdom of rare profundity, 'strictly speaking the millennium will begin on December 25th 1999, exactly two thousand years after the birth of Christ.'

'Trust a Hindu to put us right on the Christian calendar,' Jim retorted with a hint of sarcasm.

'My family are actually Christians, and have been for

166

several generations,' Raj corrected him with a benevolent smile, unperturbed by a familiar inaccurate presumption of his heritage.

'You sure it's not Christmas Day, 2000 that the millennium starts?' asked Martin provocatively, enjoying the opportunity for office banter.

'And of course, isn't it proven that Jesus wasn't born in December?' Charis pointed out. 'So that means—'

Mike resumed his chairman role with more vigour than he had shown thitherto. 'I am not sure that this discussion, however fascinating, is getting us anywhere. What we have is two young people, well, youngish, who have an interesting story about how they met up out of the blue and why they both got interested in a Duclos. Even if it's a forgery, it's well worth airing, especially with this major exhibition coming up next year. There is still time to include them in the series beginning after Easter.'

For a group that had seemed eager to press on with business at the beginning and avoid prolonging an extra meeting unnecessarily, the exchanges were notably more animated. Jim ventured the opinion that neither of Mike's proposed new participants seemed to bring anything of merit, save the man's unusual first name. Charis countered that the intrigue they brought to the party would easily outweigh any lack of sparkle in their personalities or background. Martin voiced the view that the couple's tracking down of the painting in a barn in north-eastern France spoke of a spirit of adventure and there must be something in their characters to attract viewers.

And this Irish lass sounded a fiery character with some determination to find out about this potential masterpiece.

167

Brian mentioned the chance art trip in Constable Country as a superb opening to any show, even if this Bear character was embellishing the encounter in his account.

'I don't think so,' Raj asserted, having responded to Mike's summons on Friday to read the application completed from Switzerland by the young Irishwoman. 'Some subtle enquiries I was able to conduct on Friday afternoon seem to back up his story.'

'Subtle enquiries?' queried Martin.

'I rang this Constable Centre place. They are indeed currently displaying paintings by Duclos, and they did have a visit from Princewood School some weeks ago.'

'I hope you didn't reveal who you work for,' said Mike with an edge of alarm in his voice.

'Of course not,' countered Raj. 'I know better than to give the game away.' As a sea of faces stared at him, he felt obliged to add nonchalantly, 'I just said I was an art teacher at a school in Suffolk. I made up the name. I said I had heard a party from Princewood had been there recently and asked what their visit consisted of, as I believed we had similar students.

'Helpful lady on the other end. Confirmed just about everything we've been told about this Bear teacher.'

Mike decided it was time to step in. 'I think we have got to make room for this couple. I will take the rap if it goes pear-shaped.' Aside from sighs of frustration from Jim, there was no discernible dissent. 'The big question is… who drops out of the list to make way for them?'

'Not the chap from Dumfries with the three golden retrievers. They sound so sweet!' exclaimed Charis quickly. 'If they don't appear, that would be close to a resignation issue for me.'

'And definitely not the couple in the caravan in Dorset. Or the bus driver from Rochdale.' Brian was equally adamant. 'We can't dilute art for the people to let this couple in.'

'Don't worry, Brian,' said Mike. 'It will be one of the more middle-class applicants.'

'So long as we don't lose Marjorie and her ladies who lunch from Sussex,' Brian inserted another plea. 'Finola would have a field day buttering them up.'

For the first time, the show's main protagonist spoke up. For someone whose on-stage persona was decidedly sparky and effervescent, she was particularly laid back. 'You're not wrong there, Brian,' she said quietly with her rich Glaswegian vowels. 'Putty in ma hands.'

Mike took charge and suggested two possible pairs of participants, both quite well-to-do, one of which was to be told that, sadly, they had not been selected on the list for this series, but their names would be kept on reserve if they were still interested. After a brief discussion, it was agreed that retired accountants David and Dawn from Cheshire would join the ranks of the disappointed applicants and would almost certainly never learn how close they were to appearing on *Fame or Forgery*.

'Good,' Mike summed up with a confident smile. 'We can get the letters out this afternoon. Cheryl can write an invitation letter to the "Duclos couple" and amend the original letter to the Cheshire couple to put them on the reserve list.' The secretary, who was taking minutes of the meeting, acknowledged her upcoming role in the process with a nod while noting down the change.

'Just a second, Mike,' Jim said, gazing at the production manager accusingly. 'You make it sound as if it's all a done deal.'

'Well, we have agreed to include the new couple, and

169

someone has to drop out,' Mike explained simply.

'I mean it's as if you've already decided you want this pair in, come what may.'

'If you put it like that, Jim, I was prepared to dig my heels in if I had to. But as you all have been so accommodating, I didn't really need to. But—,' Mike felt compelled to add, 'just so there is no misunderstanding, Cheryl has already typed the invitation letter which will be sent straight after this meeting.'

Jim sucked in another pensive intake of breath before issuing a warning. 'If the whole reputation of The Double F Show falls apart because of this one show and we get loads of complaints about involving art world professionals and favouring elitist education—'

'I know, Jim, on my head be it. The thought did occur to me over the weekend more than a few times.'

Fortunately for the harmony of the rest of the gathering, Brian interjected by recalling sticky moments in The Double F Show's history and how they had learned from mistakes.

'Whatever happens, it can't be as bad for complaints as when we got the valuation wrong for that Japanese pottery and had to apologise to that couple who thought they'd won a fortune.'

'Or when we dismissed that seascape as too damaged for display two or three years ago only to find out later that it would survive and it ended up fetching a good sum at auction,' Charis added.

'Yeah, thanks to the free publicity we gave it,' Brian commented ruefully.

'But even in our rare setbacks there has been a silver lining,' Mike emphasised by way of conclusion. 'And there will be definite gains in this one, win or lose.' He started counting on his fingers as he listed the benefits of the project. 'First, we will be expanding on to the continent, with pre-show interviews in Switzerland and appealing to our growing Irish audience with one of their own featured. Not to mention tapping into the resources of public schools. What's not to like?'

As there was no challenge to his assertions, the Production Manager turned to the presenter for her view. 'So, Fee, any initial thoughts on your line of questioning in the pre-show visits?'

Finola did not need to ponder before answering. 'Och, I think that's a fairly straightforward one this time, don't you, Mike? I'll just do a wee bit of probing on the old flames getting together angle. If they bite, we can make the most of it. If not, we can work it in somehow or other.'

Whilst the remark drew some amused grins around the table, not all were enamoured of the possible unscrupulous tactics envisaged. Samantha was conscious of the tendency of the show to twist its emphasis to make its participants more colourful than they were in reality, but though her artistic instincts longed for the art to speak for itself, she reluctantly accepted the need for some more aggressive merchandising of their product. Raj felt a slight chill at Finola's last sentence, but in his relatively junior position maintained a dignified silence. The others were happy to allow the star of the show's wishes to be carried out and, Jim's warnings notwithstanding, there was a decided consensus as the meeting broke up to strive to make the revised set of guests on *Fame or Forgery* a major success.

Chapter Fourteen

Seeking Approval

The reunions that shaped the end of the long summer break and indicated the beginning of another school year consisted of three stages for Bear. There had been the occasional pub visits with Mac and casual conversation in the last week of the holidays with a couple of colleagues when he visited the school to check on post, sort out stationery and tidy up his classroom. Then, on the eve of the staff training day that itself preceded the beginning of term proper, an informal gathering at The Anchor Inn took place. Finally, further news was exchanged during the training day with those colleagues not present at the previous night's social.

The Anchor Inn was the teachers' pub of choice, situated on the main square of Princewood. Whilst they were aware that underage drinking undoubtedly took place, staff also knew that The Anchor was off-limits to pupils, none of whom would dare risk being seen at the town's most prominent hostelry. The traditional informal gathering of some twenty staff had enabled the exchange of holiday experiences. Peter Walt on was intrigued to know of Bear's ventures on the Calais-Bâle line, Rachel Rhodes was grateful for the photograph of the Rhine's three-country border, and Head of Games Stuart Prentice waxed lyrical about a trip to the Italian Lakes, hinting at a possible rugby tour to the region. Alan

172

Cartwright, modern linguist with a particular fascination for grammatical curiosities but an even more insatiable appetite for obscure refereeing controversies, engaged a few of the rugby coaching fraternity with one of his conundrums towards the end of the evening. Bear, who assisted with the coaching of the Under-16 B team, was often drawn into such discussions. On this occasion he had made his excuses early to ensure a good night's sleep before the training day.

At coffee break the following day further holiday experiences were shared. Inevitably, Claudine was eager to learn of Bear's Basel adventures. He was polite and succinct, deploying a commendable journalistic economy of expression to communicate the events of the fortnight.

'A very enjoyable stay, thanks, Claudine. Good to see my friend Tim after all this time. Saw a fair bit of Basel and other places in Switzerland. Lovely weather. Hope to go back one day.'

He was guarded in not wishing to reveal anything about the painting issue, or his unexpected reunion with Ciara. Since one could not be mentioned without the other, both topics remained unexplored. Not that someone as inquisitive as Claudine was put off, however.

'No sign of romance over ze long 'ot summer, my Grizzly Bear?' she asked in a provocatively maternal tone. The divorcee from Bordeaux had lived in Britain for some twenty years now yet had never shaken off her Gallic flourish in addressing more spicy topics of conversation openly. She engaged more naturally with male members of staff than with her female colleagues, a trait that Bear had found unnerving at first, before he realised it was simply Claudine's way.

'No, nothing of that nature, Claudine,' Bear replied

173

unconvincingly, hoping on two counts that his French colleague would not pursue the topic. She had a disarming knack of unlocking secrets with careful, unthreatening questioning.

'Your friend in Switzerland didn't introduce you to any young ladies, then…?' she asked casually. Fortunately, before he could answer, John Billington sidled up to them both with an obvious observation to make from the proceedings of the first hour of the day.

'Well, Bear, how does it feel?' he challenged, dunking his custard cream biscuit in his coffee. 'Are you put out, nay, even enraged that the Head has stolen your thunder, or are you honoured that your words have been used to propel Princewood School to even greater heights of glory?'

'What are you talking about, John?' asked Claudine, puzzled.

Bear, however, had no need of the explanation the Head of Physics supplied to the French teacher. Indeed, the historian had smiled uneasily as four or five faces had turned in his direction half an hour earlier during the Headmaster's inspirational beginning of academic year speech. After the formalities of reviewing public examination results and a brief report on progress with building improvements issued by deputy David Wilkinson, Stephen Rawlinson had set out his vision for the school for the forthcoming academic year in his annual "call to arms".

Princewood School's headmaster was known for his use of clichés, mottos and watchwords which he imparted to teachers and children alike. Each year he would include in an address to his staff a motivational principle that he wished them to follow and occasionally emphasise to pupils over the

174

course of the months ahead. The previous year he had encouraged them to put no limits on what could be achieved. They were to climb every mountain, and once they had reached the top, to grasp the new exciting challenges that would suddenly be visible, to go 'to the end of the world... and beyond'. He had paused theatrically to emphasise the final few words. Now, twelve months later, he sought to consolidate his ambitious message and find a slogan that would focus minds on the goal of making Princewood the leading co-educational independent school in the region. His words, as ever, had been carefully chosen.

'I want to emphasise what is an often-underrated value today, and that is the value of... persistence,' he had declared, again pausing before delivering the key word. 'The Bible says that if we seek, we shall find and if we knock on doors persistently, eventually they will be opened. Few men demonstrate this principle as powerfully as Abraham Lincoln...' At this point the handful of teachers who had attended Bear's assembly in July struggled to resist the temptation to steal a glance in his direction to gauge his reaction as his pearls of wisdom were exploited.

Sure enough, the celebrated American President's tortuous road to greatness, illustrated forcefully by Bear and his class some weeks earlier, received another airing in edited form.

'It's fine,' Bear said after Billers had finished explaining the context to Claudine. 'It's not as though they were my words originally. I got the idea out of a book.'

'Nothing new under the sun, eh?' remarked Billers jovially. 'Still, the Head Man is true to form. We wouldn't have it any other way, bless him.'

175

Bear acknowledged the veracity of his colleague's observation. Whilst Stephen Rawlinson was not renowned as the most dynamic or visionary of headmasters, he had a reputation for being a safe pair of hands and a good judge of character. He had been astute in a couple of appointments of heads of department in the past few years and was particularly skilful in marshalling his resources, both human and man-made. Thus, it was unsurprising that he would exploit a colleague's ideas for maximum benefit to the school, even if that teacher was not acknowledged publicly as the initiator of the bright idea.

In fact, Bear was not especially put out by having his thunder stolen. He was more concerned with other remarks the Head had made in his motivational address. He had urged the staff to keep up the good work and concentrate on applying the traditional good habits of education, emphasising that quality will make itself known, often through word of mouth. Even 'in this day and age' (a favourite Rawlinson phrase) and with the proliferation of media outlets, oral communication is still the number one channel of transmission. Any involvement with the media, he reminded staff, is to be channelled through deputy head David Wilkinson. Stephen cited an example of an independent school not so far away that had ha d its fingers burnt by a television documentary that had meant to be complimentary but turned out to include veiled sarcasm about privilege and outdated practices. Bear had taken a sharp intake of breath at this point. He knew that there was a strong possibility that a request for media involvement concerning an ongoing art project might be landing on the Head's desk very soon. He wondered how it would be received in the light of the comments just expressed.

***

That process of seeking a line manager's approval had already been undertaken at the Neue Basler Kunstgalerie. In fact, events had advanced significantly in the remaining weeks of Bear's summer holiday. While he was catching up with family in Cumbria, competing in the social mixed doubles tournament at his tennis club in Princewood, indulging in the occasional trip to London and making the most of the down time, Ciara had been attending to the administration of verifying the painting removed from the Alsace farm building. After her serious discussions with Bear on the Saturday before his departure, she resolved to come clean immediately with Ernst to explain what she had been engaged in during her hastily requested day off. She had not looked forward to approaching him that Monday morning.

'Well, I must admit I did wonder,' her boss said, removing his spectacles to face her when she began by saying she needed to explain why she had asked for leave at relatively short notice. 'Not that it's any of my business,' he added amiably.

She had related the sequence of events slowly and deliberately, stressing that she was keen to follow up a lead on a missing painting and had unexpectedly met someone after a long absence who could assist in the search. She winced at her clumsy choice of words and worried that the removal of the potential masterpiece might have implications of a criminal nature. Ernst, however, had a reputation of being implacable and few things seemed to ruffle his feathers. He was not about to make an exception now.

'So what you're saying is will the farmer notice it's missing? Possibly not,' he answered his own question. 'But if we want to publicise the work, whether it proves to be a Duclos or not, it's not a risk we can take. We need to have a word with him.'

And that is just what they did, arranging a return trip across the border with a French-speaking colleague to accompany Ernst and Ciara. The farmer was understandably taken aback at the audacity of intruders on his land removing items of value. Any shock and anger he began to express, however, was swiftly dismissed by grudging admiration for the honesty demonstrated by the gallery trio. Ernst's reassuring tones persuaded the landowner that considerable positive publicity for the intrusion would be forthcoming. They were able to shake hands amicably at the prospect.

In truth, the farmer confessed that he had been meaning to clear out that basement in his barn for years. He even agreed for a forensic examination to take place to detect any additional trace of nineteenth-century artwork. Ciara's relief was palpable after the farmer was softened further with the promise of compensation for any visits to his property in the interests of art. He was amused by the prospect of television companies being attracted to his barn not just to pursue a possible story on lost artwork, but to stage a documentary on the retreating German armies and what they took with them or left behind.

Ciara was not slow in making her next move. Whilst she knew that the month of August was likely to be a quiet one in terms of the gallery pursuing new projects, given the absence of key personnel on holiday, any delay in her plan would permanently derail this once-in-a-lifetime opportunity. Ernst suggested that he was prepared to initiate a valuation process and try to assemble the country's leading experts in the field of nineteenth century landscape painting, at least three of whom were based in Basel. However, there was no rush and he expected significant meetings to be held in September or October. That gave Ciara some leeway and she ensured that she had composed her initial letter and posted it before departing with a friend on a week's break in Majorca.

On her return she was excited to notice a bulky envelope emanating from Manchester and did not even prioritise unpacking over examining the contents eagerly. It was as she expected, although the questions were more searching and personal than she had anticipated. Name, address, contact telephone number, age, occupation, details of the work of art she would like to submit for inspection, all very normal and predictable. Then she was asked to supply a full account of how she came across the work in question. No problem, she thought to herself, she had done so already in her initial letter, but she would nevertheless have to be careful in how she phrased the account. No impression of breaking and entering into agricultural property, just an innocent ramble that happened to incorporate an inquisitive wander into a concealed basement.

Just what anyone might do on a hot summer's afternoon on a day off. From that point the questions took a different course. What sparked your interest in art? Who inspired you to take an interest in art? What are your earliest memories of being struck by artistic beauty? What would it mean to you if you were accepted as a participant on the show? It was then that Ciara realised that, even allowing for her excitement and ambition to fulfil a dream, due time and forethought was

179

required to ensure the application form was filled in accurately and in accordance with the sender's mood. Three days later, after several scraps of paper had been discarded, the response was dispatched.

The relief at having completed the form did not translate into any sense of assurance of success of her project. If anything, her anxiety levels rose noticeably as she contemplated the possible reaction and discussions in Manchester as her answers were scrutinised by the relevant panel. For goodness' sake, Ciara, she told herself more than once, it's not as if you're applying for a job, your next make or break career move. She even drew an amused smile from Silke when she told herself to snap out of it rather more audibly than she intended. Yet she could not dispel the notion that this may be her one chance of achieving an ambition that had been stirred in her for a few years now. If rejected now, she would probably never get another opportunity as more deserving applicants would almost certainly be given preference.

A fortnight had passed when, one late afternoon towards the end of August, she noticed the familiar postmark with a thinner envelope. Her heart sank as she assumed that the thinner contents represented a rejection. She gritted her teeth as she reluctantly opened the envelope to survey the single sheet therein. As she digested the simple message, she stared open-mouthed as the essential phrases impressed themselves on her consciousness... we are delighted... next series of 'Fame or Forgery' invite you to participate... please confirm availability... shortly be in touch... congratulations... very much look forward... She was grateful that she was alone in her flat at the time as any other occupant would have been

180

scared witless by her high-pitched shriek of delight and amazement as she absorbed the news.

It was a good half-hour before she composed herself sufficiently before making a telephone call to the United Kingdom. The recipient's reaction was to match her own of earlier in the evening.

'Bear speaking.'

'Hello, "Bear speaking", are you free to speak?'

'Oh, hello, Ciara. I suppose so. How are you? Is something up?'

He did not need elaboration for her next words. 'Bear, guess what? We're on!'

Chapter Fifteen

Literary Inspiration

'There is nothing like art to sharpen man's inherent competitive instinct, to bring out the best and often the worst, of one's desires. The constant search for refinement, for the distinct edge of uniqueness to stand out from the crowd has always been a powerful motivating factor in creative endeavours.' Thus claimed the provocative back cover blurb that Ciara O'Malley had got round to studying thoughtfully, some three weeks after receiving her gift. She nursed a glass of claret as she decided she should make the effort to digest the contents of the book. Her sister had presented it to her in recognition of Ciara's hospitality in showing the city of Basel to Roisin, her husband and two young children during a two-night stopover at the end of their summer holiday in Switzerland.

Whilst intrigued by the title, Ciara was not immediately in the mood for subject matter that resonated with her work. The month of August had seen her spend a week in Majorca with her friend Vanessa from Limerick and that had refreshed her after the awkward yet surprisingly successful attempt to persuade Ernst of the merits of verifying the value of the painting discovered in Alsace. Her role as unofficial family tour guide at the end of August had been enjoyable but draining and she had not found the inclination to open her sister's present for a while. Now, on an unremarkable weeknight in mid-September, she decided at least a token perusal of some admittedly not unfamiliar topics was warranted, if only to forestall any potential embarrassment at the next family gathering.

Her low expectations of *Where Artistic Temperaments Clash* were, to her agreeable surprise, proven ungenerous as she tucked into the first offering, a well-documented account of the feud between Leonardo da Vinci and Michelangelo. Her familiarity with the great artists' backgrounds did not prevent her warming to the author's wit and irony in depicting the rivalry from the viewpoint of each protagonist. With each chapter, the writer attempted to present a tongue-in-cheek, scientific, psychological assessment as to why two prominent figures in the art world fell out. In this first chapter, the author concluded, Leonardo and Michelangelo fell out because they were stable mates, both hailing from Florence. Being challenged to paint the same hall in competition with each other did not help, but their real problem was that they both wanted to be their home city's top dog. It did not matter how much the world is your oyster if you are not flavour of the month at home. Hence, the deep insecurity in both great masters. Author's diagnosis: stable rivalry.

The next pair of antagonists were Caravaggio and Giovanni. Caravaggio's *Amor Vincit Omnia* was met by a painted response by Giovanni that Caravaggio claimed to be blatant plagiarism. Such protestation merely succeeded in encouraging Giovanni to produce a second version which included his rival's face being attached to the body of the devil. Caravaggio's response was to turn to verse, creating a series of comic poems mocking his rival, declaring his

183

intention to use Giovanni's paintings as toilet paper. Giovanni took his opponent to court on charges of libel and Caravaggio spent a few days in custody. Author's diagnosis: inability to let the public decide, innate insecurity on the part of both painters.

'Ah well, that's the Italians for you,' Ciara said to herself with a knowing smile, so easily worked up and passionate, before instantly berating herself for the stereotype she was normally meticulous in avoiding. She expected further feuds to be dominated by the fiery Mediterranean temperament when she was surprised to notice, as she flicked through, a chapter on Turner's rivalry with Constable. Less likely rivalries and disputes were being explored and the anecdotes shared, even if some were apocryphal, with engaging humour. Ciara acknowledged that from the earliest chapters the book had entertainment value. She was about to set it aside for the evening when she spotted one of the later chapters and decided to read on.

'Band of brothers, eh?' she thought to herself as this particular chapter heading captured her attention for the next half-hour. She correctly deduced a tinge of irony in the description of the handful of painters that belonged to the Barbizon School. Initially, the information supplied was already familiar to her. The group of artists took its name from the village of Barbizon, on the edge of the Forest of Fontainebleau, where many of the painters gathered. She nodded in recognition as the thrust of the school's purpose was explained in the appreciation for sketches in natural settings. The increased facility in painting outdoors thanks to the invention of the small portable easel and of portable paints in tubes, around 1840, encouraged the development of the group congregating in the forest scenery outside Paris.

The chapter started to grip her attention as certain characters in the movement were introduced. Jeannot and Pierrot came to the fore with growing frequency and their works received special mention. 'Why do the French use nicknames that actually make the name longer?' she pondered 'Then again, we do call Tim Sheldon "Timbo", so maybe it's a universal human tendency to stick a tag on every label.' She did not dwell long on such niceties; however, as the phrase "intellectual theft" caused her to read on. It would have surprised her to learn that she was not the only person captivated by the subject matter that week.

**

Not for the first time in recent days, Stephen Rawlinson availed himself of a convenient gap between appointments to further his research. The history of art had never been a particular chosen topic of his, but he thumbed the tome recommended by Christine Walmsley carefully and digested the information of the era targeted.

It had been a fruitful morning so far. After two well-briefed and reliable sixth formers had performed an impressive and informative conducted tour of the premises, he was able to entertain prospective parents that morning in the knowledge that their view of Princewood School was overwhelmingly favourable. Coffee, biscuits and reassuring answers to the remaining questions that the visitors had withheld from their guides added to the conviction that this was the desired destination for the first of their three offspring. Provided, of course, that their son passed the entrance examination, which, given his reports, seemed a formality. Having parted company with the new customers amiably, Princewood's headmaster congratulated himself on a rewarding morning's work, both financially and in building relationships.

There was no vanity in such an assessment. It was one of Stephen's strengths to be a sound judge of character and he showed strong empathy with people, from the wealthiest of parents to the school catering and grounds staff and the youngest of children. The stress of certain aspects of administration he was careful to delegate to his deputies, in itself a tribute to his reading of personality, as he had appointed both David Wilkinson and Angela Banks during his tenure.

His next task that morning promised to be slightly more delicate. Not in terms of what to say to the next person to enter the headmaster's study; he knew what he was going to say. He was just concerned to convey the correct impression to that particular member of the teaching staff of his interest and commitment to the scheme proposed, without sounding too easily swayed by the demands of the modern technological age. With some twenty minutes before the scheduled meeting, he returned his gaze to the story of French nineteenth-century landscape painting to be as knowledgeable as possible before the imminent discussion with his next visitor.

Sure enough, at the appointed time his secretary Margaret Fisher ushered the teacher in question into his study.

'Bear, come along in. Take a pew,' he said, indicating one of the armchairs adorning the room.

'Good morning, Stephen,' Bear replied, sensing a twinge

186

of nervousness, so much so that he almost addressed the other as 'Headmaster', a habit he had long been urged to curb by the school principal himself. Bear sensed he was somehow guilty of some offence he needed to explain, when he was the one who had requested the interview rather than being summoned.

Small talk did not, mercifully, extend beyond a polite enquiry as to how things were progressing in the History Department before Stephen addressed Bear's proposal.

'Thank you for your proposal and for forewarning me,' he began.

'Forewarning?' queried Bear.

'About an imminent approach by Millennium Pathway Productions. I received their formal request yesterday. They said you would be contacting me to ask permission for the programme.'

'Ah… good,' Bear replied hesitantly before adding, 'they seem to be on the ball.'

'They place strong emphasis on art for the people, I notice. They seem keen to stress that they take art to places hitherto unreached.'

'I believe the idea is to give everyone the chance of fame. Hence, the title of the show.'

'I'm not sure it's fame we should be seeking,' Stephen responded, then checked himself, lest his assertion be deemed pompous. 'Of course, if the filming presents the school in authentic light, all well and good, and I welcome the opportunity to extend cultural experience beyond the… er… usual parameters.'

'It will certainly achieve that,' Bear confirmed, but was immediately wary of sounding too enthusiastic and surfing the latest wave of popular culture. He qualified his remark: 'A

187

visit to Princewood would certainly be seen as a positive contribution in that respect.'

Stephen continued his gentle questioning. His main concern was to be seen and heard to be thorough. He was eager for Bear to be aware that any decision taken was considered with evidence for both sides weighed meticulously. 'I confess I am not familiar with "The Double F Show". A misleading sobriquet, I would suggest. But Christine assures me of its validity. She tells me the interest was sparked by your trip to the Constable Centre in the summer?'

'That's right,' Bear confirmed. 'My friend in Basel had reason to believe a contact had left the painting in a village in Alsace when fleeing the allies towards the end of the Second World War.'

'Indeed,' acknowledged the headmaster. 'As you mentioned in your note to me, and Millennium Pathway were again thorough in confirming the details. Their letter says that you found it in a barn. Was that with the farmer's permission?'

Bear repressed the instinct to reply 'not exactly' but adeptly sidestepped the question. 'Yes, he was happy with us taking it away for analysis.' (Albeit retrospectively, Bear inwardly confessed with a remorseful but fortunately inaudible gulp.)

Stephen paused to view the production company's letter that he had studied thoroughly over the past twenty-four hours. He was reluctant to give the slightest impression of acting precipitously. His response was measured. 'It sounds a fascinating story, and all the more so if the painting is genuine, of course. The Barbizon landscapes are quite impressive, and the revolutionary use of the outdoor environment is striking. Of course, these techniques are most aptly acknowledged by our participation at the Constable Centre since its inception.' The headmaster congratulated himself on his selection of phrases, borrowed half from Christine, half from the art history book she had lent him. He continued, 'my one concern is the way modern media can distort, for the best intentions...'

'Distort...?' Bear asked, slightly puzzled.

'I wouldn't want the school to be seen as looking for publicity at all costs.'

'I'm not sure I follow you...?' Bear asked, somewhat disingenuously, knowing from his brief viewing of The Double F Show, how the production team was quite comfortable with going over the top.

'What I mean is, Bear, that we might attract new clientele but need to protect and nurture core markets. Art for the people might be a bit of a jump. Do you know the presenter, this Fiona lady...?'

'Finola,' Bear corrected. 'Not really. I've only seen the show once and she is quite a character but can also be quite discerning... in her knowledge of art, that is.'

'Good, because I wouldn't want anything to compromise the core principles and ethos of the school.' The sentence was delivered at a deliberate, controlled pace, emphasising the need for care to be the guiding principle as the venture proceeded.

Bear felt it prudent to stress the terms of any agreement for Millennium Pathway Productions to film on the premises of any participant in the show. 'We have a veto over what is shown, but they do insist that I give a couple of minutes talking to camera about my interest in art, which they edit.'

Stephen nodded to confirm that he was aware of this condition. 'What would they see of the school?' he asked.

'From what I gather there are no holds barred, but we can refuse content apart from my monologue. They say that is authentic and can be edited, but not endlessly doctored. They want my feelings to be genuine and not rehearsed.'

'Puts quite a responsibility on your shoulders, then?' Stephen suggested with a paternal smile.

'I'm up for it, Stephen,' Bear replied, forcing a reciprocal smile that camouflaged his wariness with the role he was landed.

'Well, then, Bear, so am I. They say they want to come down to Suffolk in the next couple of months, so let's try to agree a date in mid-October, this side of half-term, with the autumn leaves still on the trees. Must have the school looking its best!'

The discussion was concluded amicably, and Stephen allowed Bear to take his leave, reflecting that the history teacher was certainly well equipped for the challenge of the media intrusion. The head teacher was left with much to ponder, however. It was all very well saying we can veto stuff, but we want something to come out of the visit and if all we see is Bear talking, it will look as if we have something to hide. He considered putting deputy head David Wilkinson in charge of showing the film crew around and contemplated the challenging days ahead. Would it be an exaggeration to say that the visit of Millennium Pathway could make or break Princewood School?

Chapter Sixteen

Breaking New Ground

'I tell you, it's all about privilege,' the self-appointed preacher resumed his discourse once the trio found open-air seating at which to consume their coffee and bacon sandwiches. The pleasant mid-October sunshine encouraged them to remain outside for the half-hour stop at the motorway service station. 'All they're interested in is getting more punters through the doors that can pay their obscene high fees.'

'But it works both ways, Jim,' film editor Martin Beckworth replied. 'When this programme comes out, we will start to access sections of the population we never dreamed of reaching. Sections with buying power.'

'Huh,' Jim snorted. 'We're a godsend to them, not the other way round. And don't expect some of these moneybags to be sudden converts to The Double F Show. They'll turn their noses up at the likes of us.' He bit determinedly on his bacon sandwich as if to underline his discontent. His colleagues did not respond immediately as the deadening drone of motorway traffic thundering past provided an oppressive backdrop to the conversation.

'Well, as Dev says, "whatever our personal views"...' Martin could not resist mimicking their boss's tones, as he knew Mike Devenish's measured counsel would wind the sound engineer up. 'We need to be discreet and not advertise our purpose too overtly.'

'Or we may have a repeat of the West Highland Terriers from Cleethorpes on our hands,' chipped in cameraman Colin.

'You're not wrong there, Col,' Martin acknowledged with a chuckle. 'When word got out that The Double F Show was in town, the whole street was out in force following us about. Or at least that's what it felt like. Got the dogs all agitated and looked for one dreadful moment as if we had to abort.'

Even Jim raised a grin at this recollection. Unsurprisingly so, as Martin recalled the incident as one of the sound engineer's finest hours. The film editor continued, 'but good old Jim saved the day by sweet-talking the animals. Don't know how you did it, Jim, but it calmed the beasts down and they were as good as gold after that.'

'And we had no end of requests to bring the dogs back on the show,' recalled Colin.

The conversation successfully diverted Jim from his repeated rant about the inequity of private education, for which his two travelling colleagues were relieved. 'I can't remember,' he said. 'Did our West Highland fella turn out to be a winner?'

'No, his pottery turned out to be a forgery. But he won the hearts of the nation,' Martin said.

'Hmm… I can't see us winning many hearts from our trip to Princewood School. I tell you, they have everything to gain and The Double F Show has its whole reputation to lose.' Jim needed little encouragement to reprise his pet theme.

The trio finished their snacks with the other two taking care not to fuel Jim's passions as conversation turned to their destination. Only Colin was familiar with Suffolk, having an aunt, long deceased, who used to reside in the county. Martin, being a sailing enthusiast, was curious to look at the boats adorning the River Frame but doubted whether there would be sufficient time for any form of sightseeing. Millennium Pathway's chosen crew for the following day's filming had a mission to perform, targeting one half of a pair of future participants on *Fame or Forgery*. The three colleagues returned to their van and exited the service station to resume their journey southward before later heading east to England's flattest region. Discussion duly returned to the individual to be featured on the morrow. Colin, who had not been present in the original preparatory meeting chaired at short notice by Mike, asked about the teacher's credentials.

'He's a history teacher, this Hoskins fellow,' revealed Martin. 'Also coaches games. We chose Thursday as a good day to visit Princewood as it seems our friend has a busy teaching day with a full morning of lessons and games in the afternoon. So we should get our money's worth. He'll be kept on his toes all right.'

'The poor beggar doesn't know what he's letting himself in for,' Jim remarked.

His comment needed no response. His two co-workers both knew one of the principles of The Double F Show was to allow full access to a participant's working life, even allowing a whole day at their place of employment to delve into the motivation and temperament of the would-be famous owner of a work of art. It was signed into the agreement that there would be no holds barred in finding out what makes Bear Hoskins tick. Despite this licence to explore, Jim was still dissatisfied.

'What I can't understand,' he announced as the van tore through Cambridgeshire on the last stages of their journey, 'is why we have to do this filming in two stages. Why can't we get both of them together in one spot? Can't this Irish lass come over?'

'You know full well why, Jim,' Martin responded patiently to his fellow passenger while Colin drove on impassively. 'They work in different countries, that's how they met up again after all these years. That's all part of the intrigue. And it will give an excuse for The Double F Show to go abroad for the first time.'

'I know, I know,' Jim conceded. 'It just seems double the expense for probably very little return, having to arrange a crew to go over to Switzerland to interview her separately. It had better be worth it.'

***

Jim would have been taken aback to know that there were others involved in the planned visit who felt similar misgivings, if not as vehemently vocalised. Stephen Rawlinson was well used to consultations in his office with parents, both current and prospective, pupils and teachers, and was also experienced in regular dealings with the public with visiting speakers, local politicians and businesspeople making occasional visits. He had never before, however, had the occasion to welcome a television film crew to the hallowed grounds of Princewood School. Nor had any of his predecessors in office. Today was destined to break new ground in the illustrious history of the renowned protestant dissenters' grammar school that had evolved over two centuries to become a co-educational independent school with an enviable reputation for academic success.

194

Yet Stephen was conscious that an image must be maintained and sometimes a risk had to be taken to maintain one's profile. Such a day had come.

Instinctively, he straightened his already immaculately positioned tie as he scanned once more the last letter from Millennium Pathway Productions. Someone called Devenish said that the company were more than happy with the date and the fact that their interviewee, Mr Hoskins, had a full teaching morning, giving the filming crew ample opportunities for still and motion pictures. He confirmed that the three-man crew would be travelling down from their base in Greater Manchester and staying in a local hotel overnight ready for an early start the following day. The suggested arrival time of nine fifteen a.m. gave the crew sufficient time to size up the grounds (Stephen was not sure he was comfortable with the term 'size up') to determine optimum angles for filming. The headmaster's offer of a tour of the grounds before making contact with Mr Hoskins was gratefully accepted.

The headmaster had considered whether he should diverge from customary practice in how visitors' tours were conducted. Usually, two senior pupils were selected to show guests around, and answer whatever questions the visitors chose to ask them. Often prospective parents would be accompanied by their offspring, so a rapport could be established with his or her contemporaries from the outset. Even for visiting dignitaries with no interest in sending children Princewood's way, sixth-formers were presented with the honour to represent the school in this way. For a moment, however, Stephen had contemplated taking the tour himself or asking one of the teaching staff to show the film crew the grounds, lest anything be detected by the guests that might tempt them to sensationalise the experience for viewers of The Double F Show. He quickly dismissed the idea as cowardice and resolved to keep the visit as normal as possible. Too much care, he reasoned, betrayed caution and insecurity that these media people would pounce upon mercilessly. Princewood School had to appear relaxed and a community at ease with itself. The desire to favour democracy and give pupils their voice had to be visible rather than the cold efficiency of an unfeeling scholastic machine. Had he exercised greater vigilance in vetting the pupil guides chosen for the tour, he might have spared a member of the history department considerable angst and the day might have proceeded more smoothly.

Just before 9.15 a.m., three individuals entered the waiting area outside the head's study. Clad in royal blue polo shirts with the initials MPP marked on their chests and the accompanying logo, 'pioneers in broadcasting excellence' emblazoned boldly below, their uniformity was impressive. Headmaster's secretary Margaret invited them to take a seat as soon as Martin announced the reason for their visit. They assumed the vacant seats on a three-seat sofa, adjacent to an identical item of furniture. This sofa was already occupied by two teenagers of about seventeen. The girl seemed to be suppressing a cheeky grin as if she was looking forward to engaging with the visitors. She nodded and said, 'Good morning,' to which the trio replied in kind. Her partner, a tall, curly haired, bespectacled youth whose glasses hid any obvious expression, added a mumbled greeting, but exhibited no more than vague curiosity at the guests. He seemed less excited by the duty they had been assigned to perform that morning.

A brief telephone ring was answered by the secretary and Margaret ushered the three representatives of the production company into the headmaster's presence. The sixth-formers were left to speculate further as to the identity of their guests. Three gentlemen needed to be shown the buildings in order to prepare a documentary related to the history of the school had been David Wilkinson's explanation which was certainly economical with the truth. In their different ways, the two teenagers could scarcely have been better chosen for ferreting the real purpose of the visit out of The Double F Show trio.

Ten minutes had elapsed when the headmaster's study door opened and Stephen Rawlinson appeared with his visitors, pointing out the waiting guides who rose promptly to their feet. 'Sarah and Matthew will show you around. I look forward to seeing you shortly and then, let battle commence!'

The visitors expressed their thanks as the headmaster took his leave. Jim spoke first in addressing their guides. 'I assume you must be Sarah?' he said, addressing the girl. 'And I suppose you must be Matthew,' he added, turning to her fellow guide.

'That's right, well worked out,' Matthew Bourne replied drily. He was one of those rare individuals who could deliver such a sentence without any obvious emphasis and even the slightest hint of sarcasm, even when it was intended.

Sarah Blake took the lead and invited the visitors to follow them as they sauntered away from the main administration building. Jim was ready with a few quips, thankfully devoid of the usual carping about private schools, and Colin soaked in the features of the premises thoughtfully, alert to any interesting camera angles that might present themselves.

Martin decided to elevate the level of conversation in a pause between the explanations of points of interest the two guides delivered. 'So what do you two study?'

Since both mentioned that art was amongst their A-Level choices, Jim chipped in by saying they were focusing on art during their visit. The naturally curious Sarah probed them as to their intentions. 'So what sort of a programme is it?'

'It's a programme about the history of art affecting independent schools,' Martin said, producing a prepared line.

'So you will be meeting Mrs Warmsley or Mrs Porter today? They are our art teachers.'

'Maybe, but it's Mr Hoskins we'll be meeting up with shortly,' Martin replied.

'Oh, but he's a history teacher,' Sarah asserted. 'Although he did join us on an art trip last summer…'

'That's right,' added Matthew with immaculate timing, 'Mr Hoskins has an interest in art. It is thought he did some modelling in his younger days.' Matthew's deadpan delivery bemused The Double F Show trio whose bewildered looks indicated they were not entirely sure whether the student was joking.

'Sshh, Matthew!' Sarah admonished with a broad grin before clarifying. 'We don't know what he got up to in his youth, but he knows a thing or two about art, we learned when we visited this place in the summer.'

'In fact, he is quite a poser is Mr Hoskins. The way he holds a board marker pen in a dramatic pose is quite something,' Matthew added. 'You'll enjoy meeting him.'

A gentle twenty-minute intermittent verbal joust ensued between the teenage guides and the three visitors, punctuated by discussions amongst the crew to note possible sites and

198

angles for filming later in the day. The Millennium Pathway trio, with Jim to the fore, were curious to extract any less than official information about life in a private school that could not be gleaned through orthodox channels, ready to pass on to artistic editor Samantha any spicy details that would attract high viewing figures. Sarah and Matthew in turn were keen to elicit any indication from their unusual guests as to their plans for the day. She was not averse to throwing in the odd provocative question; he confined himself largely to the script, but they were aware that as the visitors were hardly future parents of pupils at the establishment, they could be freer in their choice of topics. Matthew quite casually pointed to The Firs, unofficial label for an area of conifers slightly back from the drive leading up to the main building. The main smoking area, with ample cover from patrolling duty staff, was his description, adding that they hadn't received that information from himself.

When the two sixth-formers deposited their charges outside the headmaster's study at the end of their tour and had been thanked for their hospitality, the three Double F Show representatives exchanged thoughtful glances, as much to say that they had been in the company of two very shrewd young people. Much longer in their presence and the real motive of Millennium Pathway would have been obvious and the word would have got round the school.

Not that such an eventuality would have been a problem for the programme's publicity, but any intrusion by the public, in this case a student one, would be a distraction the trio could do without. Their relief was short lived, as Matthew and Sarah compared notes on returning to class on their guests' movements, both equally puzzled as to why the three men had

199

wanted to look at the sports fields for a programme focusing on the history of art.

Stephen Rawlinson was happy to receive his visitors once more and announced that they had time to set up in Mr Hoskins' classroom for the last lesson before morning break. He offered to take over guide duties for this last section. It soon became apparent why the headmaster was eager to assume such a role. As the party strolled along one of the main corridors of the nineteenth-century building, Stephen was able to point out the imposing portrait of the school's founder, James Bromwell, gazing down in a benevolent avuncular fashion on all passers-by.

Colin took the headmaster's pause at that point as the hint that was intended and started to operate his portable camera to film the artwork.

'Would you like to say something to the camera about the artwork, Headmaster?' Martin asked. 'That would be really helpful.'

'Oh... of course, certainly,' Stephen responded with feigned surprise and ensured his position did not obscure the masterpiece he proceeded to describe, with details of both the painter and the dignitary depicted. He continued by indicating a series of other portraits of leading figures, mainly former headmasters, in Princewood School's past and Colin obediently captured Stephen's confident explanations on camera. Stephen was careful to throw in a reference to the school motto *per ardua ad astra*, roughly translated as 'the sky is the limit' or literally as 'by hard work to the stars'. He tried to sound natural in underlining one of the school's core values as that of persistence and considering the limited rehearsal time he had carefully put in, carried the performance

200

off passably well. He was keen, above all, not to sound pompous but dynamic and forward looking as the new millennium edged ever closer. Jim confirmed by consulting his recording device that they had the headmaster's clear diction recorded for use in the programme.

If Bear or Stephen feared the disruption of three visitors armed with television camera on site would have on pupils' concentration, initial signs were that the children were taking the occasion in their stride. It was a changeover in lessons as Stephen handed the crew on to Bear, and Martin informed the historian that they would stay at the back of the classroom for this lesson and Colin would do some discreet filming towards the end. And the Year 7 session on the Norman Conquest proceeded without incident. The explanation of a documentary being made did excite the youngsters, and a few heads were turned as Colin adjusted his position occasionally. Yet for the most part the class was attentive, and Bear was relieved to conduct proceedings as planned as the crew acquired some footage that might find its way into the scheduled edition of The Double F Show. It was after break time that the calm started to unravel.

Inevitably, more pupils spotted the strange visitors accompanying Mr Hoskins to the staff room for mid-morning coffee. While Bear introduced the trio to the art teachers and Christine engaged them in chat about the merits of the Constable Centre and looked forward to them visiting her department before the day was through, a lively discussion was taking place in the sixth form common room.

'Who are those blokes in blue tee shirts?' asked the loquacious Freya Thomson to no one in particular.

'No idea,' offered Mark Saunders. 'They seemed to be

filming something.'

'And they have MPP on their shirts,' added Sally Sewell. 'What does that stand for?'

'Millennium Pathway,' declared Sarah Blake confidently, having had the advantage of seeing the guests up close. 'They're doing some documentary on art history.' She revealed to a cluster of a dozen students that she and Matthew had escorted the guests around the school earlier.

'Millennium Pathway Productions?' asked Deputy Head Boy Oliver Brown urgently. 'They're the lot who do The Double F Show!'

'No!' a couple of students familiar with the programme uttered in amazement.

'That can mean only one thing,' concluded Oliver. 'Someone is being filmed as a future guest on the show. Must be one of the teachers. Who were they concentrating on?'

When Sarah revealed the identity of the crew's target, the excitement level was raised several notches and spilled over from the sixth form to the younger years. A peaceful conclusion to the day's filming was no longer an option.

Meanwhile, the crew tried to reassure Bear that they would continue to keep a discreet distance throughout the morning. Discreet, that is, apart from Jim's occasional difficulties with sound and Martin's penchant for seizing certain phrases. The first lesson after break during which a Year 8 group were being initiated into the drama of the Crusades included one of Bear's classic 'what if' questions. What if you were on a ship bound for the Holy Land, charged with liberating Jerusalem for Christendom? How would you feel being away from home for months at a time, perhaps never to return? The question had provoked a thoughtful response from the class, but also a polite but intrusive enquiry by Martin for Bear to repeat the question at the end of the lesson, much to the pupils' amusement. Jim had performed a sound check and the background noise of chatter in the corridor had been sufficient to muffle the original question.

The suppressed giggles of the departing class indicated they had enjoyed the experience, although not as their teacher had intended. Martin encouraged Bear that they had some great footage already, but they wondered if they could ask Bear to include a particular comment towards the end of the final lesson before lunch. There was no time to explain what the teacher was required to say as the Year 11 class was about to begin and 18 fifteen-to-sixteen-year-olds trooped in. Warily, Bear agreed to set five minutes aside. For the next forty minutes he waded through some sources of British history in the 1920s and introduced the background to the General Strike. The film crew, whilst still in receipt of various backward glances, were relatively passive with Colin making sparing use of the camera. At five minutes to one, Martin issued a signal with a thumbs-up to indicate that the moment for the targeted comment had arrived. The film editor gesticulated to the notepaper that Bear had set aside on his desk at the beginning of the lesson. Bear picked up the note and read the script.

Conscious of murmurs of amusement from the class, he ad-libbed adroitly. 'We have an exciting change of plan that will involve eager participation from one of you, at least,' he said confidently, but struggled to hide his bafflement at the request. With limited time before the lunch bell, however, he launched into the question the crew had been directed by artistic director Samantha to ask:

'Louis XIV once said, "*L'état, c'est moi.*" Can anyone tell me what that means?'

Even the supposed French scholars in the class, when put on the spot, struggled to produce a credible answer. No problem, announced Martin, and he instructed Bear to pass the sheet to a pupil who was to say the chosen response. Struggling to keep both a straight face and to avoid giving the impression that he was reading from a script (which, of course, he was), a wiry, bespectacled boy raised his hand and pronounced: 'It means that all power lies in the hands of the monarch.'

'That's right...,' was all the response Bear was required to utter as he was assured the film would be cut at that point. The lunch bell mercifully curtailed the lesson and Bear breathed a sigh of relief. The hilarity in the students' demeanour was more restrained than that of their younger counterparts earlier, but no less apparent. Bear thought the day was descending into farce, but the crew encouraged him that he was doing brilliantly.

'All the makings of a Double F-Show classic,' Martin commented.

'And in classy surroundings,' added Jim, strangely warming to the challenge.

Bear was bemused as he was left to entertain the visitors over lunch, when they had the opportunity to meet Christine properly and engage in more authoritative chat concerning art at Princewood. Bear was largely silent, left reeling from the last lesson. It was supposed to be Britain between the wars, nothing to do with dictatorship or absolute monarchs. Why couldn't they have come after half-term when Hitler, Mussolini *et al* were on show? Or tomorrow's Year 9 class on the Napoleonic Wars? Or even earlier that day when the Lower Sixth was looking at Charles I and the monarch's interpretation of the Divine Right of Kings? Had the crew not been waylaid by Stephen Rawlinson's eagerness to capture the portraits of the school's past luminaries, some of that more relevant lesson would certainly have been captured. It then dawned on Bear that the request for the famous Louis XIV's quote was designed to connect with references to Duclos' *Flight of the Huguenots* as the despotic French monarch expelled the religious dissenters from his kingdom in demonstration of absolute power. Nevertheless, Bear struggled to fathom out where this most bizarre of days was heading. He did not have long to wait.

Martin took charge of proceedings and asked if Bear could say his piece while seated on an outdoor seat with an imposing oak tree in the background. The seat was moved some twenty yards from its usual position to accommodate best use of the autumn sunlight. Bear was fully aware of what 'his piece' entailed and was more than prepared. He was to explain how he came to be interested in a potential lost Jean Duclos painting, how he met Ciara again after several years' gap, and how they came across their find in their outing into Alsace. There would be no questions to answer; these would occur when Finola herself took to the stage at the studio on the chosen day. What Bear said today would be providing the background; Ciara would be delivering a similar brief speech in Basel at some time that autumn.

With a short window available before Bear had to change for his games session, he was eager to complete this part of proceedings without delay. Since it was still lunch break, there was no shortage of pupils milling around, including several sixth-formers who had been part of the discussion earlier in which the real purposes of the trio's visit, and Mr Hoskins' involvement, had been deduced. Others, of course, had since learned of the cause of the excitement. So it was that Bear's quiet monologue in front of the oak tree had an audience of some thirty pupils who intruded as close as they dared, close enough to hear, at least. Bear was thankful that the speech was deemed acceptable after one take, although he did wince later when he realised he had been a shade too definite in his emphases. He had stressed rather too forcefully that Ciara was 'just a good friend' and that they had met up again quite by chance. Did I really use that little word 'just'? He wondered. He feared he had and that it would come across as if he had something to hide.

He excused himself from the filming team as he left to change for his Under-16 B team rugby practice, having been warmly congratulated on his speech. The disturbing thing was that the three visitors genuinely seemed to believe it and were not simply putting on sales talk. He feared he was likely to be a figure of much mirth by the time the programme was put together.

The opportunity to see their future F Show participant on the games field was too good to overlook. The crew had been instructed to spend the whole working day getting to see how Mr Hoskins ticked, and so they followed the rugby practice that Bear shared with the A team manager, Rob McAllister. Part of the session was set aside for each team to practise some set moves before a game for the last half-hour. As thirty boys were put through their paces in various passing manoeuvres, Colin tracked Bear's movements closely from the touchline. After ten minutes, Martin sidled up to Bear, now resplendent in his Princewood School Physical Education tracksuit. A few words of praise to finish things off would go down very well.

Apparently, they had most of the key elements recorded – questioning, encouraging, exposition, challenging, directing – but the crew just needed a visible, audible instance of Bear issuing praise to a pupil, nice and short and sharp. The rugby field was the ideal place. Something brisk and punchy.

No problem, thought Bear. He summoned two players apart from the group and asked them to pass the ball between them while running past the cameraman with Bear himself in the background. At the given moment when the pass was delivered, Bear would utter, 'Great pass, James!'

The first attempt, almost inevitably, was a flop as the pass went to ground. Certainly not a great pass. The second was executed correctly, but Bear forgot to add the player's first name.

The third attempt was dropped and the fourth was a forward pass as the overeager recipient ran into an offside position. By then the selected duo had dissolved into helpless laughter and had to be replaced. Finally, at about the twelfth take, James's hoped-for great pass had been supplanted by 'Super pass, Archie!' and that remark was to find its way into Princewood folklore.

The appreciation of the Millennium Pathway trio continued, and they expressed to his face and to the headmaster, how Mr Hoskins had the makings of an excellent participant for *Fame or Forgery*. On Mike Devenish's repeated instructions, the show's nickname was not used. Over tea and biscuits in Stephen's study, to which Bear and Christine were invited (the latter for an expert final opinion on how to present Princewood's artistic heritage, but perhaps as an apology for not involving her more), an informal de brief concluded that the filming had been completed to the visitors' satisfaction. Stephen was relieved that the day's events had passed without serious mishap and the guests took their leave.

'It will be a long day for you by the time you get back to Salford,' the head remarked sympathetically.

Bear was about to reflect on what had felt like the longest day in his teaching career, but any relief at reaching its end was tempered by Martin's parting shot.

'Today will seem like a picnic when we do the final shooting in the studio when Finola comes into her own. She'll enjoy meeting you. That's a test of stamina all right. We'll see you then, Mister Hoskins. All the best!'

Chapter Seventeen

Crisis Management

When Mike Devenish thrust the tabloid in front of the two co-workers invited into his office at short notice, he had expected a sharper reaction. As neither responded with the appropriate level of concern, his normal composure and legendary patience were stretched beyond usual limits.

'Oh, yes, the French baggage handlers,' acknowledged artistic director Samantha Higgins simply, confirming that she was familiar with the story.

'It's dragging on a bit,' Martin Beckworth ventured. 'What about it?'

At least the two visitors to Mike's office that morning did not need to have 'it' explained to them. The headline reinforced a comparatively minor item on the news that had grown in significance. 'French baggage handlers' strike wrecks Brits' half-term plans' was a succinct description of an industrial dispute at France's airports that was intended as a warning shot across the bows to their employers. If the demands were not met at this relatively quiet time of year, then a more significant holiday season may yet be targeted.

'What about it?' Mike echoed Martin's question rather more vehemently. 'This strike has only gone and wrecked our plans, not of a half-term jolly, but of a crucial trip over to Switzerland to check out our Miss O'Malley.'

'Really?' returned Samantha quizzically. 'It's the French we're talking about here; the Swiss never strike.'

'Normally, absolutely not,' agreed Mike. 'But as our destination is Basel-Mulhouse airport, which happens to be a few miles inside France, it won't be the Swiss we need to worry about. That's the problem of visiting someone on a border.'

'Living dangerously, life on the edge,' quipped Martin before it dawned on him that the issue carried some gravity. 'So we can't do the filming at her gallery next week, you mean?'

'That is precisely what I mean, yes,' Mike replied with his customary calm restored now that his visitors were on the same wavelength. 'There are no flights available to any airport in the region that will take our equipment at such short notice.'

'Do I take it that we can't rearrange her slot?' Samantha asked gingerly.

'We're taken up with filming all the way to Christmas,' Mike replied with an exasperation that was still searching for a way through the impasse. 'This was our one opening before the end of the year. If we can't get the filming with our Irish friend done now, we may have to scrap the programme.'

Martin was about to offer the observation that it was a risk they always knew they were taking, given the late decision to insert new participants on The Double F Show schedule, but decided discretion was called for. He was sure his boss did not need reminding. He and Samantha looked on sympathetically striving to offer a solution. Before they could do so, Mike stepped in with a warning.

'Whatever you do, don't tell Jim. Otherwise, he'll suggest

axing our friends Bear and Ciara and bringing in the dreadfully dull Cheshire couple instead. I can just hear him say "I told you so" even if he didn't (tell me so, that is).'

'Come to think of it, where is Spencer this week?' wondered Martin.

'On leave until Wednesday, and when he returns, he will be expecting to head out to Switzerland for the next little expedition. He will have to be disappointed.'

'Yes, he was sounding a bit chirpier than last time,' Martin observed. 'Looking forward to a nice little autumn jaunt on to the continent. More his cup of tea than a stuffy private school.'

'I suppose we need to think a bit outside the box,' Samantha suggested. 'How about bringing Miss O'Malley over here?'

Mike shook his head. 'The whole point is to capture them in their normal working environment which in her case means the gallery. It would look really manufactured if we made an exception and did the pre-show filming anywhere else. It would look as if we had something to hide.' As neither of his enlisted supporters responded immediately, he added, 'There are a few people in MP, our esteemed sound engineer included, who are not exactly happy at us using a "professional" for a show supposed to be about bringing art to the people. It would look contrived if we weren't seen to be up front in showing her at her real workplace.'

'I suppose postponing is not an option?' ventured Martin, a proposal that was met by a withering look from the production manager. 'Of course not. Silly question,' he added quietly, remembering the Barbizon School exhibition that was the impetus for the late alteration to the filming schedule.

A heavy silence descended over the threesome as they searched their brains for a solution. Mike felt the impulse to break the pensive mood with dark humour. 'Young Raj will be most put out if we can't so through with this show. He's produced a real dossier on the gallery in Basel, what questions to ask, what to look for; he even has a fair idea of this Ciara O'Malley's job. He's really got stuck into this project. I'd hate to break it to him that all his labour may be in vain.'

'He's a good lad, that Raj,' commented Martin jovially. 'He's so dependable and good humoured, always has a pleasant little aside to throw in. You know, the other day while he was... wading through some research on Basel, I suppose... he said life would be so much easier if we transported the whole show to Switzerland. The Swiss would sort all logistical difficulties out, with their efficiency and immaculate timing. If only...' Martin added with a rueful grin.

'Hang on a minute,' Samantha interjected, turning earnestly to Mike. 'I think Raj may be on to something.'

'What do you mean?' queried Mike wearily.

'I mean, why don't we still do the pre-filming of Ciara in Switzerland, as planned and even do the actual show over there? That way we could film everything nearer the time, as in ... all in one visit?' Samantha spoke deliberately as if every part of a mental jigsaw was fitting into place. 'We could postpone the filming to the last possible moment and do it all over two days.'

'Or even one day at a pinch,' Martin surmised. 'So long as this Ciara has a change of clothes to make it look as if it's being done on two separate occasions.'

Mike's response was automatic. 'But we've never done a

final shoot outside Salford, let alone abroad.' He realised, though, that the sentence he started to utter as an objection ended up more as a cautious enquiry as to the feasibility of the radical new proposal.

'Got to be worth looking at, Mike?' Samantha challenged. As the production manager was slow to respond, she put the crucial logistical question to him. 'When would be the last date we could film to get everything ready for the series in April?'

'Well...,' Mike made a mental calculation. 'No later than mid-February.'

A few minutes later the informal meeting broke up with an improbable plan to investigate a radical shake-up of The Double F Show's filming schedule being established.

***

'Is this some kind of joke?' Paul Schlessinger stared at the headed letter paper he had just been scanning. He directed his gaze earnestly towards Monika, taking care to deposit his coffee cup on its saucer while his wife nonchalantly buttered herself a bread roll.

Not unnaturally, Monika could do little but shrug her shoulders from the other side of the breakfast table that morning until he reached across to show her the document in question. On reading the contents, Monika smiled to herself. Clearly, she found the sub stance more amusing than her husband.

Paul, however, was not in a mood for jokes. Humour had been in short supply over the autumn in the Schlessinger abode in Hirschingen and even through the normally busy pre-

Christmas period. Sales of even the most popular lines at Schlessinger Glas had stagnated. 'Plateaued' was the assessment of one of his middle managers. Slumped, less generous but quieter commentators on the shop floor had decided. The niche that Paul had hoped to carve out for his company in 'leisure glassware' had not materialised and his business was not receiving favourable reviews. The article in the *Badischer Wirtschaftsspiegel* was less than complimentary. *The change of direction made by Paul Schlessinger since inheriting the reins of the glassware concern from his father has not paid off,* the reporter for the estimable regional economics monthly had noted. Paul had received the visiting reporter in October on the latter's tour of traditional kitchenware goods manufacturers in the region and found his perfectly polite questions intrusive. His explanation of average sales figures as representing a period of consolidation had felt awkward, as though he was desperately seeking an unconvincing alibi to a crime of which his interrogator knew him to be guilty.

'What do you find so amusing?' was Paul's predictable question.

'Not exactly amusing, it just looks like a fun evening,' responded Monika amiably. 'I can't say I've ever heard of Millennium Pathway Productions. Who are they... American?'

'British. They want to do some show in a studio, something to do with the Stadtgalerie. Let me have another look.'

Monika handed back the sheet and Paul relayed the finer details which neither of them had thitherto grasped. 'They are filming a show in English about art, providing art for the people and they need to assemble "a discerning clientele", whatever that means. I am invited to be part of the studio audience on the night of filming as they are distributing free tickets to family members of those related to the participants, and also to friends of the gallery. Hah! I'm not sure if I fit into either category!'

'Friends of the Stadtgalerie?'

'I suppose ...' muttered Paul as he re-read the details carefully. '... or maybe not?' He looked up quizzically before clarifying. 'The Stadtgalerie is hosting the event, but the NBK is issuing the invites. Maybe it's a joint partnership for the greater cultural good of Basel,' he voiced the last remark with measured sarcasm. 'Anyway, it seems we have two free tickets to attend and need to confirm our attendance by the end of the week to guarantee our seats.'

'*Hmm*... sounds interesting. So, are you going to treat me to a cultural evening out, darling?'

Instinctively, her husband knew that barring genuine prior engagements, this was not an invitation he should be turning down. He suspected a television studio shoot would be a vulgar affair, with manufactured laughter and applause and the audience obliged to play a full part in the whole pantomime. He had never come across either the television programme or the channel and was unsure of any similar show existing in Germany, or Switzerland, for that matter. 'Art for the people' sounded a very egalitarian slogan, yet it seemed that the audience was to be composed of the great and the good of the cultural life of the Basel region. That meant visitors from Germany, like himself, and probably from France as well. He pondered at the English language element. Presumably the supposedly educated were invited as they would be able to understand proceedings better, and hence participate in an informed manner. Why he should be chosen for such an occasion he could not fathom. He surmised that as a CEO of a company specialising in artistic products he would be seen as a discerning customer. He concluded reluctantly that his attendance would do his company's profile more good than harm. His reverie was interrupted by his wife raising her voice with a further question.

'We're not doing anything that evening, are we?' she asked, and answered her own question by consulting the calendar hanging on the kitchen wall.

Paul agreed to confirm their attendance but not without a certain unease. His next trip over the border to their West Switzerland branch could include a slight deviation to check out the Basel cultural scene. No harm done by making sure there are no nasty surprises in store, he thought. The recollection of his last visit to the Stadtgalerie impressed itself strongly on his memory and the sense of a connection between the two would not be easily repelled.

***

Bear was curious to see how Ciara would react to the ordeal that he had experienced a few months ago. When she emerged from the gallery into the biting February late afternoon, it was clear that excitement, rather than relief, was the dominant emotion. Of course, she had not had to endure having dozens of schoolchildren noisily following her every move, as Bear had encountered back in the autumn. Yet he suspected the same pushy production team had been filming, eager to extract the optimum image to present to the voracious viewing public.

'Well, stranger,' she said as she entered the familiar surroundings of the Café Engelchen.

The comforting strong aroma of freshly ground coffee was a beckoning antidote to the winter chill as she approached his table. 'Not quite such a long time on this occasion, eh?'

They hugged warmly and Bear genuinely received the sense that she was pleased to see him. Having flown over the night before and prevailed upon Tim a second time for his hospitality, he had ascertained that she would not be free until the end of the working day. It had proved to be a busy day for her, as Bear fully expected. Yet there was an energy about her movements, an excited fidgeting, a struggle to keep still even as they took their seats opposite each other. How much Ciara was captivated by the thrill of the experience of the two days she was imbibing, and how much she was sparked by meeting Bear, he could not discern. Clearly, the former had a marked impression on her, as she soon voiced her enthusiasm.

'It's so good to see you. Isn't it exciting?' she remarked, grasping each of her hands into a fist in an effort to control her passion. 'We're going to be on The Double F Show! And tomorrow we'll meet Finola herself! Actually, meet Finola Flowers… in person! I can hardly wait!'

Ciara had to check whether her companion shared her passion, and he assured her that he was very much looking forward to the filming the following day.

'How was it today?' he enquired.

They paused while the waitress delivered the cappuccinos they had ordered, which gave the gallery employee time to draw breath before launching into an account of the proceedings of the day. She described the ordeal of the

217

monologue she was required to deliver, explaining how gobsmacked she was that someone from the past had suddenly shown up in Basel, and even more astounded to hear the following day of his interest in a particular painting. She hoped it didn't all come out in an incoherent surge, but the filming team assured her that they loved her passion. On being questioned by Bear she revealed that a jokey Scouser called Jim was part of the team and a fairly quiet cameraman called Colin, she thought. Bear nodded with an amused smile at his recollection of the crew he had encountered a few months back.

'They had a tour of the gallery,' she disclosed. 'Especially the Barbizon paintings on the second floor. Looks like they're making a big thing of it.'

Before Bear could offer a comment, she continued, 'and they did a few informal interviews with people in the office. They asked Silke what she thought of me as a colleague and she said I had a good sense of humour, in English, that is. And Ernst, whom I've never heard say more than two words of English, had clearly prepared himself. He came over all thoughtful (they let me watch that bit as they filmed) and said, "Ciara is very hard working and full of good ideas for exhibitions." He delivered the line perfectly with hardly any accent, as if he'd been practising.'

Bear was somewhat unsettled by the heightened state of preparation by the NBK employees. 'Do you think anyone in the gallery knows the outcome? I mean, whether the painting is a genuine Duclos or not?' he asked, curious.

'I don't think so, seeing as no one from the gallery is on the expert panel judging the work. If anyone has been tipped off, they haven't let on.'

'It'll be interesting to see how much footage they use. I gather our Head got in on the act just before they came to me in October.'

'Got in on the act?'

'Apparently, according to one of my colleagues who happened to be passing, the Head was waxing lyrical on the portraits of the school's eminent founding fathers, throwing in a few artistic terms. All in front of the camera.'

'He sounds a bright man, your headmaster.'

'Let's say he does his homework well.'

The mention of the original scheduled date for Millennium Pathway to come to Basel caused her to shudder momentarily. Her next remark had the sense of a confession. 'I tell you, I almost died when they said they couldn't do the original date and that they would "let me know". Let me know! Two weeks I was agonising before the solution was found to come to Switzerland at this time of year.' She checked herself as another surge of excitement coursed through her. 'Isn't it exciting, Bear?' she said as her eyes lit up. 'We're actually going to be on The Double F Show! With Finola herself!'

Bear recalled the events of the autumn, of a fortnight of fending off pupils and colleagues' questions about The Double F Show. When is it happening? Can we get tickets for the studio filming? When do you get to meet Finola? What did you say about Princewood? He had to confess he was also now feeling a flow of excited anticipation on the eve of the studio shoot. His face emitted a restrained expression of excitement across the table. Ciara grabbed his hand to stir his enthusiasm further.

'It's okay to be excited, Bear!' she assured him. 'You are

219

allowed to feel goose pumps on the eve of such a big day. Our lives may never be the same again!'

She looked at him intently, still holding on, and managed to elicit what sounded like nervous laughter from him; she turned her gaze away momentarily to survey the café scene and patted his wrist affectionately in affirmation, only to seize his left hand with her right hand once more. Bear felt pleasantly stirred by the lingering physical contact which he had not been expecting. Her explanation for the action was deliberate and delivered in a soft but firm voice.

'Just don't look now, but I think we need to keep holding hands for a moment if you have no objection. Just smile sweetly and I will explain gradually.'

Bear knew from experience of going out with Ciara that when she occasionally took time to slow her speech down, she expected to be granted full attention and was not amused if she had to repeat herself. He was quick to sense the reason for her request. 'This is a bit of déjà vu, isn't it?' he replied, in equally measured tones. 'We've been here before, haven't we? I mean, not in the café, but haven't we had a similar conversation a few months back?

'We have. On that occasion you warned me of a certain gentleman eavesdropping.'

'Oh, what's his name…?' Bear struggled to remember the strange encounter in the curry house over the German border, but within a few seconds he was plugged into Ciara's wavelength. It was as if they read each other perfectly to realise what the need of the hour was.

Their eyes were fixed on each other as they were conscious of a silent complicity that required loyalty and rigorous singing from the same hymn sheet. It was no surprise a matter of seconds later that a familiar burly figure left the seat he had occupied on entry to the café not a minute earlier to approach their table purposefully. He stopped to smile at what appeared to be two lovers locked in intimate conversation and caress. He was uncertain whether to interrupt such a private moment, but now that he was so close to them it would have seemed strange simply to walk away without engaging in some form of conversation.

'Well, good afternoon,' the newcomer announced cordially. 'Long time no see, isn't that what you say in English?'

He was met by broad, contented smiles by both occupants of the table, as if there was an unspoken agreement to defy him with politeness.

'I don't recall...' Bear began.

'Paul Schlessinger. We have a common interest in art... we met across town back in the summer. In the Stadtgalerie.'

'Oh... So we did!' Bear exclaimed jovially, as if a light bulb had been switched on and he hadn't thought about art or galleries for months.

'And now we meet in a café over the road from another art gallery,' remarked the glassware executive with a hint of menace, yet retaining a cordial smile.

'What a small world!' Ciara beamed at Paul Schlessinger before gazing lovingly at her table companion, adding, 'isn't it, darling?'

'It sure is, sweetheart,' Bear responded, matching her searching look with reciprocal intensity that seemed to unsettle the third participant in the exchange who sensed he might be intruding on a rare intimate moment.

'I didn't expect to see you over here in Switzerland in

February. Unless you're into winter sports. But you're a long way from the Alps if you fancied skiing,' Paul jested.

'No, I've not come over for skiing,' Bear said, turning momentarily to Paul before readopting his besotted expression looking deep into Ciara's eyes. 'It's my half-term holiday from school and it was the only time we could get together.' He squeezed her hand affectionately for emphasis and the determination to maintain hand contact throughout the encounter seemed to be forging an unusual bond between them.

Realising there was no obvious way of prolonging the conversation to his advantage; Paul politely took his leave and decided not to stop for a quick coffee before returning from his detour into Basel back over the border. It was a good minute before the pair released their grip and burst into a helpless fit of laughter.

'What is Timbo going to make of us?' Ciara speculated, as they prepared to head to their host for the evening for a 'lower-key' soirée with Tim and Sarah.

'He'll certainly say we want to be careful,' Bear jested before adding, at least half-seriously. 'And he won't be far from the mark.'

Chapter Eighteen

Fame…or Forgery?

The customary broad sweep of the scene captured a wide range of facial expressions. Had the cameraman so desired, he could have slowed even more his careful encapsulation of the surroundings in the studio for the evening. As it was, Colin did not dwell on every face in the audience, but he was sure that attentive editing would yield some valuable results that would accentuate the atmosphere building. Had he chosen to pause as he directed the instrument's gaze, he would have detected various clues in the countenances of those present as to their state of mind as the evening was about to unfold.

He would have noticed the good-humoured banter of a Swiss businessman turning round to a neighbour in the row behind him, happy to share a wisecrack with his acquaintance. He would have noticed the same individual engaging in conversation with another friend in the row in front as the former enjoyed very much being the centre of attention. Had the cameraman lingered, he would have captured the same businessman waving in acknowledgement to another acquaintance and his wife some four rows back. Such recognition was possible as the exhibition hall in the Stadtgalerie had been turned into a studio for the night with a mobile platform seating some two hundred guests ascending to the ceiling the further back one looked. The German business executive being saluted returned the greeting but immediately sighed as he settled himself down to what he sensed might be an uncomfortable evening, the eager expectancy of his wife notwithstanding.

He would have seen the speculative, intrigued exchange of ideas of a younger couple who had been invited by friends and were fascinated to see how they coped with the occasion. He would have taken in the nervous excitement of a young woman in the front row striving to remain composed as she knew the summons that she had so much been looking forward to was imminent. The face of the young man seated next to her betrayed similar levels of anticipation despite his resolve to stay calm and focused. At the end of the front row, a gentleman with a clipboard with notes to consult retained a pensive gaze as he realised that the moment of perhaps the greatest gamble in his broadcasting career was upon him. Throughout the audience, the cameraman could have stopped at numerous places and recorded the amused countenances and gesticulation of attendees to the event picking up the object left purposefully beneath each of the seats. Yet Colin did not need to dwell on each image to know that, one way or another, this would be a night to remember.

Had he so chosen, he could have fastened on to the same young man in the front row rising to his feet as the man with the clipboard approached, apparently with some instructions. The latter placed a reassuring pat on the other's shoulder in response to some remark by the former. At this point, the young woman also stood up and joined in the conversation. Clipboard King consulted his watch and delivered so me cheery aside to the pair of them. The young couple, if they could be described as such, looked at each other with intense excitement before retaking their seats. The cameraman, happy to sweep across the auditorium to garner pre-show footage, deliberately did not focus on any one individual. He was distracted for a few seconds as a confident-looking gentleman, smartly dressed in jacket and bow tie, relayed a message into his ear which he acknowledged quietly with few words and a nod.

If the German businessman had been looking that way, he might have guessed that the subject of that brief conversation was himself, that the smartly dressed one was identifying the man in the seventh row to the cameraman. At that moment, however, the business executive's attention was sharply drawn to the young couple conversing with the clipboard holder. So there *was* more to yesterday's meeting than some intimate romantic encounter, he told himself, recollecting the baffling scene in the café the previous afternoon, wondering why he had met the man twice in a matter of months, both times in the proximity of an art gallery. And here they were again, this time seated in the front row of a soon to be televised show, presumably with leading roles to fulfil.

At the improvised sound desk towards the back of the auditorium, the engineer allowed himself a moment to take in the audience that was filling up. Definitely not the average raucous Double F Show crowd, he noted with an amusement that easily dislodged his initial disdain for a clientele drawn solely from the region's bourgeois elements. He grudgingly acknowledged that Mike had shown boldness in arranging the venture at such short notice, and he found himself mentally tipping his hat to the production editor for making the gamble, win or lose.

Standing in between the first two rows a short woman

whose long pale blue dress and white scarf accentuated self-assurance and harmony with her surroundings was engaged in humorous discourse with a couple in the audience. Her beaming grin was punctuated by diplomatic half-cackles which were designed to jolly along the customers. She was a past master at how to work an audience, and while she had never yet faced a group with so little socio-economical breadth before, Finola Flowers was determined to be seen to be enjoying the occasion. Inwardly, she wondered what had possessed Mike to take the show to such a location, but she was determined to maximise the opportunity for publicity in the process.

At a signal from Mike, the bow-tied gentleman strode to the front of the auditorium as some of the lights were dimmed. The temporary studio had filled up by now and was hushed as the individual addressed them. Speaking in a toned-down German bereft of most of the Swiss vowels for the benefit of visitors from across both the nearby borders, he welcomed them all as participants in a great adventure, thanked them for attending and issued the obligatory instructions in the unlikely event of a fire. He wished them an entertaining evening and reminded them that the rest of proceedings would be conducted in English and handed over to Mike Devenish.

The clipboard specialist smiled broadly as warm applause greeted his approach to the front of the gathering. Mike was an old hand on such occasions but had worked hard at practising the adjustments he had to make for this different type of clientele. His speech was more deliberate to allow for the delivery in a second language to the majority of his hearers. He had to ensure he explained the essence of *Fame or Forgery* more precisely to attendees who had probably never seen the show before. He had to remind himself that all those in front of him were here because of an invitation, not because they had applied to come and been the lucky ones whose names had been drawn by ballot. Exporting the show to the continent was going to require diplomacy and skilful crowd management, he sensed.

His opening remarks explained the ideas behind the show – art for the people, not just the connoisseur, no holds barred in visiting the participants at their place of work, being prepared to take in good part any ribbing that came their way from Finola. The audience gazed back at him in genuine interest, almost visibly communicating a collective sense of excited curiosity that suggested that they were about to experience a unique evening in their lives. Mike then teasingly announced that there was a possibility that by the end of proceedings our two participants might come away having discovered a rare masterpiece and their lives might never be the same again. What Mike had to say next could have derailed the whole process and punctured the atmosphere at a stroke.

'You may have noticed that some of you are fortunate enough to have something under your seats,' he announced. Indeed, several spectators already held up the objects in question.

'Hey up,' noted Jim Spencer from the sound booth. 'This is the moment.'

Mike produced one of the objects from a jacket pocket as he bent down to place his temporarily unwanted clipboard on the floor. He then issued the invitation, 'If you have one of these, give it a shake like this...' He proceeded to shake vigorously. Those in possession of the object shook with gusto and the ringing of fifty cowbells filled the auditorium. 'That's brilliant,' he declared once the noise had died down. 'I can just feel myself on a Swiss mountain somewhere in the Alps. I tell you, the folk back in Britain will love that.'

He then produced a second item and asked those blessed with such an instrument to make a similar noise. A smaller number, but no less enthusiastically, responded with the sound of klaxons.

'I don't believe it,' muttered Jim. 'He's got them eating out of his hand.'

The sound engineer had not been alone in suspecting that the Swiss public would not take kindly to national stereotyping and resorting to trite images. He had a grudging admiration for the production manager's boldness in taking a few risks, although he did feel the complimentary glass of vintage port on arrival was taking things a bit far. At least it's got them in a relaxed mood, Jim had to acknowledge. When Mike asked if anyone could yodel and invited them to perform on his signal, several were only too happy to demonstrate their art. Anyone not falling into any of the three above categories was asked to contribute with heartfelt applause at the right moments in the show. The exchange of amused glances across the audience, even some giggles, confirmed the best hopes that Mike had entertained, that the traditionally staid, polite Swiss, along with visitors from across two borders, were up for something different that evening.

It was Mike's 'enormous pleasure to introduce the inimitable Finola' and the petite Scotswoman glided confidently to the centre of the stage to the recorded strains of 'Fin-ola!' resounding from Jim's box, as was customary for her entrance. Mike warned the audience that they would have trouble understanding their Glaswegian hostess, to which she responded with a playful admonishment for his impertinence. A couple of minutes of banter ensued in which Mike allowed Finola to share a few experiences of the show to the uninitiated audience, and then asked her if she was looking forward to the evening.

'My word, I should say so. What an atmosphere!' she gushed. 'I felt like Heidi up on the Alpine pasture when I heard those bells. They're in fine form here in Basel, I tell you.'

An appreciative raucous acclamation from bells and horns was the response not just to Finola's compliment but to a prominent card held aloft by one of the film crew with bold images of the objects that could be deployed at that juncture. This was a process that was to be repeated several times during the evening and the pattern was well set.

From there the show began to unfold as first the audience was treated to a pastiche of the character of the city of Basel in the form of a two-minute film, its history, culture and artistic heritage. Finola then exclaimed how privileged The Double F Show was to be coming from such a cultured city as they were to consult some distinguished experts to decide if the work of art they were going to encounter was to lead to the 'joy of fame' or the 'disappointment of forgery'. First, she declared, a long way from Basel is the town of Princewood, and it is here that tonight's journey begins. The film footage with voiceovers introduced the riverside surroundings and the elegance of the eighteenth-century buildings of the illustrious private institution, Princewood School. Stephen Rawlinson was shown pointing out the depictions of his noteworthy predecessors and heard offering his prepared words of wisdom

229

on the school's artistic traditions.

The audience was intrigued by the décor and seemed to be taking in the setting with full attention. The focus then turned to Bear's account in front of the oak tree by the sports fields as he related the visit to the Constable Centre, his mild interest in Duclos' missing painting and his casual acquaintance with the Barbizon School through someone who was just (yes, he had slipped in that unfortunate qualification) a friend. Bear cringed as he recollected what he perceived to be, if not a faux pas, then at least a clumsy utterance that might well be pounced on by younger hearers once the show was broadcast later in the year.

Cameraman Colin was poised to direct his instrument to the front row of the audience as Finola addressed the gathering with a few transitional remarks, zoning in on the interest sparked by the sixth form artists' day trip the previous summer and Bear's final comment that he had arranged to visit a friend in Switzerland in the summer holidays. Colin was well used to Finola's next remark, a cue that varied little from programme to programme as she mused, 'So what, you may well ask, happened next? We're delighted that the man himself is here in Basel again to tell us. I give you… history teacher and art sleuth, Mister Bear Hoskins!'

The camera picked up Bear rising from his seat with a nervous smile to head towards one of two sofas installed just to the audience's left of the stage. Cue another round of boisterous bell ringing and klaxon honking. Finola gestured for him to be seated as she occupied the sofa opposite. As the interview began, Bear felt strangely at ease. For all her flirtatious flamboyance and playing to the gallery, a pun that Bear had unearthed in rehearsals earlier that day, she was a consummate professional. She had talked of having to be 'in character' during the filming, but her guests needed to be themselves. She had asked each of them, Bear and Ciara, what question they would like to be asked first when she took up the story following each of their recorded monologues. Whatever they wanted to be asked, she would ask. She was as good as her word.

'So Bear, when you arrived in Basel on your holiday, was there anything unusual?' asked the presenter.

Bear had already offered his reply in rehearsal and was encouraged to stick with it. 'There was the fact that Tim had vastly improved his cooking skills since I'd last seen him. And there was this dinner party he arranged on my second night.'

'What was so unusual about this occasion?'

'I met someone I hadn't seen for eight years. And if Tim had pronounced her name properly, I would have been warned. I'm sure he did it on purpose,' Bear jested.

Finola skilfully teased out of Bear something of how he had first met Ciara before suggesting that they all heard from her. There followed on the screen a brief tour of the NBK with Ciara's monologue, recorded the previous day, with contributions from Ernst and Silke. Ciara's fondness for The Double F Show came across as she mentioned how frequently she accessed episodes despite living in Switzerland. Otherwise she concentrated on explaining her work at the gallery and the excitement she gained from setting up exhibitions and seeing them through to a successful conclusion.

Once the introduction to a day at Ciara's workplace was completed, Finola was ready to whip up the audience's enthusiasm once again. 'Well, folks, let's find out what

231

happened next as these two old friends (they're no' old at all, they're just bairns really!)… as these two old friends met up again. Ladies and gentlemen, put your hands together for ace history of art specialist and exhibition organiser Ciara O'Malley!'

Again the outpouring of participatory zeal in the form of klaxons and cowbells filled the atmosphere. Yet whereas Bear had to overcome a certain wariness in front of the camera, Ciara's nervousness was simply in meeting a star she had admired from afar. The relaxed conversation they had had with Finola had calmed her somewhat, and she even followed up the presenter's suggestion with a cheeky conspiratorial smile in Bear's direction to show the audience how much they were up for the challenge of the evening. Bear returned the grin rather more sheepishly and noticed in doing so that his companion was much more naturally in character.

After Ciara was seated, Finola issued the agreed opening question. 'Well, Ciara, did you know that young Bear was an art afficionado?'

'I knew he knew a bit, mostly stuff I taught him,' the Irishwoman delivered her pre-arranged response. 'But I had no idea that he remembered so much about the Barbizon School.'

'The Barbizon School? Tell us all about them.'

That was the cue for Ciara to explain the origins and aims of that group of painters and how they had strayed into conversation at the café the day after the unexpected meeting with her erstwhile partner. The revelation about Bear's casual reference to Gisele's mention of a mysterious missing painting and her own professional involvement in checking it out saw Ciara take centre stage for a few minutes, punctuated by a few cues from Finola. She explained the task assigned to her to investigate a Wehrmacht officer's bequest, unaware of the stirring this turn of events was causing in a section of the auditorium. On hearing *The Flight of the Huguenots*, Paul Schlessinger knew his growing unease throughout the evening had been justified. Monika patted his elbow sympathetically as she realised that her father-in-law's mysterious wartime experiences were going to be revealed. Of course, Gerhard's name had not been mentioned yet, so no one else in the audience was minded to turn in the direction of the glassware executive, but Paul took a deep breath as he sensed the occasion was not one when he could hide in the background in comfortable obscurity.

Bear was largely silent until Ciara mentioned the planned trip over the border on the off-chance that the cache might have survived half a century of central European winters, dust and natural decay.

'So ye had a wee outing, then? Was it a fun trip?' teased Finola, now less charitable with her guests as they had relaxed and overcome any nerves. 'Did it bring back memories of your student days, reignite old passions?'

Bear stepped in with a pre-rehearsed answer. He was determined not to be trapped again after his 'just good friends' comment inevitably left him open to interested knowing looks and retorts by the Princewood School community. 'It certainly revived our passion for art and for discovering the past,' he said thoughtfully and with an authority that surprised himself, and even the presenter.

Finola, conscious of the regular UK televisual audience rather than the invited visitors in the live studio, decided she could not overlook the opportunity to tease out details of the guests' relationship. 'And ye say ye had nae seen each other for… how long was it, eight years? It must have been very special to get together and relive some experiences on the road.'

'It was a very special search that had a very significant ending,' Ciara answered, solidly backing her co-guest by steering clear of the banter to get to the heart of the matter.

It became apparent that Ciara's determination to give a clear presentation of their experience was overcoming her awe at being on a sofa opposite someone she had revered for a few years now. The refusal to respond to the flirtatious banter supported Bear's deadpan approach and would have derailed anyone less professional and adroit in repartee as Finola Flowers. The presenter would have been amused if she had been able to see Mike Devenish's reaction at that point. Here, at last, Mike observed with relish, were two participants on The Double F Show prepared to stand up to Finola, in the nicest possible way. This was going to make for excellent television, he thought, revelling in the prospective viewing figures.

'So what was it like working your way through all those villages in northern France on a hot summer's day?' persisted Finola. 'Did ye enjoy working together? Did it stir up a few flames of days gone by?'

Bear was aware that their hostess was sticking to a pre-arranged script to draw out any revealing aspects of his relationship with Ciara, whether current or historical. He was just as prepared, however.

'Our passion for the truth was certainly stirred up and we were focused on the ultimate goal, even though we took time to find the right location.'

'We were fired up by the possibility of unearthing a masterpiece, Finola. That was our passion,' explained Ciara supportively. Despite the reverence she felt for the presenter through watching countless episodes Ciara was well familiar with the Scotswoman's tactics to spice up conversation and she was determined not to succumb.

The guests were allowed to finish their account of the discovery of the painting in the Alsace barn without significant interruption, at which Finola announced that it was time for a commercial break. Her promise to be right back and urging of tele-spectators not to go anywhere, was reinforced by the enthusiastic accompaniment of bell and horn. That afforded the studio a momentary breather during which Bear and Ciara turned to each other. He shrugged his shoulders as if to say that all they could do is respond honestly and she responded with an assured smile as if to say that she was feeling comfortable with the occasion and appreciated his part in making her feel that way. The transmission of such feelings was genuine. She felt his steadying influence on proceedings that had backed up her zeal and willingness to experiment.

She was appreciative of Bear being there supporting her on what could be the most significant night of her life. She had time to cover her mouth to conceal a giggle and as Bear attempted to ascertain the cause of such mirth, quickly suppressed it as Finola had received the nod to continue the filming; she waved him away as much as to say that the explanation for the passing thought would have to wait.

For the next part of the show, both guests were relieved to take a back seat as two experts held court. First, to join them at the end of the sofa and be interviewed by Finola was Martha Wächter, introduced as a historian specialising in the wartime occupation of north-eastern France. She was described as an Englishwoman married to a local who had spent the last twenty-five years, half her lifetime, studying living conditions in that period. For the next five minutes the invited expert explained the severities of wartime shortages, the likely conditions of most farms in eastern Alsace and how possible it might have been to have stashed away an object the size of the painting in question undetected for so many years. She acknowledged that it was unusual but given hidden recesses and the evolution in farming methods and changes of owners, it is perfectly conceivable that parts of an agricultural building, especially below the surface, may have been left unattended through being deemed surplus to requirements.

Finola drew Martha into outlining the likely movements of the Swabian regiment in those confused days of late November 1944. The historian indicated the likely escape route across the Rhine and how the unit would have been minded to steer well clear of Strasbourg if they had received notification of that city's fall.

'Is there any evidence that the unit received such a word?' asked Finola.

Martha paused before elucidating. 'It is apparent that the unit's commander was able to make radio contact with a mobile headquarters and was advised in no uncertain terms not to stay the night in the barn, and instead to cross over the Rhine without delay, a situation made more pressing by their lack of fuel.'

'Now it seems the commander had several items of plunder he would have had to leave behind, including the painting we are discussing tonight. He was obviously a lover of art. What can you tell us of this man?'

As a black and white photograph of a young Wehrmacht officer appeared on the screen to the side of the sofa party, Martha introduced the temporary custodian of the alleged masterpiece. It did not go unnoticed in the auditorium.

'His name was Gerhard Schlessinger. He survived the war and a few years afterwards set up a successful glassware manufacturing business in Hirschingen in Baden Würtemberg. He died about eighteen months ago.'

'Which is where Ciara comes in again,' continued Finola enthusiastically nodding to the gallery employee, 'as this is the very gentleman whose bequest she had the privilege of handling. The very same ex-German army officer who left the painting behind in a barn somewhere in Alsace.' She allowed herself time for the briefest of dramatic pauses before resuming. 'Now I don't know if you're aware, Ciara, Bear, but we have a special surprise for you both because in the audience tonight is none another than Gerhard's son, the current CEO of Schlessinger Glas, Paul Schlessinger!'

Bear and Ciara looked at each other in momentary alarm but were so entrenched in the pantomime of the occasion that they forced cheesy smiles as the camera swung round to capture a bemused Paul Schlessinger. He could hardly evade attention as several close to him had turned to make encouraging gestures as soon as they heard his father's name mentioned. Through gritted teeth he knew that any publicity had to be good publicity. At least he was forced into a corner now and had to make it so. He was relieved that the camera did not linger on him and Finola expressed the hope that they would perhaps hear from Paul after the show. There was still much to get through and they needed to press on.

Finola drew the conversation with Martha to a close and

thanked her for her insight. Then she rose to her feet and faced the camera head on. This was clearly a regular feature of the show as the background detail behind the work of art was concluded and the moment of truth, the verdict as to whether the find would lead to fame or forgery, was approaching. Before that the presenter invited her audience, live and televised, to join her 'next door'. She left the lounge area on the audience's right to walk across to the other side of the stage where a robust plastic round table was located with an envelope perched prominently on a metal support that enabled the imprint of the words 'Fame or Forgery?' in clear bold black type to be visible to the first few rows of spectators. Yet this object was not of immediate concern to Finola who skirted round the table, half-turning to the audience as she walked, saying that there was one more person we needed to talk to.

She approached a contrived wall at the back of the set where a fair-haired gentleman in his mid-fifties awaited her. He stood to the right of some elegant navy-blue curtains and Finola positioned herself on the other side.

'I'm privileged to be joined by renowned Basel art expert, Max Klammer. Max, welcome to *Fame or Forgery*.' It was indeed the jovial individual that Bear had come across at the Stadtgalerie the previous summer and whom Ciara knew from various cultural engagements in the city.

After Max returned the greeting, Finola invited him to perform an important ceremony before sharing a few thoughts. Max nodded agreeably and grasped the curtain pulley and the curtains parted to gasps of excitement from across the studio. The space was occupied by a striking landscape painting with a family in eighteenth-century dress

238

stopping at a village with mountains in the background seemingly seeking shelter for the night. Finola stressed that Max was not one of the expert panel assessing the genuineness of the work of art but was being asked to give his professional independent view as to the chances of the work being really that of Jean Duclos.

Max's assessment was measured. 'Of course, careful analysis in a laboratory will reveal the pigments, the particular type of paint used, and the exact brushwork deployed. From what I have seen in the last half-hour there is a strong chance that the Barbizon School is involved. The fact that it is not pure landscape, that the artist has used human figures, is a slight deviation from the main thrust of the school's work, but we need to remember that Duclos was his own man and did not always follow the exact guidelines that others in the school would stick to.'

Finola teased out some non-committal, speculative responses from Max that were designed to whet the appetites of viewers still further before the final climax. As Max was thanked and withdrew from the scene to sit alongside Martha on the sofa, Bear and Ciara were beckoned to join Finola in the 'Decision Room'. As had been rehearsed earlier that day, they stood behind the round table with the crucial envelope in front of them. As Finola had warned them, she delivered an agonising summary of the highlights of the journey they had been on to reach this point, stringing out the details so that the experience would remain in spectators' minds for as long as possible. Then she posed the time-honoured announcement and question, 'We've almost reached the end of our journey. This is the moment of truth. Will it be fame or forgery for Bear and Ciara?' Then, inevitably, after the briefest of pauses,

'We'll find out after a quick break!'

A few seconds were taken up with hand signals to verify the sound was in order before Finola resumed the tortuous path towards the show's conclusion. She repeated the enormity of the moment and posed the essential question again. She paused to milk the tension with trademark presentational skills before picking up the envelope. Bear and Ciara smiled uneasily, both conscious that they had a few more seconds to act out their roles. It would be a blessed relief to know the answer, whether favourable or not. Finola continued, 'within this simple envelope we have the answer. A team of experts from the Swiss Institute of Art have collated data and explored every aspect of the painting's character and quality to verify whether it can truly be attributed to Jean Duclos.'

Slowly and deliberately, Finola removed the contents of the envelope and began to read out loud from the single sheet:

'Dear *Fame or Forgery*, it has been a great pleasure and privilege to examine this painting at length and judge its credentials. It is an especially humbling honour in view of the significant anniversary this year of the founding of this illustrious and influential school of painters...' Ciara bit her lip as she struggled to master her frustration at the long-drawn out process as the niceties were expressed. Finola had warned them both that they were probably going to be cursing under their breath at this point, saying, 'Get on with it, woman!' and that they should just remember that it was all part of the act. Bear managed to maintain a rigid grin borne more of nervousness than any pleasure in the moment.

Finola resumed after her dramatic pause. 'We have looked at the subject matter, in particular the background landscape and human figures included in the foreground. This latter feature is not a regular aspect of the Barbizon School that focuses primarily on the built and natural environment, but it is by no means excluded to incorporate human form. We have closely analysed the brushwork and variation of shade and tone in comparison with other works of Jean Duclos. Our laboratory have analysed samples of the paint used and of the canvas to ascertain the likely date of composition. Our examination has been thorough and painstaking. After much discussion and analysis, it is our unanimous decision that we are sadly unable to attribute this work as a genuine painting by Jean Duclos.'

An audible gasp of disappointment was emitted from the audience as both Ciara and Bear knew what was coming next. They had rehearsed the moment carefully that afternoon and had been advised to answer the question as honestly as they could at that moment. There was, Finola had assured them, no wrong answer so long as it came from the heart.

She turned to the two participants. 'So Bear, Ciara... how do you feel at this news?'

Chapter Nineteen

The Re-emergence of a Tragic Hero

It is unusual for stunned silence to be entirely appropriate in broadcasting that relies on conversation, but if ever such a point could be reached, that moment had arrived. Of course, they were prepared for what both conceded was the likelier outcome. The y had prepared responses and even had them vetted by Finola, yet there seemed no escaping resorting to clichés.

'Well, that's the way it goes. You have to take the rough with the smooth,' Bear uttered.

'That's show business, I suppose,' Ciara added.

They each expected to be allowed to elaborate, to be asked if they had enjoyed the experience of being on The Double F Show and to be allowed to sign off with expressions of gratitude for the whole experience, for the 'journey' they had been on and how they wouldn't have missed it for the world. To their surprise, Finola turned in the direction of Mike Devenish and on receiving a thumbs-up signal to indicate it was fine to continue, she took up her discourse again.

'However, before we finish, there is more to the letter…' Bear and Ciara braced themselves for a routine dissection of the artist's work in which the key aspects of forgery were outlined. They were correct in that assumption, at least partially.

Finola ensured she delivered the next few sentences even more deliberately than usual.

She quoted again from the Swiss Academy of Arts' letter:

"There is evidence of a forged artist's signature that has been inserted at a slightly later date that initially caused us to question the notion that Duclos was the artist. Microscopic study of the proportions and combinations of colour, as well as the fine deployment of shade used by the painter of this piece bear all the hallmarks of another artist working in the Barbizon area at around the same period of the mid-nineteenth century. It is, therefore, our unanimous conclusion that The Flight of the Huguenots *that we have had the privilege to examine was authored by none other than Antoine Caussade."*

There was a second's pause that seemed to last much longer. Faces turned to one another in wide-eyed amazement. Ciara put both hands to her mouth in astonishment and Bear puffed out his cheeks. Finola grinned broadly in the direction of her two guests and was about to ask for a reaction but was immediately hindered by a thunderous ovation with the whole audience rising to their feet. Bells and klaxons sounded as the applause rang out; even the odd yodel filled the air as the acclaim continued for some thirty seconds. No one seemed to know whom they were applauding. It was just a simultaneous outpouring of joy at such a rare find.

After a plea for silence, the applause died down and Finola asked the fortunate pair how they felt for a second time. They were even less eloquent than their utterances a few moments ago.

'It's... amazing,' Ciara managed to say, seemingly in shock.

'I'm speechless,' Bear uttered.

Finola took up the reins again to lead the show adroitly to a happy conclusion. She was determined that they would not have to do any extra takes in these final moments so that no audience or participant reactions would appear contrived by having to be repeated. 'From their reaction I am sure I don't need to remind anyone here why this is such tremendous news. But, Max… if I can invite you to come back…,' she said as the Stadtgalerie employee returned to the table. 'Perhaps you can explain to the viewers why the news of the real artist is so significant.'

Max was only too happy to outline the short and tragic life of Antoine Caussade, thought by many to be the most brilliant of the Barbizon painters, at least in terms of potential. He had died in a climbing accident, aged just 27, after producing several stunning landscapes. It transpired that while Duclos was lodging with a third member of the Barbizon fraternity, he was caught *in flagrante* in bed one afternoon with the wife of his landlord by Caussade who was carrying out an errand. It was widely acknowledged, Max related, that Duclos had bribed Caussade to secure the latter's silence about the affair. When word started to get out about the liaison, Duclos suspected that the younger man had split on him and it was rumoured that Duclos was responsible for the mysterious fatal climbing misadventure. None of this was ever proven, Max emphasised, although Duclos did leave the Paris area soon afterwards and lived in relative obscurity in the Lot-et-Garonne, in the south-west of France for the rest of his days. His earlier promise as a painter was never fulfilled, although in some of his correspondence he hinted at a painting depicting some Huguenot travellers. This work had never

244

been unearthed, until today, Max added with conviction.

The conclusion of the night's filming was conducted in a celebratory atmosphere. The most unexpected outcome had delighted the artistic fraternity in attendance and even those less acquainted with art history recognised the name of Antoine Caussade. There was no need to whip up the spectators as Finola took them through the concluding ritual.

'So after a painstaking few months we can say that for Bear and Ciara it has been a night of... fame!' Bells, klaxons and yodelling appeared on cue. Finola had to raise her voice above the euphoria as she issued the closing greeting, spiced with a prepared remark that had been intended for Duclos to be declared the author of the mystery painting, 'What a start to this anniversary season for the Barbizon School! Join us next time on The Double F Show when we will find out if another participant will be heading for fame... or forgery!'

Sustained applause rang out as Mike Devenish approached the front to announce that the formal end to proceedings had arrived, and to thank everyone again for their attendance and enthusiastic participation. Amidst the excited hubbub of chatter, Tim and Sarah walked down to the front to congratulate the pair on their success and said they would catch up with them later. The Double F Show had hired the use of a bar adjacent to the Stadtgalerie for an after-show party for the company and guests. Bear and Ciara were ushered around the corner to pursue the celebrations, but not before noticing a familiar face being the centre of attention. They could not hear what was being said but the content of the discussion was eminently guessable.

'I don't believe it! Fassbender's here...,' observed Paul Schlessinger. 'Just when I hoped to retreat gracefully...'

'Not a chance,' emphasised Monika with a whisper. 'Don't you realise this is your big moment? You can bask in your dad's glory,' she urged as the individual pointed out strode towards them, notebook in hand. 'Perhaps show a bit of emotion, you know, how overcome you are with joy?'

'Evening, Herr S. A few thoughts on the evening, perhaps?' Dirk Fassbender had an engaging manner, polite to the point of obsequiousness as if to say any story he would deliver would be written as a service to his interviewee. From past experience, however, Paul knew that if he was less than transparent the journalist was more than prepared to draw his own conclusions, often less than favourable.

'I am just... overwhelmed,' the glassware executive replied, genuinely searching for a suitable adjective. Once he had started down the road of proud son suddenly discovering the depths of his late father's largesse and humanity, there was no stopping him. Even the hardened hack Fassbender seemed stirred as Paul seemed to be holding back tears as the latter expressed his thoughts. No, he had very little idea of what his father got up to during the war. No, he never spoke about it much. Yes, of course he knew of his father's love of art. Of course, in his own poor way he had striven for years to maintain the traditions. And yes, the unexpected bequest was typical of Dad; he was so proud of him. If Fassbender and a couple of other journalists who had gathered were hoping to stir up controversy with a few barbed remarks and thinly veiled sarcasm, they were sorely disappointed. Paul Schlessinger played his part to perfection and curiously, felt all the better for it.

The after-show party was proving much more of a celebration than the employees of Millennium Pathway could have dared anticipate. Naturally, whatever the outcome, they were determined to adopt a positive mood at the end of the two days' filming and invited a few carefully selected local dignitaries from the cultural and business spheres to join them in their private bar for the remainder of the evening.

Memories of the next couple of hours proved hazy to Bear and Ciara in the months ahead. There seemed to be a succession of well-wishers coming up to them to utter some observation on either the evening's proceedings or their respective video presentations. They graciously accepted congratulations yet could only wonder in bewilderment at being the recipients of such praise. The find had been a real stab in the dark, indeed a last throw of the dice at the end of a long summer day, when the starlings had performed their wondrous demonstration of togetherness to guide them to the treasure.

Finola had made a point of chatting to them informally and proved to be the picture of serenity in contrast to her on-screen persona. She seemed glad to have finished her performance and returned to normality.

'I hope you guys did nae mind me hyping things up a bit,' she said. 'Ye know, asking a few questions about old passions. It's all part of the act, ye know.'

They both said it was fine, they knew they had to play along with the banter.

'I thought ye did brilliantly,' Finola continued, 'made for great telly the way ye kept sticking to your passion for art. Can't wait to see how it all looks when we've put it all together.'

Mike was full of congratulations, tinged with a degree of apology, when he approached the pair shortly afterwards. He had learned just before the show that there was an unexpected twist but couldn't let on. Even Finola hadn't been tipped off until the last moment. He gave a ringing endorsement for their authentic stoic disappointment at the initial verdict and the joyous disbelief when the attribution to Caussade was disclosed. Jim Spencer went as far as putting a fraternal arm on Bear's shoulder, assuring him that he was a real 'class act' and that would come across when the show was broadcast.

The procession of well-wishers was unabated. Even if Ciara and Bear had wanted to extricate themselves from each other, they had no such opportunity. Their drinks were readily replenished as everyone present seemed to wish to pay their respects to the golden couple.

Fortunately, the press was not admitted to the function, so the brief comments they had voiced to an eager reporter by the name of Fassbender immediately at the close of the filming had to suffice.

The peculiar nature of the couple's regal status prompted Bear to observe with amusement, 'Anyone would think we were newlyweds, the fuss they're all making!'

This remark had caused Ciara to splutter over her cocktail, which she carefully placed on the table at which they were seated before playfully admonishing her fellow celebrity with a slap on the wrist.

It was another ten minutes, after they had been introduced to one of the patrons of the NBK and been engaged in Barbizon-centred conversation, that the pair were able to resume conversation with each other. This time Bear's curiosity needed to be satisfied.

'What was it you found so amusing earlier, you know, during that break, the one before the historian lady joined us?'

he asked. 'It looked like you might give way to a fit of giggles.'

'Oh, that!' she exclaimed, struggling to control a laugh at the recollection. 'I was just thinking of the contrast between meeting up with Paul Schlessinger in the café yesterday, and then being interviewed by Finola tonight.'

'Well, what of it?'

'Well, on the first occasion we did everything possible to pretend we were still going out together, and on the second we did everything possible to pretend we weren't!' She let out a hearty laugh, which Samantha Higgins reacted to by remarking how pleased she was that Ciara was enjoying the evening. The artistic director was happy to avail herself of the opportunity to engage in conversation with someone familiar with Basel's cultural life.

Bear was a spectator for the next few minutes. That was probably just as well, as he was unsure how to react to Ciara's last remark. He could have dismissed her reference to their response to Finola as a slip of the tongue, but he was relieved not to feel obliged to press her for an immediate explanation. Perhaps it was the drink talking on her part as she had consumed a few that evening, more than usual. Yet he was drawn to the conclusion that there was authenticity in his companion's remark. It was an utterance that remained with him for the remainder of the evening.

***

The ten thirty appointment the following morning was scarcely beckoning. The nursing of hangovers and gentle recovery from the partying of the night before were the priorities for many in the Millennium Pathway party. Bear had a couple of hours spare before his flight home, whereas the majority of the television production company were heading back overland. Yet important concluding business had to be conducted and both participants from the show needed to be present. The booking of a training room at the NBK ensured Ciara did not have to travel far. Bear thanked Tim for the second time in a few months for his hospitality on leaving the latter's flat and headed in the direction of the gallery. He had expressed regret not to be visiting the same premises again, having received Tim's bombshell a couple of weeks earlier. Bear said how much he was looking forward to returning to Basel in the summer for Tim and Sarah tying the knot and wished him all the best as he prepared to move into Sarah's residence on the other side of the city.

Mike and Samantha had invited the successful participants in *Fame or Forgery* to an informal chat to discuss how to proceed, what was euphemistically known as 'after care'. In normal circumstances, when the show was filmed at the television company's Salford studios in the early afternoon, there was time for any such debriefing once the spectators had dispersed.

Clearly, this was not going to be so manageable with the evening performance on this unique Swiss adventure, so the post-show chat was arranged for the following morning, irrespective of the result. Normally, Samantha would provide some encouraging tips on how to detect real works of genius to participants whose outing had ended in forgery. Occasionally, Mike would steer overjoyed successful customers to knowledgeable people in the art business who could assist them to make best use of a potential windfall.

This conversation looked a degree more complex than either of the typical scenarios. As it transpired, the discussion was relatively smooth.

'So... what happens now?' Ciara asked with characteristic but not unfriendly directness across the training room table once Mike had thanked them both for taking time to attend the meeting.

He outlined the fact that in most cases where the participant or participants on The Double F Show had been successful, where the 'Fame' verdict had been announced, the role of Mike and Samantha was to direct the lucky winners as to the financial and artistic guides who could enable them to maximise their good fortune. Matters were not, however, so straightforward in this instance.

'Why is that?' asked Bear.

'It's a matter of ownership,' Mike explained. 'Whilst *The Flight of the Huguenots* is a genuine work by an acclaimed member of the Barbizon School, namely Antoine Caussade, it is unclear who has right of ownership.' He paused as his hearers sat up attentively. 'As Captain Schlessinger, as he was at the time admits, he stole the painting and intended to take it home across the Rhine. It stayed in a farm building for some fifty years. The farm has since changed hands and the previous farmer is believed to have died. I gather attempts are being made to trace his family. The question is, where was the painting stolen from?' he asked rhetorically.

'Some large house serving as a temporary German army HQ in the Champagne region,' the history teacher supplied.

Mike nodded. 'The owner was a French Jewish financier, Pierre-Yves Rosenbourg, who for obvious reasons did not hang around when the Germans invaded. At the end of the

251

war, there were some small articles of value hidden in a basement. Possibly the more enticing stuff was gobbled up by his uninvited house guests over the next few years. It looks as if he was hoping to return after the war.'

'But he never did?' Ciara prompted.

'He has never been traced. It is quite possible that he used his not inconsiderable wealth to arrange a change of identity and a ticket out of Europe. So if he's still alive, unlikely but possible as he'd be well into his nineties by now, he can't be contacted, no heirs that we are aware of and no one who can claim possession of the painting.'

'So we don't know the rightful owner?' Bear asked.

'Interestingly,' Mike continued slowly, keen that his emphasis should not be lost, 'there is no record anywhere of Rosenbourg ever buying the painting in the first place. He may have acquired it by dubious means, or simply stumbled across it, as you yourselves did last year.' Mike's next pause was brief, and he proceeded to forestall any unnecessary interruptions with entirely predictable prompts. 'The French heritage organisation Institut de Patrimoine National has a claim as they now own Rosenbourg's rather grand house and use it as a kind of centre for historical research. The Germans could conceivably claim the painting for themselves as the area was German territory at the time the painting came to light... seriously, the legal experts say that even with the Occupation, they could argue they were in lawful possession of the artwork. And if the rights of a painting left behind in Champagne can't be sorted out, there is a wrangle over Alsace too. The region belonged to Germany even before the Second World War, so there is an argument that the German government could request it be housed on German soil.'

Bear and Ciara exchanged astonished glances at such a suggestion.

'But that's not going to happen,' Mike assured them. 'Whilst there might be a case for saying "finders, keepers" and arguing that you two could be deemed the rightful owners, as the painting has been recognised as stolen property in what is effectively a confession by Gerhard, it will have to be restored... to someone. As no individual has been contacted who might be the required recipient, some cultural organisation in either France or Germany could end up having ownership. There would certainly be some eager competition, but for one thing...'

'Which is...?' Bear felt compelled to ask the obvious again.

'As you know, Gerhard asked specifically in his bequest for the proceeds, if at all possible, to be forwarded to the cause of peace in Europe to, in some way, atone for the horrors of the conflict that he was a part of. Now we know that the painting never was his to bequeath to anyone, but as the statement is part of a series of documents filed under bequests as requests to be carried out on his demise, the statement about the proceeds or benefits from displaying the painting going to peaceful causes would need to be made public.'

A further pause gave Mike time to deliver his final emphatic blow. 'Which means that no organisation in either France or Germany would risk the international ignominy by being seen to snatch at a gift to humanity by someone who, by all accounts, did everything he could to redeem himself in the rest of his long life, except, of course, disclosing the business of the painting until he was too old and frail to do anything about it. Which means... I don't know for certain, but I would

253

strongly suspect that an agreement will be found for the painting to remain on Swiss soil, housed, possibly, within these four walls.'

The last sentence hung in the air for a few moments and was never far from Bear and Ciara's thoughts as they discussed the events of the past two days before he left for the airport.

As were the next few words that Mike Devenish was obliged to utter which required a signature from both of them.

Chapter Twenty

The Unofficial Secrets Act

'I must say, you were very calm today.' Bear's words as they settled down to a valedictory early lunch in the Café Engelchen before his return flight were instinctive, issuing from a compelling observation during the 'after care' meeting.

'Calm? Me?' Ciara replied, somewhat perplexed, as she took a sip from her cappuccino.

Her bewilderment was not misplaced. Calmness had not been a quality Bear had readily associated with her during their courting days. She had usually been the one with the unorthodox idea, the unusual outing, the sense of the unique, and had often needed Bear to rein her in if her creative ideas looked unworkable. If anything, during those days she had admired, and vocalised, his soothing presence and ability to make a quiet suggestion to adjust a plan slightly and bring about a pleasing outcome. By contrast, his speculative 'what if' and 'I wonder how (insert name of any historical character) must have felt' remarks had given her opportunity to reflect and temper her enthusiasm with perspective.

'Yes, you were completely calm as Mike was explaining about ownership rights, and why we're unlikely to become millionaires,' he clarified.

'Well, I never thought that was going to happen. We were just the two people who came upon a find, rather dubiously, at that. Mind you, who can tell what fame awaits us once the show is broadcast?'

'Three months! It will be a challenge to keep everything under wraps for that length of time… but it has to be done,' he said. It was clearly a time for reflection and the exchange of impressions on recent events. He felt unable to let his initial thought go. 'And it wasn't just today. Last night when we got the disappointing initial verdict, when it looked like a complete forgery—'

'As opposed to just a skilfully forged signature,' she interrupted.

'… you took it all in your stride, as though you suspected it. And when the final verdict was given… all right, you expressed amazement, but it was as if you weren't completely surprised.'

'Well, I do work in the art world, you know. We get surprises, good and bad, unexpected finds and frauds from time to time. The thing is to expect the unexpected.'

'But you never used to be so calm, able to accept things so easily.' She shrugged. 'Call it mellowing with age, I suppose.'

He was persistent. 'Did you have a strong feeling in advance?'

Her hesitation told him all he needed to know. She realised she had to come clean.

'Last summer, a few weeks after you left, I read a book, a present from my sister,' she began. She then explained the contents of a relevant chapter in *Where Artistic Temperaments Clash*. The chapter heading 'Band of Brothers' was certainly less than applicable as the scheming developed for Duclos to maintain his illicit liaison and of necessity, to buy Caussade's silence. From her reading she had strongly suspected that Duclos had been the master forger and opportunist. It was a surprise, she added, that the affair had remained a secret for several months, before and after Caussade's untimely intervention.

Bear took a few moments to absorb the disclosure before responding, 'Talking of secrets, how did you feel about signing the Unofficial Secrets Act?'

'It will be a challenge, for sure,' she conceded. 'Though probably harder for you than for me. No one knows about The Double F Show over here. I don't suppose it will cause much of a stir.'

'In this famous artistic city? Are you kidding? Especially if the painting does end up in Swiss hands, possibly in your gallery.'

'Which is why Mike was definite in ensuring the press was under a three-month embargo from reporting on last night, until the programme is aired.'

'Let's hope they stick to it. I'm not sure the tabloid press in Britain would be so scrupulous.'

The document that they both been required to sign was an agreement not to disclose the outcome of the filming, whether they had earned fame or been victims of forgery, until after the broadcast, scheduled for three months from then. How the euphoria in the Stadtgalerie auditorium of the previous night could be contained was an unknown, but the audience had been requested not to pass on word of the event until the show was broadcast in May. Of course, a few murmurs did get out, but not sufficient in the pre-internet age to create ripples back in the UK. Mike Devenish proved very adept to dispelling rumours of some great art find in Switzerland or eastern

257

France and said if he heard any further details, he would be most interested as background detail to one of their stories. There was one awkward moment when a journalist for *The Arts Quarterly* rang his office in Salford and asked about a potential discovery of a Barbizon School artist's work somewhere in Switzerland. He was not sure if his rebuttal that if the story were true, we would all know about it by now, was that convincing.

Three months in which they could not reveal anything about the show. Bear was glad that half-term was to follow immediately after his appearance in Basel. His pupils were unaware of the reason for their history teacher taking a couple of days off. They knew about his imminent appearance in *Fame or Forgery* sometime in the spring or early summer but nothing about the dates for filming. Mac and the ever-inquisitive Claudine had extracted from him that he would be returning to Switzerland for this visit, although with the latter he had hinted at pursuing some romantic interest and having been given special dispensation by Stephen Rawlinson to be absent, an important family event to which he was invited. That was true, to Tim and Sarah's wedding; he hadn't been strictly dishonest, just inaccurate in the date by about five months. He doubted whether Claudine had been convinced and he would have to do further dissembling on his return to school.

Yet such was the nature of a school community that, whatever the hot topics that command the attention of the student or teaching body, within days there is always another burning issue to supplant it. Bear was strangely confident, despite the temptation to reveal all, that he would have the determination to maintain silence until the climactic day of the

258

broadcast, when, they were to discover, they were to be honoured by having a show to themselves. Almost invariably The Double F Show included two stories, but on this occasion the extraordinary venue and circumstances warranted devoting the whole hour to this one tale of two erstwhile flames meeting up after an eight-year interval. What Bear and Ciara were unaware of was the delicate diplomacy needed to disappoint an enthusiastic couple of would-be participants from Cheshire to postpone their appearance for another six months. Finola herself was prevailed upon to sweet-talk the disappointed duo with their Japanese ornamental vase conceivably from many dynasties ago, to appear as 'top billing' in the next series.

Bear smiled to himself as he recalled the determination of the pair of them to deceive Paul Schlessinger in the same café scene a couple of days ago, and in an Indian restaurant the previous summer, and to defy Finola's attempts to inject romantic connections the night before. He concluded that with that team spirit, they should both be able to hold to the terms of what Mike Devenish jokingly referred to as The Unofficial Secrets Act. Naturally, Ciara asked what he found so amusing. His response was guarded.

'I was just thinking we had developed good teamwork all the way through the adventure, especially throwing Paul Schlessinger off the scent,' was his incomplete explanation.

Inevitably, this remark sparked reminiscences of the past few months. The events were recalled in a flurry of comments: the visit to Constable Country, Gisele's talk that drew the initial inspired answer from Bear, Chas's bizarre observations on starlings, Tim's soirée, their meeting after eight years, the unexpected common interest in a painting,

Paul's creepy behaviour, finding the painting after some help from further starlings, getting it over the border safely, awkwardness of dealing with the farmer, the application to The Double F Show, the tension about being accepted, the baggage handlers' strike nearly derailing things but enabling the show to be rearranged, the show itself with its unpredictable final twist. They spent a good hour in exchanging memories.

When it was time for Bear to make his way to the airport, they were able to look forward to meeting up again in July for the wedding, but both knew that the closing exchange of pleasantries seemed limp in view of the momentous journey they had been pursuing. A journey, indeed, that still needed to be seen to its successful conclusion. They were able to encourage each other to maintain vigilance until the date in May when their find would be revealed to the general public. The Unofficial Secrets Act became a mutually voiced watchword, a cover for what they both suspected they were feeling but did not quite feel able to express. They embraced warmly as he departed via the airport bus.

While her companion had a week's grace before answering questions on his second visit to Switzerland in a year, Ciara was immediately left with a less intrusive press to handle but a much more sensitive art fraternity who would pounce on any morsel of gossip. She was shielded by Ernst from the occasional brazen reporter who had heard whispers of a significant evening at the Stadtgalerie, but when accosted a couple of times in the street by emissaries of certain periodicals she was able to bat them away with an assured 'no comment', curiously resolved under no circumstances to let Bear down. After the first two weeks of denials, the secret proved easier to maintain and she found her experience of keeping forthcoming exhibitions under wraps until the designated time to release information invaluable in the process.

***

A short drive to the north of Basel, over the border in the picturesque town of Hirschingen, similar concerns were afflicting the peace of mind of another party to the Unofficial Secrets Act. In this individual's case, the agreement was genuinely unofficial as he had been merely asked not to divulge the outcome of the strange British art programme before it was broadcast. On onelevel that was a simple task, as there were few, if any, in Paul Schlessinger's circle of friends who had an interest in British television, still less on what was usually, he perceived a crude form of popular entertainment. Those who had attended that evening were certainly suitably entertained but not sufficiently close to the drama to remind Paul of the responsibility of keeping a secret with any intensity.

Of course, Dirk Fassbender was poised for his story and was counting down the days until that certain Wednesday in May, the day after the transmission, when all would be revealed. Paul was questioned about something that happened 'on a night out in Basel' by someone who sounded like a journalist at a business forum a few weeks later, although he introduced himself as a sales manager for an electrical goods company. 'Just an evening discussing art' was Paul's bland response.

How he wanted the period to come to an end and to be

261

able to front up and say how proud he was of his father and how he wanted to continue in these honourable traditions. He knew he had to put on something of a front, but as the weeks progressed, he seemed to be acquiring a passion for the traditional ways and crafts he had inherited but had moved away from in his business.

'You're doing really well,' Monika had congratulated him in mid-April. 'Not long now.'

It was as if Paul wanted to show the world how he could persist in keeping a secret for several weeks and then shock the business and cultural world across the three countries border by demonstrating emphatically his pledge to return to the traditional designs of Schlessinger Glas. It was a conviction he had reached with peculiar ease. There had been the initial struggle to put on a brave face that evening at the Stadtgalerie and pretend to be moved by his late father's desire to advance the cause of peace. Once he had uttered such platitudes to Fassbender's demand for an immediate reaction, he realised it was going to be much easier to ride the tide of goodwill than to fight for his own floundering vision of the Schlessinger glass empire.

It was thus with a mood of celebration that Tuesday evening in May that he took Monika out to their favourite restaurant in town. When she gratefully accepted the gesture, she gave him a quizzical look as though wondering why he had chosen that date.

'Is there some cause for celebration I don't know about?' she asked provocatively. 'It's tonight! Nine o'clock our time, eight in England, they will be broadcasting you know what. You knew that!' he admonished playfully.

'I know,' she replied with a cheeky grin. 'But I needed

262

you to say it—' She paused before adding, 'you know, this whole process, these past weeks have been like a religious conversion for you.'

'And I guess I've seen the light,' he said. 'When Fassbender's piece comes out tomorrow, it's going to be the start of a hectic few days.'

'A bright new era for Schlessinger Glas,' the human resources assistant manager declared as the CEO led her out to the car for the last evening before the new dawn.

***

Millennium Pathway was used to keeping secrets, to avoiding disclosing details of programmes, but of all the parties involved, they were the ones finding it hardest not to give the game away. Of course, living around the Salford area where the show was broadcast meant that several of them were bound to encounter friends and associates who would raise the upcoming series of *Fame or Forgery*. It was not a simple matter to deflect inquiries as to the content of the shows.

One of the hardest aspects was sharing, or being sparing in sharing, the details of the filming in Switzerland with colleagues who had stayed at home and were eager to learn of the success of the trip. The official line was that it was a 'fame' but as usual, 'keep it under your hat'. The excited gestures exchanged between those who had been present in the Stadtgalerie as the weeks progressed, however, indicated that something significant had taken place. Colleagues were not slow to pick up on the discernible sense of anticipation as the relevant episode's transmission drew nearer. Even the normally cynical Jim was caught off-guard with a couple of 'not long now' comments.

Mike had weathered one uncomfortable moment when his neighbour remarked that someone at the golf club could have sworn that he saw a Millennium Pathway van in northern France when the golfer had been returning from business interests in Normandy. Fortunately, his neighbour was well used to Mike's enigmatic comments as a new series dawned.

'Well, Bill,' he had said, tapping his nose to denote that secrecy was called for. 'We might be branching out soon, but that would be telling, wouldn't it?'

A hastily arranged pep talk of all those who had travelled to Switzerland on the eve of the final weekend before transmission saw a call to arms by the production director. He congratulated them for not allowing any 'drip feed' of information about the unusual programme with the strange couple of old flames meeting up after years apart. He implored them to maintain vigilance to maximise the drama of the occasion when the artistic world would sit up and take notice at the unique find and MP's credibility as a serious player in the art world and as an entertainment provider would reach unprecedented heights. The promise of a major all-expenses-paid luxury dinner, not to mention likely pay rises, would be fulfilled if they could respect the Unofficial Secrets Act for just a few days more.

Chapter Twenty-One

Reigniting the Flame

'I don't know how you managed it,' Rob McAllister remarked to his drinking companion. 'I take my hat off to you, whatever comes out in the next hour or so. Here's to you.'

The English teacher raised his glass of beer in demonstrative salute, to which the recipient of the praise responded in like manner, albeit less flamboyantly. The express ion of a toast, indeed, was representative of their respective personalities. Rob was always ready to experiment, to attempt bold new ventures with a flourish that did not always succeed, although his staff pantomime eighteen months previously had been a notable triumph. His close friend, more reserved, conservative, yet open to adventure, was more reflective. That evening he had much to ponder.

After a pause, he confessed to a certain relief that the wait was nearly over. The last twenty-four hours had been demanding, he freely admitted. 'I was rather put on the spot when the Head made his announcement in yesterday's assembly.'

Rob was amused at the recollection. 'I never thought I'd hear the Head Man say, "Don't forget to tune in to The Double F Show tomorrow at eight". That has to be a "first"! Well, nearly there, Bear, I can't wait to quiz you when we find out the verdict. How you've kept it a secret I'll never know.'

'I nearly gave the game away to someone from church the other day. I had to explain why I would be missing from the midweek group tonight.'

'Oh, that's true,' Rob acknowledged. 'You're not known to miss your group. That must be another "first". What happened, did this person give you a grilling?'

'Not at all, it was so casual. Sheila... she's in her fifties, I suppose, and hosts from time to time... she asked if I was doing anything special and when I said you had this evening planned. I mentioned about appearing on the show and she just casually asked how it went... it almost slipped out.'

His working environment had been demanding in testing his ability to button his lip, but, in fact, once he had dismissed the last teasing queries from his tutees eager to extract which of the two 'F' verdicts applied to him, Bear had relaxed significantly. He left school that day to change for an evening at The Anchor Inn with the television channel secured by agreement with the landlord who was pleased to have a rare midweek gathering of Princewood School staff.

Now that he had batted away the excited enquiries with a deadpan 'no comment' and realised that he was to achieve something special in following Mike's Unofficial Secrets Act to the letter, he was almost nonchalant when a handful of colleagues sauntered into the hostelry over the next ten minutes.

The long May evening sunshine lent a freshness to the atmosphere following the mid-afternoon shower, and it was with reluctance that Bear and Rob vacated their beer garden seats to enter the television lounge to take up their position in front of the large screen. As they made their way into the lounge, familiar voices permeated the nineteenth-century inn.

John Billington's infectious guffaws at some anecdote were prominent. Claudine, not usually one for pub evenings, had resolved to make an exception and her shrill Gallic gasps of amazement at Billers' observation, no doubt, lent character to the setting. Full of the typical Princewood School types, Bear thought to himself, and felt comfortable in the presence of his colleagues. In all about a dozen members of staff had turned up to experience a communal occasion when one of their number became, for one night at least, a national star attraction.

As eight o'clock approached an almost reverential tranquillity engulfed proceedings as all present were eager not to miss any of the finished product, a real edition of *Fame or Forgery* featuring one of their own. All had been aware, of course, of the crew visiting the school back in the autumn and were curious to see how Princewood, and Bear in particular, was p resented. The studied hush had communicated itself to other drinkers that Tuesday evening. An especially loud greeting of the barman by a regular was met with a good humoured, polite but firm indication that that particular lounge bar was reserved for a programme of local interest. The customer took the advice in good part and stood at the back of the lounge, lingering with a view to catch some of the programme, as did two elderly gentlemen whose animated conversation was curtailed as they were directed towards the television screen to observe the town of Princewood being depicted on national television.

In the weeks and months that were to follow that Tuesday evening in May, Bear was repeatedly drawn to a stock expression to describe his feelings on witnessing the adventure of the *Flight of the Huguenots* being unveiled on screen. It usually took a few supplementary sentences to explain himself with any clarity. Yet he could not honestly wander from the statement that watching himself was like an out of body experience. Or what he assumed such a happening to feel like. He had already seen his monologue delivered from under the oak tree in October while in Switzerland in February and recalled vividly every step of the evening in the Stadtgalerie. He had mulled over in his mind the significant parts of the interview with Finola and the thoughts he and Ciara had exchanged before and after the show. He knew the outcome and now simply had to let his acquaintances in on the secret, but he had moved on, at least in terms of the relevance of the missing painting being recovered. Yet here he was, present as his curious colleagues and a few interested onlookers at The Anchor Inn enjoyed an absorbing hour following the stages of the painting's story, with an apparent sub-plot included for good measure.

John Billington struggled to maintain absolute discretion once Ciara's monologue from Basel which followed Bear's was shown and she had confirmed that the pair had met unexpectedly after such a long absence.

'Are they…?' he asked hesitantly of Rachel Rhodes, turning to a younger colleague who might have more of a direct line to rumours circulating around the possible romantic affairs of single members of staff. Rachel did not need him to articulate the rest of his question and simply shrugged her shoulders.

Bear would later confess that he felt that he was watching his own funeral, not from any morbid angst but merely from the view of someone who had moved beyond the current intriguing conundrum and had passed to another world, life after Duclos. He was waiting for his colleagues to join him and share in his knowledge of what that world was like.

It would not be true to say that he was entirely unamused as he recalled the events of the past ten months unfolding, but his amusement was more pleasure at seeing his colleagues entertained in unusual fashion. The Head's presentation of the portraits of the school's luminaries of yesteryear drew laughter as to how Stephen Rawlinson seized the moment to advertise the school in the most dignified manner possible. Ciara was described variously as 'feisty', 'spirited' and 'savvy'. 'A great foil' were the words emanating from historian Peter Walton, who had decided to join the evening's festivities with the added interest of seeing the terminus on the Calais-Bâle route, as he noted the joint determination of the two participants to stand up to Finola's provocative questioning. Comments were expressed at Finola who, for all her roguish sense of humour, was an eminently likeable character who was ever seeking to make the guests feel kings or queens for the day and to encourage them in their pursuit of art, whatever the outcome of the programme.

As the show drew towards its conclusion, Bear was taking the experience in his stride.

There was just one word that remained with him throughout, that would not leave him. It was the word he had feared was an indiscretion and could come back to haunt him, or at least be the source of teasing. In fact, when the monologue was shown early in the proceedings, his anticipated sense of embarrassment and awkwardness did not surface.

'We are just good friends,' he had said of the person who was about to be introduced to the televisual audience. Yet his remark did not come across as an awkward qualification, to suppress any rumours that may have been aroused. The emphasis on 'just' communicated exactly the right tone, meaning 'simply', in all simplicity and, dare he say, purity, free from any constraints or obligations. It was a liberating 'just', showing there was no encumbrance, no need for intensity in the relationship and lent a strength to the bond that, he noted, was backed up by the subsequent encounter with Finola, as well as other instances not seen on screen that night.

There was general amusement as Bear and Ciara were not persuaded to elaborate on any passion outside their interest in art, and Bear was conscious that no one knew the answer to Billers' unfinished question, nor needed to know.

It occurred to Bear momentarily that some of his colleagues might have thought he was putting on an act by referring to being 'just good friends' and that the whole experience of appearing in the show was an act. But the thought soon passed. They were all absorbed in the experience of televisual theatre and not prepared to cast a verdict on any relationship between the two participants. Had the last few months been all an act, he asked himself? Divorced from reality? Or was reality to be gained in discovering yourself, however trivial the content?

It then dawned on him that, as the final exchanges of that memorable night in Basel were transmitted, a fine piece of drama, in its way a work of art, was being enacted. As Finola was reading the initial verdict amidst considerable hush in The Anchor Inn, Bear struggle d initially to keep a straight face. The groans of disappointment that followed the apparent rejection of his and Ciara's efforts were palpable. Pained, deflated expressions on several faces were cut short, as they were keen to hear what their colleague's reaction was.

'Philosophical,' observed Billers of Bear's acceptance of defeat. 'What a shame!' exclaimed Rachel sympathetically.

'That's the way it goes sometimes,' muttered Peter.

The refocusing on Finola's explanatory speech was pursued by the inn's audience grudgingly, as though eager for the dull formalities to be concluded at the end of an enjoyable but seemingly disappointing evening. As she delivered the final words to produce the real verdict, the explosion of joy in the lounge was delayed for a few seconds of suspended belief before being released. Cheers from strangers in the pub celebrated the fact that the town of Princewood, through an intrepid traveller and his Irish lady friend, was firmly on the map.

Rob was warm in his congratulations. 'Put it there, mate,' he said, offering Bear his hand which he firmly accepted. 'I am even more amazed how you kept that secret for three months, especially such an ending. A masterpiece of storytelling with a twist at the end. Incredible!'

'Thanks, Mac,' Bear replied. 'I'm glad it's all over.' He was about to accept Mac's offer of a final pint in celebration when he suddenly remembered the tip-off he had received from Mike as the final credits were being played, to the accompaniment of the jolly Double F Show signature tune. 'Wait—'

He gestured firmly to his friend not to cast his eyes away from the screen as the music faded. Finola reappeared on the screen, now no longer in the Stadtgalerie but seated at a park bench somewhere, an ordinary everyday scene to try to entice further participants to chance their arm on the show. What she

271

was about to impart Bear knew in content, if not in exact wording as he had not been present at this recording.

'Perhaps ye'd like tae know what's going to happen to *The Flight of the Huguenots*,' she began. 'Yes, it was fame for Bear and Ciara, but they knew, or at least I suspect they knew all along, that they could nae keep any proceeds from it.' She proceeded to explain the legal tussle that could ensue between two countries and the mystery of the heirless Monsieur Rosenbourg, the lack of a decisive claim to the masterpiece. 'But Ciara, at least, is going tae see a wee bit more of the painting... eventually...'

Bear's calm as he listened to the explanation of the painting's future was apparent to all patrons of The Anchor that evening. He knew of the decision for Gerhard Schlessinger's wishes to be respected and for the masterpiece to be housed on neutral territory, the Neue Basler Kunstgalerie to be its permanent home. Eventually.

'Well, let the tour commence!' exclaimed Billers enthusiastically as Finola finished her announcement and the final credits rolled.

'What a wonderful idea!' gushed Claudine. 'I will 'ave to make an effort to get down to London. 'ow long ees it being exhibited there?'

Bear understood maybe six months, to see out the rest of the anniversary year. He could scarcely believe that the arrangements to transport such a precious cargo to supplement the Barbizon collection could be made at such short notice and could only imagine the frantic negotiations behind the scenes to ensure the painting was displayed in the National Gallery a few weeks hence. And after a tour of European capitals and art centres, *The Flight of the Huguenots* was to enjoy its resting place in Base 1, city of such distinguished art heritage. He had been party to such revelations before that evening, and his role was simply to enjoy his colleagues and friends gradually learning of the final dénouement.

The impression recurred to the historian as he sipped one obligatory final pint in his honour was that the night had truly been one akin to attending one's own funeral, and he voiced that passing thought to the assembled company.

'I'm told weddings might be the better analogy, not that I can speak from experience, of course,' suggested fellow bachelor Rob. 'Friends of mine tied the knot last summer and said the actual day was almost more of a celebration for friends and family, whereas they , the happy couple, had gone through the rehearsal, gone through the whole experience the day before, and could relax as they just glided through the day.'

Rob's views were not universally supported, as a couple of the married colleagues testified to anxiety and less than smooth experience of nuptials, but for Bear, there was one word that resonated yet again that he could not get out of his mind. Amid the general chatter that fascinated and enthralled the Princewood School staff, the curious, delightful series of events of the past months that had been summarised, the intriguing characters of Ciara, Finola, Mike, Max, even the enigmatic German businessman whose father had championed the cause of peace in Europe, one question was never far from their lips. It was Claudine with her natural inquisitiveness who voiced it.

'So, Grizzly, what ees 'appening with your Irish friend? Are you going out wiz 'er?'

'I can only give the same answer as I did last October,

273

Claudine. We are just…,' he replied and was happy not to finish the sentence. There was a gentle contentment in the tone as if economy of words conveyed all the meaning necessary.

The gathering broke up as closing time approached, and the assembled teachers went their separate ways. Bear returned to his flat, a brisk ten minutes' walk in the mild late spring evening. His natural curiosity stirred him to consider making a phone call, a notion he immediately dismissed on the grounds that the intended recipient was an hour ahead and probably already retired to bed. On turning on the light, he was not surprised to note that his answer phone showed a message, presumably from a friend who had seen the programme and wished to offer congratulations. As he prepared to press the button to play back the message, however, he instinctively knew who the caller was. The harmonious Irish lilt was instantly recognisable.

'I had to ask you how it went. It's been so strange waiting all day and not being able to see the show until I get sent the video. But I'm sure you came across well. I hope I did… but aren't we just a great team?'